─────────────── ★ ───────────────

The woman lay on her stomach, her head facing toward me. The exposed hand rested by her cheek. I had a sense of déjà vu, as if I'd come across a corpse in the woods at some other time or place in my life. It felt familiar in a way that finding Lillian hadn't, which was odd, because that was an experience I'd actually had before.

I wrapped the sleeve of my sweatshirt around my left hand again and slid it under her wrist. The arm stuck out of a brown leather sleeve. It was stiff, resistant to being lifted. I noticed the nail beds were a dark blue under the iridescent polish. I felt for a pulse with the fingertips of my right hand. As soon as I touched bare skin, I knew I was touching death.

─────────────── ★ ───────────────

"Bravo to Marcuse for this entertaining and engrossing puzzle."

—*Publishers Weekly*

"An intriguing, spiffy first mystery. The characters are full and quirky, the New York ambience honest and affectionate, and the details and shadings just right."

—*Booklist*

Forthcoming from Worldwide Mystery by
IRENE MARCUSE

GUILTY MIND

Irene Marcuse

The Death of an Amiable Child

W❂RLDWIDE®

TORONTO • NEW YORK • LONDON
AMSTERDAM • PARIS • SYDNEY • HAMBURG
STOCKHOLM • ATHENS • TOKYO • MILAN
MADRID • WARSAW • BUDAPEST • AUCKLAND

for the old people

THE DEATH OF AN AMIABLE CHILD

A Worldwide Mystery/September 2002

Published by arrangement with Walker Publishing Company, Inc.

ISBN 0-373-26433-X

Printed in U.S.A.

Acknowledgments

Bear with me, I've got a few people to thank—

All my draft-readers—Janet Jaffe, for finding the order in chaos; Judy Morrison, Judy Woodruff, Joyce Willis, Sally Taylor, Andrew Marcuse, Lois Alexander, Christine Shook, Cathy Schechter, Aaron Marcuse-Kubitza; my parents, Peter and Frances Marcuse, especially my father for sharing a work space with relatively little friction. Read it again, guys—the ending's changed! For editorial polishing—Kathy Saideman, Liza Nelligan, Michael Seidman; and of course my agent, Sandy Dijkstra.

For technical advice—Claudia Beck, RN, MS, ANP; Richard Decherd, RN; Dr. Patricia Carey; and my legal eagle, Douglas Reiniger, to whom I owe more than a mere thank-you.

And most of all my husband, Philip Silver, for his total confidence that I could accomplish what I intended. All the best lines are yours.

Hey Tabitha—now do you believe this is my job?

ONE

As if Monday mornings weren't bad enough, this was the one after the April change to daylight savings time—my least favorite day of the year. I resent the hour they steal from me, and I don't forgive them until the October day they give it back.

I had my keys in the lock going out the door, the strap of my daughter's backpack over one arm. Clea bounced down the hall to the elevator. She was back in two seconds, tugging at my jacket.

"Mama, the lady smells nasty," she whispered.

"What? Did you push the elevator button?"

"I think she peed her pants." Clea tugged again.

Damn. Between Clea's school uniform and grabbing a bagel for the road, we'd actually had a shot at being on time.

"Okay, let's have a look." I sighed and handed her the backpack. Clea put it on and allowed me to run my hand over her head to check the cornrows I'd braided yesterday. The parts were straight; her hair glistened. Being white myself, I take care that my black child's hair looks good.

The lady is a small, elderly white woman who on occasion spends her nights in our building. We refer to her as "the lady of the landing" because she sleeps in the three-foot by five-foot landing where the stairs pause and turn between the twelfth floor and the roof. We were used to seeing the small mound of her feet tucked under her coat in the morning. Clea always went up a step or two for a closer look; I always whispered her down. She's like a cat, Clea; if it's there, she has to see, to sniff. But she's only five, and this time she'd sniffed out more than she understood.

Cautious now as a New York child should be, she stayed close to my side. The smell wasn't strong, but she'd gotten it right: the lady had soiled herself.

"You stay here." I used my no-arguments voice to keep Clea at the foot of the stairs while I went up for a closer look.

The lady's bed, a blue wool blanket folded in half to protect her from the chill of the marble floor, was bunched up near her knees. She lay on her left side, facing the wall under the window. The coat she usually slept under was draped at right angles across her hips, as if a casual hand had wanted to soak up the urine and keep it from spilling down the steps.

One bare foot hung over the top step, toes pointing down. I touched the skin of her calf. It was cold and stiff. I knew there was more wrong with the lady than incontinence.

I closed my eyes for a second and took a deep breath. I'm a social worker. My clients are elderly people, and this wasn't the first time I'd found one of them unexpectedly dead—except this one was practically on my doorstep, with my child not ten feet away, and Clea's needs came first.

"The elevator's here!" Clea announced.

"Let it go." My voice was sharper than I intended. When I turned around, Clea's thumb was in her mouth. Her eyes were big, but at least my body was blocking her view.

Okay. I knew what to do, I just had to calm down and reorder my priorities. Not scaring Clea was high on the list. I went down the stairs, picked Clea up, and settled her on my hip.

"It's okay, Bopster. The lady's sick. We have to go back inside so I can call an ambulance to take her to the hospital." I carried her down the hall.

She wrapped her arms around my neck. "Why did she poop in her pants, Mama?"

"Remember when you had diarrhea and you couldn't hold it? Sometimes that happens to grown-ups, too." I unlocked the door, deposited Clea on the couch, and turned on the TV. "Look, there's Mr. Rogers. I'm going to help the lady. I'll be right back."

Clea took a bite of her bagel, her eyes already tuned to her television neighbor. I went out and locked the door behind me. I didn't want Clea wandering out into the hall.

OUR BUILDING IS an old co-op on 111th Street, with no doorman to keep uninvited visitors out. The hallways have the feel of a noir movie, the floor a linoleum checkerboard of square tiles in black flecked with gray and gray flecked with black. Fixtureless fluorescent lights give a greenish cast to the pale gray walls, the darker gray doors. A patch of early sun from the east window above the landing where the lady lay added a grace note of natural light. The closed doors of my neighbors exuded silence as usual at this time of day.

The lady of the landing had been sleeping in the stairwell on and off for several months. She was a constant rebuke to me, a reminder of the limits of my profession and my ability to help those who might need, but were unwilling to accept, my assistance. If we saw her when she was awake, as we occasionally did in the evenings when she entered the building, she refused to speak to me. Clea might get a half smile, but that was it.

I knew only her first name, Lillian, because my elderly neighbors, the Wilcox sisters, provided the blanket she slept on. I'd tried to talk with her, to find out why she was homeless and where she spent her other nights. Lillian met all my overtures with silent resistance, until finally I got the message and stopped trying to provide assistance where it wasn't wanted. Social work has its guidelines, and chief among them is the right of client self-determination. Where I work, our clients come to us voluntarily; if someone doesn't want our services, we can't force the issue.

As the months went on, I started thinking of her more as a neighbor than a client; she was always clean and unobtrusive, never spoke unless spoken to. Apartment dwellers coexist, exchange pleasantries in the halls, pretend not to know more than we're told. Although I kept a professional eye out for her, I allowed her the respectful privacy due a neighbor. I'd made myself available; Lillian knew she could ask me if she ever needed help.

I paused at the foot of the stairs, breathed in social worker, breathed out neighbor. Anyone who works with the elderly encounters death, sometimes closely. In my two years at Senior Services, I've found the bodies of three people who died in their apartments, two others who survived more than a day on the floor before being rescued. Unpleasant doesn't begin to describe the experience. I've had to learn a measure of professional detachment in order to respond with practical efficiency.

I climbed seven of the eight steps to the landing, trying to ignore the smell. I put one knee down on the landing and leaned over for a closer look. I had enough experience to know that amount of blood does not necessarily correspond to severity of injury, but—I had to back away. I raised my head to the window, the bright blue sky. I took a few shallow breaths to regain my composure before I looked down again.

There appeared to be an injury of some sort just above her right ear. A dark clot of blood was matted in her white hair. Dried blood was smeared around her shoulder, on her right hand, streaked like rouge across her cheek. Her nose had bled, leaving brown rivulets in the wrinkles around her mouth. Her head rested in a sticky maroon stain.

Her eyes were open, staring at the wall.

I reached for her arm, prepared for it to resist being moved, but instead it was limp, heavy, cold to the touch. I slid two fingers under her wrist, feeling for a pulse. The thing that distinguishes death from sleep is stillness, a halo of silence that surrounds a body when it's no longer breathing. Death may be hard to comprehend, but there's no mistaking it. The lady of the landing was dead.

I tried to remember the last time I'd seen her. Not yesterday evening when we'd come home around six; maybe Saturday—

yes, around midnight. My husband, Benno, and I had gotten a baby-sitter and gone to the movies.

When we came down the block toward home, we noticed her ahead of us, drifting down 111th St. like a wraith in her black wool coat and old-fashioned black felt cloche. She bent to unlock the door and gave a quick glance over her shoulder before slipping into the building. We hung back, giving her time to get in ahead of us. She was proud; if we'd come in with her, she would have walked the twelve flights up rather than ride the elevator with us.

Now her clothing lay in a pile between her body and the wall, as if the same careless hand that had draped her coat over her hips had shaken the garments out before dropping them. On top of the heap were her hat and her white cotton gloves, one thumb and an index finger mended with precise stitches of black thread.

She was wearing a slip, yellowed satin with a band of lace at the neckline. The strap of a brassiere bagged underneath. Lillian had been on the emaciated side in life; in death she seemed already skeletal. Her skin was dry, waxy; her shoulder, elbow, ankles were knobs of bone barely covered by shiny skin.

Her right leg stuck straight out, the toes pointing into the corner. Between the puddle of black clothing and her foot were a pair of shoes, patent leather with a small bow of grosgrain ribbon. The stockings she tucked neatly into each shoe had been removed and lay crumpled in a fold of blanket. Next to the pile of clothing was a brass key with a spade-shaped head, like the key to our building. It was threaded onto a chain, a string of little metal beads like the cord to a light-pull.

I backed down the stairs, leaned against the wall, and tried to get a grip. Neighbor and potential client, I'd felt a responsibility to Lillian. Keeping elderly people out of nursing homes is a major part of my job. I arrange for the services they need to live as independently as possible in their own apartments—cleaning, shopping, home health aide, transportation, medical care.

I stared at the gray wall, told myself there was no way I could have known she would die here. I'd done all I thought I could do at the time. If Lillian believed sleeping in a stairwell was better than being institutionalized, well, it had been her decision to make. I knew I was rationalizing. Her death upset me, shook my confidence in my ability to correctly assess and respond to a client. A fellow human being.

I became a social worker when I already had a fair amount of life experience behind me. What I learned in grad school, besides how to make it look good on paper, was to recognize an emotional reaction and not let it interfere with the needs of a client. Of course, the hardest thing for a person in the mental health field to do is apply professional expertise to personal situations—take the divorced marriage counselor. Here I was, facing a situation I would have handled competently if it arose in the course of my job. On my own doorstep, I was behaving like an amateur.

I'm experienced with the drill: police; EMS; official determination of death; undertaker or morgue; next of kin tracked down and notified. It was time to get going. Familiar as the routine of unexpected death was, it still made for a rough morning.

CLEA WAS mind-melded to the TV. I don't usually like to use the electronic baby-sitter, but at the moment it was a blessing. Her eyes barely flicked in my direction when I came in.

I washed my hands, twice, and put on rose-scented hand lotion to counter the smell of Lillian's body. It did nothing to erase the taste of death from the back of my throat.

I took the cordless phone into the bedroom and called, in this order, my husband, my job, the Super, and 911. I wanted to get Clea out of the way before the official business of death got under way, and a few more minutes wouldn't matter to Lillian.

Benno, a self-employed cabinetmaker, has a shop near Canal Street. Riding the red heartline of the Seventh Avenue IRT, he'd be home in half an hour. I knew the police would want to talk to me, and I figured it would be better if Clea went to work with him rather than being late to school after the tragedy in the hall.

My job was no problem. Lillian's death qualified as a client emergency, so instead of being late I was actually signing in early.

The lengthiest call was to the Super, Barbara Baker, who lives in the basement apartment. Barbara's forty-four, two years and two days older than I am. She's the first friend I made when I moved to New York, still my closest friend, the person who taught me to cornrow Clea's hair.

"Hey, Anita, what are you doing home at this hour?" Barbara said.

I told her. She clicked her tongue at the news.

"That's a hard way to go, alone like that. I told you she would've been better off—"

"You don't have to rub it in, I feel bad enough. I can't imagine what happened to her. I honestly thought she was safe here, at least I could keep an eye on her."

"Well, you did your best, you and your soft heart. Me, you'd think I would have listened to the people who pay my salary but no, Protective Services turned her down, so I had to get filled with the spirit of Christian charity. You see where acting from your heart gets you? But what an awful thing to happen."

At one point, I'd called in PSA, Protective Services for Adults, the agency of last resort. As far as they were concerned, while Lillian may have been a nuisance to the building, she was a danger neither to herself nor to others, so they declined her case.

"It's my fault, Barbara, not yours. I should have tried harder to get her to trust me so I could find out why she was here in the first place. Even the police couldn't keep her away for long. I don't think anything short of hiring a night guard would have worked."

"Yeah, right, I forgot, I'm a Super, not a doorman. I got blamed for her being here in the first place, Anita, you think now she's dead they won't find a way to blame me for that, too? You watch.'' Barbara hung up the phone.

New York-born, Harlem-bred, Barbara has an excellent grasp of building politics. She's lived here for decades; her husband was the Super until he had a heart attack last summer. Although the co-op's Board of Directors voted unanimously to give her the job, Barbara is now at the mercy of a newly elected board whose current president is opposed to a woman Super.

I dialed 911. After I gave the preliminary information, the neutral, unshockable voice put me on hold. The first time this happened to me, I was appalled: even 911 makes you wait! But I learned that the dispatcher was relaying the initial call to police and EMS, and would get back to me for details. 911 came back on the line. I went through it all again and was informed that the ambulance would be there in approximately fifteen minutes.

I put the phone down. This was life imitating work. I sometimes think I spend half my time on the phone; they should give social workers phone implants along with our MSWs.

Mr. Rogers's voice still soothed from the living room. I joined Clea on the couch and opened my arms for her to climb into my lap. I sniffed her little-girl smell, part hair cream, part milk. Whatever had happened to Lillian, I wanted to keep it from touching Clea's world. Mr. Rogers said he wished he had a neighbor just like me, closed his door, and disappeared into TV land. Clea graced me with a piece of her attention.

''What happened to the lady?'' she wanted to know.

''You were very smart to see that something was wrong. The lady's sick, and an ambulance is coming to take her to the hospital. I called Dad, and he's coming home.'' Clea's still young enough to be distracted away from a subject I'm not ready to discuss. ''Since you'd be very late for school, we thought you could go to the shop with him instead. Does that sound like a plan?''

''Okay. Can I go see the lady in the hospital? I'll bring her a bear to make her feel better.''

So much for changing the subject.

"That's a good idea, Bopster, but she's not ready for visitors yet." Along with smiles, the lady of the landing favored Clea with an occasional gift—a stuffed cat left by the door, a chocolate bunny from Mondel's. Clea was about to launch another question when *Sesame Street* came to the rescue. She wiggled out of my arms and turned her attention back to the set. I sighed. Just as well she was absorbed again.

Benno's keys jingled against the door. Clea was off the couch and swarming up his legs before he could get inside. "Daddy, Daddy, the lady pooped her pants and I smelled it!"

I couldn't help it; I laughed. It was either that or cry, I was so relieved to see Benno. He put his arms around me. I rested my head on his shoulder, Clea sandwiched between us.

But only for a minute. The wail of sirens rose from the street and brought her squirming out of our embrace and over to the window. She struggled to push it up so she could see out past the child safety guards. Clea loves action, any kind of action; sirens and flashing lights put her into ecstasy. Her heart's desire is to ride in an ambulance.

"Are they taking the lady to the hospital? Can I go with her? Please, Mama, please, I'll be quiet and I won't get in the way!"

I opened the window and lifted her up for a better view. It was a police car, not an ambulance.

"No, Bopster, you can't go to the hospital. Dad's taking you to the shop, remember?" Her little head drooped with disappointment.

"Come on, chief assistant cabinetmaker, we'd better get you out of those school clothes and into overalls." Benno took her hand to lead her into the bedroom and winked at me over his shoulder. Clea wouldn't stay down long.

I kissed him through the air and went out to the hall.

I RECOGNIZED THE PAIR of uniformed cops who got out of the car; they'd responded on two of the other occasions I'd called 911 after finding a client's body. Growing up in Berkeley, California, I learned to have a healthy disrespect for the guardians of law and order. Inez Collazo, a petite Puerto Rican woman with a wad of honey-colored hair tucked under her cap, and her green-eyed Irish partner, Michael Dougherty, however, were both sensitive and smart. Seeing them gave me hope that the morning would be manageable.

"Hey, it's the social worker," Dougherty stepped out of the elevator. "This another one of yours?"

"No, this is personal. I live here."

"She live here too?" Dougherty climbed a few steps up for a better view. "What's her name?" He pulled his pad out of his back pocket and flipped it open.

"As far as I know, she's homeless. Sometimes she spends the night here. I think her first name is Lillian."

Michael frowned. "So what's she doing sleeping in your stairwell?"

"I don't know, Michael. Maybe she thought it was safer than a shelter."

"Yeah, right," Michael snorted. "Looks like she was pretty safe here, don't it? How long's she been making her home on the stairs?"

"All winter. She started out downstairs in the vestibule, between the two doors, until they installed a second intercom and put a lock on the outer door to keep her out."

"Doesn't look like it worked. What a town, little old ladies sleeping wherever they feel like it. How come you people don't have a doorman?" Michael glared at me like it was my fault.

"This isn't the East Side, or West End Avenue. Besides, where would we put a doorman?" It's a small building, as New York apartment houses go—twelve floors, four apartments per; forty-nine units, counting the Super in the basement. We don't have a real lobby, just an alcove for mailboxes next to the elevator on the first floor.

"How did she get into the building?" Inez asked.

"She used to slip in behind a sympathetic resident."

"Such as yourself," Michael put in.

"Yes, I was one of the ones who let her in. Some people slammed the door in her face. Go ahead, sue me. I give money to homeless people on the street, too, and I don't care what they spend it on, either."

"A regular charity ward," Michael muttered. "She take her own clothes off, or we dealing with a sex crime here?" He used his pen to gently raise the coat covering Lillian's torso. He bent over for a look, winced, let the coat fall. "Looks like she's still got underpants on."

"She used to undress and sleep under her coat." The possibility that Lillian had been raped was not one I wanted to entertain.

"No one ever tried to get rid of her? Called the police to evict her?"

"Of course we did, but you know how it goes. About a month ago, I heard a commotion in the hall. When I came out she was screaming, 'Get your hands off me, you Nazis, don't you touch me!' She calmed down when she saw me, but two of your colleagues had her in handcuffs. They said she resisted arrest by kicking at them. A little old lady in a shabby slip, mad because they woke her up in the middle of the night. What danger was she?"

"Cops don't like to be called Nazis. Was she Jewish?" Michael asked.

I had to think about it. "I suppose she could have been." I know, it's a stereotype, but I don't think of Jewish people as being homeless. "Some cops give people reason, you know. She had her clothes all neatly folded and her stockings rolled up in her shoes, but they wouldn't let her get dressed while they waited for EMS to take her to the psych ER at Bellevue. Their attitude was, EMS'll wrap her in a blanket. Which they did, and three days later she was back again."

I'd made a dozen calls to Bellevue, but it's next to impossible to get information on someone in a psych unit unless you're a family member or have the person's consent. I was about to make a trip over there when Lillian showed up again.

"So how come you people let her sleep here?" Michael asked.

"I didn't 'let' her do anything. She didn't want my help,

Bellevue didn't think she was incapacitated enough for them to keep her, and whatever she told Protective Services made them decline her case. I figured she was okay here, at least I could watch out for her…'' I stopped. I liked Michael in spite of himself, although at the moment he wasn't doing much for my opinion of cops. "I know, I should have done more. But what? Old people can be awfully stubborn.''

"You were the one who called it in?'' Thank you, Inez.

"My daughter noticed the smell, then I went up and found her.'' I put a hand on Inez's arm. "You won't have to ask Clea any questions, will you? She didn't see anything.''

"Where is she now?'' Inez asked.

"In the apartment, with my husband. He's getting her stuff together to take her back to work with him.''

"*Back* to work?'' Dougherty looked down at me. "He's been out already?''

"Yeah, he leaves about seven o'clock. I called him to come home for Clea.''

"He didn't notice the deceased at that time?'' Dougherty wrinkled his nose and added, "He didn't smell the deceased?''

Inez took a turn up the stairs to look at Lillian. "This lady does not appear to have died peacefully in her sleep. I wonder what's taking EMS so long?''

"No hurry to pronounce her, is there?'' Michael said.

"Anita, do you know anything about this key?'' Inez asked.

"I think it's the front door key for the building. What do you think happened to her?''

"She didn't live here, why did she have a key?'' Inez didn't let me divert her.

"To get in?'' I offered.

Michael was not amused. "This isn't a game, Anita. Did you give it to her?''

"No, someone in the building might have, but it wasn't me.''

"But you know who did.'' I was on the receiving end of a double-barreled cop stare.

The Wilcox sisters, feeders of parakeets and pigeons, had

taken Lillian under their wings as well. They hung a plastic shopping bag with the blue wool blanket on their doorknob every evening; Lillian returned it the following morning. I assumed they'd given her the key as well, but I didn't know for sure.

The elevator door opened. The EMS crew, two young white guys carrying a body board, shouldered their way into the hall and saved me from ratting on my neighbors.

Michael held up a hand. "Nezzie, we need to get a detective over here. Maybe you could use Anita's phone, talk to her family while you're at it?"

WE CAUGHT BENNO and Clea on their way out of the apartment. In honor of the occasion, Clea had put on her official souvenir MTA bus driver's hat. The beads on her cornrows gave it a festive fringe of pink, purple, blue.

Inez, disregarding the danger of overbalancing from the nightstick, gun, handcuffs, radio, extra ammunition, and flashlight attached to her belt, squatted down to Clea's level and saluted her.

Clea saluted back, in her glory at having the undivided attention of a real police officer. "Do you shoot people with that gun?" she asked.

"No, sweetie, I never have." Fortunately, Inez laughed. "Did you notice anything about the lady besides how she smelled?"

"She had pink polish on her toes," Clea said.

It amazes me every time. Clea sees the details, things you wouldn't expect even to register with a child. For all my careful examination of Lillian, I hadn't caught the painted toenails. But then, Clea is a nail polish expert. My friend Janis favors elaborate manicures, to the delight of Clea's little-girl soul. When she comes over, Clea greets her with fingers spread wide. Janis obliges with the color of her desire—hot pink, purple, black sparkles for Halloween.

"That's very good, sergeant," Inez congratulated her. "I think we'll have to promote you to detective!"

"Can I have a badge?" Clea pressed her advantage.

We all laughed. Clea got shy and hid her face in my pants.

Inez turned to Benno. "You didn't notice anything when you left this morning?"

"No, I wasn't really paying attention. Catherine Wilcox was just coming out of the elevator with her coffee, and I held the door for her. I was in a hurry, and she can go on."

Catherine is the younger sister, all of seventy-eight. Every morning on the dot of 7:00 she makes a run to the Mill Luncheonette for two containers of coffee, two buttered rolls, and the *Times*.

Clea pulled at my hand, wanting a closer look at the paramedics' gear. I picked her up and handed her over to Benno. "EMS is here, maybe you should get Clea out of the way while they're…" Blocking the view of what was on the landing, I finished the sentence silently. The last thing I wanted was for Clea to get another glimpse of Lillian.

Benno picked Clea up. "What do you say, kid? Let's blow this popsicle stand."

MICHAEL HELD the elevator door so Benno could carry Clea quickly past the stairs. The two men exchanged a look, sizing each other up. Michael was taller, but Benno had him beat in the chest department. Michael let it go first, with a smile, and the testosterone level in the hallway dropped. Men.

I stepped into the elevator and adjusted Clea's hat. "Be good for Daddy now, Sergeant Servi," I told her.

Benno stroked my hair back off my face. His hands are like oven mitts, quilted with pads of muscle. "You be careful, Anita of my heart." He pulled me in for a kiss. I wanted to stay with him, to let the elevator transport me back to a place where the lady of the landing was still alive and I could still help her.

I planted a quick one on Clea's cheek instead and backed out of the elevator. Benno pushed M and the door closed. Through the little round window, I watched my family disappear. My heart felt like it was descending with them.

TWO

BEHIND ME, Michael cleared his throat. Whatever feelings I had about the lady of the landing would have to wait. She was police business now. I was headed back to my apartment when Catherine Wilcox popped into the hall.

"What's wrong? Oh, dear, Anita, what's wrong?" Catherine started for the stairs.

I tucked her hand under my elbow and walked her back to where Elizabeth waited, bent over her cane in the doorway of their apartment.

I'm only five-feet, two inches, but the sisters make me feel like a basketball player. I looked down at Elizabeth's curved shoulders, the dark scalp showing through the plaits in her thin gray hair. The elder by thirteen years, Elizabeth is the brains of the pair; Catherine provides the brawn. At a combined age of 169, they're formidable, although I can see ahead to the day when they'll cross the line and become clients more than neighbors.

Inez came over and I made the introductions.

Elizabeth interrupted with an imperious frown. "We prefer not to converse in the hall, Anita. Please, come in and sit down."

Entering the apartment, Elizabeth took up her post on the far side of the dining table, strategically placed so that she had command of the kitchen and living room. She thumped her cane and demanded, "Catherine, give these young women some refreshment. I believe there's a pot of tea on the stove. And a plate of biscuits!"

Catherine and Elizabeth Wilcox are black women of the old school; anyone who crosses their threshold is offered food and drink before any business can be conducted. I've learned that no matter how politely it's done, refusing hospitality hurts their feelings. As Benno says, they don't make them like the Wilcoxes anymore, and they deserve our respect.

They're also devotees of Creative Health Foods, with its drawers of dried herbs and spices. I always have a cup of whatever herbal concoction they've got on offer. This morning's brew, Catherine informed us, was a spring tonic—blessed thistle and red clover laced with honey. It was too sweet, but it must've worked; I felt more alert after a few sips.

I watched the amazement of a first-time visitor cross Inez's face. The living room walls are pale lavender, the wall-to-wall dark purple; the windows are covered by mauve sheers under elaborate drapes. The most prominent decorative elements are a huge birdcage in front of the window and dozens of photographs in antique frames arranged on the long wall above the sofa.

Catherine had had a moderately successful career as a singer. Although she wasn't a famous name, she'd sung backup with the best. The photos, many of them autographed, were a Who's Who of elite black entertainers from the forties, fifties, sixties—including my personal heroine, Nina Simone.

The cage, shaped like a house with a peaked roof, is bird heaven for one green and two blue parakeets—Charlie, Bird, and Parker. Elizabeth refers to them as her dimestore darlings, and they have every avian toy available. Clea would spend hours watching them fly and climb, ring bells, and chew their cuttlebones, if the sisters didn't flutter with worry.

Inez left her tea untasted on the table. "You were acquainted with the deceased?"

Elizabeth's white braids and Catherine's dyed black twist nodded in unison.

"Do you know her name?"

"I believe it was Lillian Raines, Raines with an e, may she rest in peace," Elizabeth said, carefully noncommittal.

"We used to see her in Riverside Park, sitting by the grave of the Amiable Child. Of course, we don't go there anymore, you know, what with Elizabeth's legs…"

"I'm sure the policewoman does not want to know about my legs, Catherine."

Inez kept to the subject. "Do you know why she slept here?"

Catherine opened her mouth, but Elizabeth spoke first. "We wondered, of course, it's only natural. She was a lady, you know, in spite of how she lived, and a person of her breeding, well, it would not have been polite for us to inquire as to her reduced circumstances."

Inez favored her with the same skeptical look she'd given me earlier, like she knew there was more to it.

"Did either of you hear anything unusual in the hall last night?" Inez asked.

Elizabeth tapped her hearing aid, leaving this one for Catherine to answer.

"No, well, no, we wouldn't have, we close our bedroom door, and the windows, too, it's our habit from the time when I performed at night and had to sleep during the day. We use a little fan to stir the air, and then of course the noise helps me sleep…" Catherine trailed off.

"Ms. Raines apparently had a key to the building. Would you know how she got it?"

The way Catherine's hands moved, she could have been auditioning for Lady Macbeth.

Elizabeth looked straight at Inez and said, tartly, "Well, I suppose someone who lives here must have given it to her."

Inez gazed mildly back at her. It was the oldest tactic in the book: give the interviewee enough space, and she'd hang herself. Most people, confronted with silence, get uncomfortable and start inventing.

Elizabeth kept her peace.

Inez closed her notepad. "Thank you for the tea, ma'am. A detective will visit you later today. Please tell him anything you think of that might be relevant."

Myself, I was impressed by the deft way Elizabeth had managed not to answer the question. I knew her well enough to know she wouldn't lie outright, but sins of omission were evidently another matter.

Catherine gripped my arm and stopped me from following Inez out.

"You mustn't say anything about the key to the police, Anita. If Mr. Orton finds out we had anything to do with it, the building will sue us! He said we'd be responsible if anything happened because of her being here, oh, I knew we—"

Elizabeth, the voice of reason, cut her off. "What's done is done, Catherine. They can't prove it was we who gave her the key, but I agree, it's better to say nothing."

"It's awful, just awful, and to think I went out this morning, and the poor thing, lying there and me not even... Oh, I knew no good deed would go unpunished, and now..."

"Catherine, stop dithering. It's that poor unfortunate herself who was punished, and she's beyond suffering now. Anita, were we wrong to help her?" Elizabeth's face was agonized.

I knew exactly how she felt. "No, Miss Elizabeth, I think it was a good, generous thing to do, but you should tell the police about the key."

Elizabeth was politely adamant. "I prefer not to discuss such matters with the police. I don't see that there's anything to be gained by assigning blame for her presence in the building."

That gave me pause. It was like we'd all conspired to let Lillian sleep here, each of us thinking we were doing, if not the right thing, at least a good thing.

IN THE HALL, I saw the commotion had woken another neighbor. Geoffrey Tate, the building's resident alcoholic, leaned on his door frame and blinked at the scene.

From the look of him, my aversion to mornings was nothing compared to Geoff's feeling about being vertical so early in the day. He drooped like a moonflower at noon, crumpled on the vine, his chest bare, hairless except for an arrow of fine strands pointing from his navel down into a pair of bright green sweat pants. His brown socks did a good imitation of dirt, although the dull squint of his eyes kind of ruined the overall effect.

Until the crash of '87, Geoff had been a successful portfolio manager at Merrill Lynch. Now he's a successful drinker who manages, barely, to manage his own portfolio. According to building gossip, he recently came into a trust fund that keeps him in vodka, Chinese food, and women. The girlfriends seem to come and go at sporadic intervals. Benno's theory is that Geoff lures them with drugs when the dividend checks come in, and they abandon him when his funds run low.

For the past few months, however, he seemed to have a steady, a white woman with a reddish ponytail. Her main virtue, in my opinion, was the groceries she brought to supplement the Chinese delivered. Between the improved nutrition and the beard he grew as a happy solution to the problem of shaving with trembling hands, Geoff's been looking better lately.

"What the—?" Geoff ran a hand over his head, standing his brown hair on end. I must have been the first thing to swim into his vision. "Hello, Anita, is something wrong with the sisters?"

Ponytail ducked under Geoff's arm. She wasn't at her best at this hour either, but it was easy to see what Geoff thought was her main attraction: a scattering of freckles danced down into her cleavage, nicely framed by a silky turquoise teddy. She looked to be in her early thirties, a couple decades younger than Geoff. Her pointy chin and the pinch of her mouth seemed at odds with the generosity of her breasts.

"What's goin' on, babe?" She leaned against Geoff's chest, tilted her head to look up at him. Geoff put a hand on her stomach, made a circular, stroking motion. If I'd been interested, I could have seen whether her pubic hair was as red as her ponytail.

Michael came over and addressed them. "Good morning, sir, ma'am. Were you both here last night?"

Ponytail took the cigarette out of Geoff's hand and inhaled. She blew smoke from the corner of her mouth, aiming it vaguely in Michael's direction. "What's it look like to you?" she asked, pleasantly.

Geoff reclaimed his cigarette. "Hey now, don't get your back up. The man just asked a question. Of course we slept here last night. Well, it was more like this morning when we got in. I don't know, maybe three-, four o'clock. So what happened here, Officer?"

I left him to Michael and went to get my purse, lock my apartment door, try again to leave for work.

When I came out, the paramedics had been replaced by several people in dark blue jackets that had Crime Scene Unit printed on their backs. "What do you think happened to her?" I asked Michael.

"From what the paramedics said, most likely she fell and hit her head." He shrugged.

"Fell from where?" I answered my own question. "The top landing? But she never went up there."

The upper landing would have been more private, but it was also much colder—Lillian would have been lying in the path of a serious draft blowing in under the roof door. Okay, so if she didn't fall, how did she get that head injury? I asked myself. Could someone have hit her? Banged her head against the wall? The idea horrified me. She'd died right outside my door—if her death was anything but accidental—

"Why is the crime scene unit here?" I asked Michael.

As if in answer, a camera flashed and I heard the whir of a Polaroid spitting a picture. A young white guy with deep creases around his mouth handed Michael an old-fashioned cloth coin purse. "We found this in her coat pocket."

Michael snapped it open and fished out a Medicare card, a wad of bills, and a business card from St. John Senior Services—my place of employment, three blocks over in the Cathedral of St. John the Divine on Amsterdam.

"I've probably given her half a dozen of those over the past few months," I said.

Michael flipped the card over so I could see the other side. "You write this?"

Emma Franklin, it said, in spidery blue script.

"She's my boss, but that's not her handwriting or mine." Then the coin dropped. "Raines, I knew it sounded familiar. We've got a file with that name in the inactive cases." So all along I'd had access to information that could've helped me to help her, if I'd only persisted in trying to learn her last name.

"Don't leave yet, Anita," Inez said. "I'm sure the detectives will want us to follow up on this."

As if on cue, the elevator door opened. "—the names. Most of the apartments are occupied by elderly, retired people. I hope your men will not cause any undue alarm." Howard Orton, board president, a rotund man in his late sixties, addressed a tall man in a suit with plenty of gray in his short Afro—the detective, I presumed. "Now Mrs. Teague, she's in her eighties and not entirely compos mentis." Howard continued in his methodical way as they got out of the elevator.

He glanced up at the landing and turned away, rocking back and forth, then put out a hand as if for balance. I stepped up and gave him my arm for support.

I got a nod of appreciation from the tall man, but Michael and Inez got his attention.

"Thank you, Anita, I'm all right," Howard ran a hand over his comb-over, what Benno calls "the immigrant hairdo" because it comes from the other side.

I tuned into what the detective was saying. "Yes, yes, you two go to the, ah, the agency and get whatever information they may have. Come back here as soon as you're finished. I'll need you to assist with the, ah, the canvass of the building."

We rode the elevator down, Michael muttering about *bubbes* in *tchotchke*-filled apartments. The melting pot in action, an Irish cop *kvetching* in Yiddish.

COMING OUT OF the elevator, I took a quick, involuntary look up the stairs. Mr. Malinsky, second-floor resident, retired fire fighter, had a habit of lurking like a stick insect on the landing between the first and second floors, where he could keep an eye on the mailbox area. Sure enough, he was up there, an albino praying mantis with long, stiff, jointed limbs.

When he saw us, he pounced. "What's going on upstairs?" Malinsky gripped Michael's arm and stared at him through the bottom half of his bifocals.

Michael grimaced but Malinsky held tight. His hands were large, the hairs between his knuckles extravagantly curly although the hair on his head was cut short and bristly.

Inez answered his question with one of her own. "Do you know anything about the woman who slept on the landing above the twelfth floor?"

"Yes, I am aware of that particular menace to the building. I hope you've come to take her away once and for all." He let go of Michael's arm.

"What makes you say she's a menace, sir?" Inez asked.

"She has no business in this building. She blocks the stairs, which is a health hazard. She presents an obstacle to ready access to the roof in the event of fire. I have spoken with the authorities on numerous occasions regarding this situation."

Mr. Malinsky was off on his hobby horse, Lillian as threat to public safety; I'd heard it all before.

Michael made a pro forma apology for the police department's inability to keep Lillian away, then assured him that she wouldn't be a problem anymore, seeing as how she was dead.

Mr. Malinsky's face flushed momentarily red before he smiled, an unpleasant, triumphant grin. I walked away. I already thought he was a creep, I didn't need to see his delight in Lillian's death to confirm my opinion.

THREE

IN NEW YORK, April is the start of the kindest season. The air was balmy, turning the first corner of summer. It was one of those clear spring mornings that make the city seem like a reasonable place to live—or did, before today. I shivered. My cotton turtleneck and wool blazer did nothing to protect me from the memory of Lillian Raines's bare shoulder, the blood caked around the wound on her head.

We turned the corner to Broadway where the Callery pears were in full flower, up to their ankles in daffodils. Broadway had the look of a bride, the white blossoms marching down the aisle attended by pink magnolias blooming at each end of the islands between uptown and downtown lanes. At the intersection of the cross streets, a scattered mix of tulips, scarlet and yellow, bowed in the breeze.

Spring also brought the homeless population into full bloom. Being accompanied by uniforms made me not exactly invisible—the eyes of the regulars flicked in recognition, then away—but certainly unapproachable. No paper cups were held out to me; the quarters sat quietly in my pocket.

Broadway between 108th and 116th averages two panhandlers per block. They cluster here because it's a student neighborhood, a last bastion of liberals. On the upper left side of Manhattan, the spare change flows fairly freely and there's a wide variety of cheap food. You can get a double-wide slice of pizza for $1.50 at Koronet, two egg rolls for $1.00 at Moon Palace, or the recession special at Mike's Papaya—two hot dogs and a medium drink for $2.00. If you count bun, onions, and ketchup (our ex-president Reagan's favorite vegetable), it even approximates a balanced meal.

Delivery trucks double-parked, unloading cases of paper towels, potato chips, bread, juice, gallon jugs of milk. A line of people waited for coffee and bagels from the cart on the corner. Students clustered outside Tom's Restaurant, reading the menu in the window. Two women with toddlers in strollers stopped to talk in the middle of the sidewalk. It was all business as usual, but today I didn't feel part of the flow.

The smell of coffee reminded me I was operating on a sub-therapeutic dose of caffeine—that is, the dregs of Benno's cold coffee I'd inhaled on my way out the door the first time, with Clea.

"You guys interested in coffee? We could make a quick stop at the Hungarian Pastry Shop," I said.

Inez and Michael looked at each other. "I think that would be okay," Inez said. "Even patrol cops are allowed a cup of coffee."

"Yeah, they have the real thing there," Michael said. "Inez got me hooked on that Spanish coffee, and Hungarian Pastry's the only place serves it south of 123rd. If only they had doughnuts!"

"You mean you don't have croissants with your espresso?" I said, mock-shocked.

"No, he still eats like a cop," Inez answered. "Doughnuts for breakfast, Cuban sandwich for lunch. Very healthy, ham, cheese and roast pork."

"Hey, they put lettuce and tomato on if you ask."

"Which you don't!"

We walked down 112th, enjoying a full-frontal view of St. John the Divine, the rose window a single eye gazing back at us. It's the largest Episcopal cathedral in the world. Construction began in the 1800s and at the rate they're going, it should be finished around the time Clea has grandchildren.

From the Hungarian Pastry Shop, we jaywalked across Amsterdam to the driveway along the cathedral's south side. It's like entering another world, the cathedral grounds. The Canon's

Close, a fenced island of lawn shaded by tall, straight trees with an ornate stone pulpit in the center, has a woodsy feel, with clusters of daffodils and narcissus gone native, along with grape hyacinths, violets, columbine.

St. John Senior Services is an afterthought of an agency, tucked under the stairs to the south transept, in the Crypt— more commonly known as the basement. We share the cathedral's capacious lower level with the kitchen and the barrel-vaulted gymnasium, where the homeless shelter's clientele sets up their cots every night.

Our budget is as small as our three-room office. Although the cathedral's mission is to serve the needy, the elderly are not a marquee population; they don't attract volunteers and donations, as the shelter and the AIDS ministry do. If it weren't for Emma Franklin, our fierce, effective executive director, our line would have been deleted from the cathedral's budget and our space reallocated long ago.

ANNE, THE ADMINISTRATIVE assistant, was force-feeding paper to the balky copy machine. I could never decide who was more of an anomaly in the medieval architecture of the office, Anne or the copier. The machine is nineties sleek; Anne dresses like an eighteenth-century noblewoman.

Anne is nudging fifty, and her personal sense of style got stuck sometime in the hippie era. She wears her light brown hair braided and coiled around her head. Her outfits are composed of flowing layers in variations on a theme color. Today it was yellow, a match for the daffodils in a blue glass vase on her desk. The attention grabber was her vest, egg-yolk satin embroidered in silver metallic thread. It worked for Anne, and I could see it worked for Michael.

"It's about time you got here." She glanced up at us. The copier hummed and spat paper. "What's the armed guard for?"

"Good morning to you too. This is Officer Collazo and Officer Dougherty. Anne Reisen."

"Anne Reisen, Anne Reisen," Michael murmured. "Seems

to me it should be sun risin', que no?'' He spoke to Inez, but he looked at Anne.

Anne ignored him. He was not the first to have made that pun.

"Is Emma around?" I asked. "One of our clients died last night."

"No, thanks to your absence, she's out on a home visit, as is the radiant Debra." Anne did not suffer first-year social work interns, gladly or otherwise, and Debbie is not in any case one of nature's bright lights. "I have been left alone to fend off the ringing telephone. Who died?"

"The lady who slept on the landing in my building. Turns out her name was Lillian Raines and she had a Senior Services card in her pocket. These guys are here to see if we can locate her family with the information we have on her. Did you know her?"

"Waiflike white lady in a black hat and coat?" Anne looked startled. "She hasn't been in here in ages."

Anne's worked here ten years to my two, and she knows our client population as well as Emma does. She shifted her attention away from me and condescended to return Michael's smile. "You're welcome to have a seat while you're waiting." She gestured at the three folding chairs huddled around a low table.

Inez pulled her notepad out of her back pocket and sat. Michael chose the chair closest to Anne's desk and put his coffee down next to the daffodils. Prince Charming in action, he offered Anne a raisin snail. She's a whole-grain muffin woman; I didn't linger to see her response.

THE FILE ROOM is really a closet, just big enough for two file cabinets. Like the office as a whole, its main virtue is the lock on the door. I pulled Lillian Raines's file and read quickly over the face sheet.

Emma had done the intake herself, five years ago. Lillian's address was listed as 506 West 112th St.—the Maramay, known locally as the Bike Building because the delivery "boys" for the neighborhood's Chinese restaurants and pizza parlors leave the tools of their trade chained to the railing in front of the building.

It didn't surprise me that Lillian Raines had lived there. The Maramay started life as a residential hotel; we have clients who moved in when the building was in its glory days and stayed on as it became an SRO, Single Room Occupancy, renting rooms by the month to anyone able to come up with the rent. The newer tenants tend to be transitory—panhandlers, alcoholics, prostitutes, drug users; homeless people and deinstitutionalized mental patients arrive, housing vouchers in hand, from halfway houses, shelters, psychiatric hospitals. Some are clients of the methadone program above Chemical Bank on 113th; others survive off bottle deposits, panhandling, a little dealing, a little prostitution—supplemented by free lunches at Broadway Presbyterian, Riverside Church, St. John the Divine.

I wondered how long Lillian had lived there, and if she still had her room. It would explain where she spent the nights that she wasn't in my building and how she kept herself clean—but if she had a room of her own, why would she sleep in a stairwell? It didn't make sense.

I read quickly over the rest of the face sheet. Other than the basics, it wasn't very informative. Lillian was born on September 23, 1919. *Emergency Contact* was blank. Under *Next of Kin,* Emma had put two question marks—a variation on her personal shorthand that I wasn't familiar with. Almost everyone has at least a great-niece in California or a godchild's grandchild in Minnesota; if there's really no one, Emma uses a zero with a slash through it.

The line for *Referral Source* said Marilyn Dykes—the St. Luke's Hospital social worker responsible for 9B, the unit where they put the old people. *Reason for Referral:* Broken hip resulting from fall on stairs.

Translated, it meant Senior Services would have coordinated things with the discharge planner to ensure that Lillian got the services she was entitled to: Meals-On-Wheels, home health aide, physical therapy. A broken hip is so common, Emma didn't need to spell it out.

The more in-depth, confidential second page didn't add much in the way of solid information.

Initial Assessment: LR is a small, thin, soft-spoken WF who appears competent to evaluate day-to-day needs, although tangential and evasive about personal matters. Possible history of institutionalization and continuing delusional ideation re: son (see history). Not on any medication.

History: LR recently moved to New York City from N. Carolina, ostensibly to look for a son who was "taken from me as a child." At that time, her husband told her the boy drowned and she was responsible for the accident. LR admitted she was a heavy drinker but denied harming her son: "I would remember if my only child drowned." Her husband put her in a hotel (private sanitarium?) which she was not allowed to leave and divorced her. LR said the only time she "felt crazy" was "when they gave me pills." She stated that she no longer drinks, takes "not so much as an aspirin."

LR described her son as "an angelic child" who never cried "because I gave him everything." She believes her husband lied to her so he could remarry and take custody of the child. She would not tell me the name of the "hotel," or discuss the circumstances of her leaving N. Carolina. LR agreed to pay our maximum fee rather than give financial information, stating that her ex-husband had died and left her well off, but "money won't make me or God forgive him." When pressed for more information, she became agitated.

It was intriguing, but with the husband dead and no solid information on the son, I decided to leave it for Emma to decide where the line of confidentiality should be drawn.

I made a copy of the face sheet and put the file on my desk

so I could read through the progress notes and write a final entry. Before I handed the copy to Inez, I added a note to the effect that Lillian had moved here from North Carolina.

"Thanks, Anita. We'll stop off at the Maramay on our way back, show the photo around, and see if our mystery lady still lives there. I'm sure Detective Neville will call Ms. Franklin later this afternoon." Inez looked at her watch. "Hey, partner!"

Michael and Anne were deep into a discussion of the role of a cathedral in the communal life of the Middle Ages compared to the role of this particular cathedral in Morningside Heights in the twentieth century. Anne believed a religious institution could and should be involved in the secular as well as the spiritual life of the community. Michael, reluctant product of a parochial school education, argued that the church should stick to religion. It was too deep for me.

"It's been a pleasure doing discussion with you," he bowed to Anne, "and doing dead people with you, Social Worker." He bowed to me, turned and offered Inez his arm.

She rolled her eyes. "Anita, I'll have your statements typed up later today. When would it be convenient for you and your husband to come in and sign them?"

"I'll have to check with Benno, maybe early tomorrow morning?"

"Yeah, we'll be there, chained to our desks by statements from every *bubbe* in your building." Michael winked at Anne, held the door for Inez.

"THAT'S A NICE MAN," Anne said. "What do you know about him?"

"He's single, if that's what you're after, but don't tell me you of all people are interested in a cop?"

"He doesn't seem like your typical law enforcement type, does he?"

"Actually, I think he's something like third generation on the force. He told me he tried to get out of taking up the family profession, but after doing time as a sail bum in Miami he started to miss the city and the seasons. Which is why he's still a patrol cop at his advanced age.'' Michael's in his late thirties, an easy ten years younger than Anne.

''The uniform suits him, don't you think?''

''Personally, I think he looks a little too much like a TV cop. Tall, dark, handsome, that cleft in his chin.''

''Yes. And those green eyes, that wavy hair...''

I refrained from making a snide remark about flower children being attracted to men in uniforms. I knew Anne's taste in men ran to younger; she maintains that males of the species over forty are a lost cause—too many years of relating to women as inferior objects put on earth for the sole purpose of catering to the needs of men. Younger men, with fewer years of indoctrination, are more appreciative of women as independent individuals. She tells me I'm lucky with Benno—he's very evolved for a forty-five-year-old.

''Hey, don't forget these.'' Anne handed me a half dozen message slips.

I POURED MY COFFEE into a mug from our motley collection and gave it a minute in the microwave while I shuffled through the message slips.

My cubicle isn't much; enough space for a desk with a file drawer that locks, telephone, bookcase, a chair for visitors. The three fabric-covered partition walls provide visual privacy and display space for Clea's artwork. I've got my own window, though, leaded glass with diamond-shaped panes, good for an hour of early afternoon sun. The other amenity in my cube is an electric cup warmer, the perfect modern accessory for the basement of a medieval cathedral where the flagstone floor provides radiant chill and the shabby Oriental carpets do more to improve acoustics than temperature.

I opened Lillian's file to the right-hand side. Reading between the lines of Emma's entries gave a picture of an eccentric, self-contained woman who felt patronized by the agency. It reinforced my impression of her. She wore stockings and gloves; she may have slept in a stairwell, but she didn't see herself in the role of client.

There was, however, one major omission: family. Contacting family members is often the best way to help an elderly person; why hadn't Emma pursued the son, found out about siblings, nieces, nephews? Had she tried, gotten nowhere, and not written it down? Progress notes, as practiced by Emma, are brief and factual—her analyses she keeps in the confidential drawer of her memory. I figured I'd ask her about it later.

It's a fine line, deciding when and how much intervention is necessary with an elderly person. You're dealing with adults, people who've taken care of themselves for sixty, seventy years, lived through a world war or two, a depression. How do you get someone like that to admit she needs help with laundry, bathing, dressing, the activities of daily living she's been doing all her life? Add a dash of dementia, and it would take Solomon to know when to butt in.

None of which made me feel any better about my role in "letting," as Michael put it, Lillian sleep on the landing. I made a brief, final entry and closed the file. I had living clients who needed me.

One of my morning's messages was from my nemesis, Naomi Spivik, who calls every few months. I might have put her off, but she and Neil Patel, another client I did need to see, both lived in the Bike Building.

Going over there seemed like a good idea. An SRO is a closed society and cops are at the bottom of the hierarchy of outside visitors. Cooking on a hot plate is the least of the illegal activities that go on. Police are called strictly as a last resort; there's always a chance they'll get an urge to investigate a situation other than the one they were asked to handle.

Social workers, on the other hand, are at the top of the list because we're able to cope with problematic residents. We bring money and medications; we help with bill paying, arrange doctor visits, escorts, shopping and cleaning services.

If the police were flashing Lillian Raines's photograph around, the news of her death would have the hive buzzing. If

I'd failed her in life, at least in death I could make up for it by helping to locate her family. The cops might run into a stone wall but I've built up relationships with people there, and someone might be willing to say more to me than to them. After all, who would you rather talk to, a social worker or a cop?

FOUR

THE MARAMAY IS a tall red brick building of the same architectural vintage as its neighbors, but it doesn't take the fifteen or twenty bicycles chained to the railing in front to tell it's come down in the world. The limestone wreaths and garlands have been removed from the lower three floors, leaving no potential hand- and footholds that could be used to climb in— or out. The pediment above the door sprouts a scraggly dead tree. It looks like the eccentric aunt who didn't get invited to the wedding over on Broadway.

The elderly residents are like the Maramay's underlying brickwork, stable but crumbling at the edges. They get by on social security, savings, pensions; they suffer from cataracts, arthritis, dementia, weak hearts, broken hips, malnutrition, isolation, depression. Shared kitchen facilities and communal bathrooms add to their difficulties, and expose them to their less-than-scrupulous fellow tenants.

A young Hispanic woman with large gold earrings was on her way out. I caught the front door before it clicked shut and walked in. An alcove on the left housed four pay phones and a soda machine with a steel bar padlocked across its belly. On the right, the manager's apartment had Private Do Not Knock written in an annoyed scrawl on the door. The white tile floor, the Maramay's one remnant of elegance, sported an overpatterning of gray mop swirls.

The concierge's desk, a narrow room behind a Plexiglas window and a counter with a scooped-out space to pass keys, mail, and rent money, is now the manager's office. A warren of open wooden mailboxes takes up one wall; the other has a glass-fronted, padlocked cabinet where extra room keys hang in ragged rows. Everything is painted a faded-urine yellow.

The office is the domain of Frank and Edna Sprague, an Irish couple in their fifties who manage the building. They spend their time barricaded behind the window, drinking spiked coffee, arguing with the residents. The two of them resemble a pair of elongated Easter eggs topped with short, straight, iron-gray hair. Edna, the more gregarious of the two, favors flowered housedresses with large patch pockets for her cigarettes, lighter, keys, a small can of Raid. When it comes to zapping roaches, she can outdraw Calamity Jane.

I let myself in and stopped by the office for the official gossip. My lucky day; Frank and Edna were both there.

"So Anita, you the one sent those cops to see us this morning?" Frank's tone had an edge to it that told me my status as a welcome visitor had taken a nosedive.

"Well, I wouldn't exactly say I sent them. Weren't they trying to find out about a woman who used to live here? Lillian Raines?"

"Yeah, that's what they said. She moved out years ago, didn't leave a forwarding address or nothing. You here to hassle us some more?"

"No, I'm just doing a couple of home visits."

I was intentionally vague. The Spragues know almost everything about almost everyone in the building. I try not to add to their data bank, although I'm not above taking advantage of it. I rely on them to let me know who hasn't been cooking, or coming down for mail. It's information I can use to suggest services a client might be too proud to request.

In any case, I did have arrangements to go over with them, so I changed my opening gambit. "You know Mr. Patel's going in for surgery next week, and I'll be picking up his mail?"

"No problem with the mail," Frank said. "As long as he writes us a note giving permission to release it."

"That's what I'm on my way to get."

"Yeah, we just need to be sure it's all legal. Don't want

anyone accusing us of not taking care of our people, now, do we?'' Frank laughed, but there was a warning somewhere in his voice.

Edna tried to make nice. "Now I thought that was a very polite young man, kept his nose where it belonged and didn't get my other tenants upset. Unlike some of them others.''

It figured that Edna had taken to Michael as a fellow Irishman. In the gorgeous mosaic of New York City, ethnicity trumps occupation. Sometimes.

"Two of 'em came back later, knocking on doors.'' Edna raised her voice in a mocking falsetto. '' 'Did you know this woman? Do you know if she had any relatives?' They had this picture of her, dead. If I hadn't of known it was her, I wouldn't of recognized her. I don't know why they had to bother my tenants. Nobody here knew nothing about her. People here mind their own business.''

Now there was the misstatement of the year. "Did they find out anything?''

"How would we know? That cop didn't tell us nothing, he was so polite!'' Frank said. "And those other ones, 'I'm not at liberty to answer any questions, sir' and 'You'll have to speak with the detective, sir.' Sir my white ass!''

"He said they were having trouble locating her people,'' Edna contradicted him. "He took the paper she filled out when she rented the room, not that it had much on it. She was a quiet little thing unless you touched her and then, watch out!''

"That little old lady had a mouth on her, for sure,'' Frank said.

Yeah, I thought, there's a case of the pot calling the kettle black. Frank went through the side door into their apartment.

Edna took a pack of Salems and a lighter out of her pocket. "I don't think she had a soul in the world. We got to talking about kids one time, you know me and Frank never had any kids, and she told me about her sweet baby boy. From how she talked, I sorta thought he was dead.''

"Did she have any friends in the building?'' I asked.

"Nah, not that I know. She kept herself to herself, know

what I mean? She was a strange duck. I heard she had a pile of money stashed away somewhere." Edna exhaled a stream of smoke and squinted at me.

I shrugged. "Who told you that?"

Edna poked me with an elbow, like we shared a secret. "Oh, I hear things, I hear things. But I tell you, I wish everybody paid their rent on time like she did. Paid in cash, too, like clockwork the first of the month."

I GOT THE WORST over with first, and went to see Naomi Spivik. At ninety-seven, she's a child's nightmare of an old person—hard of hearing, quavery voice, skin like crumpled white tissue paper, hennaed hair with an inch of gray at the roots, and moldy green stumps of rotting teeth surrounded by a smear of red lipstick. Not to mention the dowager's hump, the cane, the strands of costume jewelry that don't hide the food stains on her dress, and the cologne that doesn't cover her lack of hygiene.

She's also a prime example of a person who treats money like we're still in the Depression. Paper shopping bags line the walls of her room, spewing dividend statements from Vanguard, Fidelity, AT&T, Ford, IBM. She could easily afford all the help she needs as well as a mouthful of gold teeth, but she prefers to think of herself as poor and put upon.

The first time I met Naomi, I tried to prioritize her needs. The more questions I asked, the more agitated she got. Her voice rose, she thumped her fist and reiterated her complaints, insisting that I didn't understand, no one understood! Finally I realized she wanted attention, not solutions, and we established a routine: I listen to her vent; she feels better until next time, when we do it all over again.

Her closest relative is a great-nephew, the executor of her will. I spoke to him once and his response was, "She's impossible to deal with, I'll straighten it out after she dies." I almost sympathized with his attitude. I couldn't get her to keep a housekeeper for more than a week, or eat anything other than wonton soup. Her most significant relationship was with a Chinese delivery man. I dread seeing her, although I will admit I'd come to admire the impulse that made her put lipstick on and pin a silk flower in her hair for my visits.

I knocked loudly and waited for her call to enter. Naomi had a habit of leaving her door unlocked during the day. I'd reasoned with her about why it's not a good idea, in this day and age, in this building. She ignored me. It was simply too much of an effort for her to get up and get to the door.

I figured I was in for a long litany of the injustices perpetrated by her neighbors. She surprised me by singing the praises of a young woman, Virginia, who'd escorted her to the hairdresser. Her hair did look better than usual, but her mouth—I could never look at her mouth without shuddering. It was hard to imagine the stumps didn't hurt, but her teeth were one thing she never complained about.

Naomi slapped her hand down on the rickety TV table next to her chair. "I said, I want you to call the police! You're not listening! I said, that young woman is a robber and a thief! I paid her but was that enough? No, she went in my handbag and helped herself. I want you to report her!"

I must have tuned out, because I missed the transition from praise to blame. It seemed the young woman had done what everyone did—stolen from Naomi. Same with the housekeepers: robbers and thieves. It was a wonder she had anything left. No, she hadn't actually seen the woman take her money, but she knew, she knew!

I started my ritual warning about her unlocked door, which Naomi squelched with a scornful, "You think just because I'm old I wouldn't notice if someone walked in here and robbed me blind right in front of my eyes?"

"What about when you go to the bathroom? Maybe someone came in then?"

Naomi fumbled at her necklaces. She located a metal chain, the same kind as Lillian's, with two keys hanging from it. "Do I look stupid? I always lock my door when I use the facilities." She held the keys up and shook them in my face.

I was afraid she'd have a stroke on the spot. I gave up on

reason and promised to call the police when I got back to my office. That satisfied her.

NEIL PATEL, on the other hand, is one of my favorite clients. Born in India before Partition, he's a courteous man with a deep, smooth voice, skin the color of milky tea, a head of thick white hair. His hands are extremely distorted by arthritis, the knuckles at such a slant to his palm that it's all he can do to grip a fairly large object.

An engineer and amateur inventor, Mr. Patel has outfitted his room with conveniences to compensate for his hands. Attached to the arm of the chair where he reads is an adjustable bookstand with a gooseneck lamp and a fat-handled pointer with a rubber tip to turn pages. He can't do buttons or zippers, so I helped him mail-order clothing that closes with Velcro—the greatest invention of the twentieth century, according to Mr. Patel. His big regret is that he didn't come up with it himself.

Mr. Patel has lived in this room for more than fifty years. He has a refrigerator and an illegal toaster oven to reheat his Meals-On-Wheels; it suits him not to have a bathroom or kitchen to keep clean. The rent is cheap and no one cares about the overflow of books, or that every horizontal surface is buried under papers, gadgets-in-progress, and potentially useful scraps of wood, metal, rubber, plastic.

Mr. Patel greeted me with a bow and inquired about my health and that of my family. As soon as we dispensed with the pleasantries, he sat down with his head in his hands.

"Anita, I am very upset." He looked at me from deep black eyes. "The police were here just now. A former neighbor of mine was found dead this morning."

"Lillian Raines?" I asked. "I live in the building where her body was found. You said she was your neighbor? Did you know her very well?"

"We were only acquaintances, because you know she was a very quiet person and I am a very quiet person. She has not lived here for many years, but I saw her only last week. We shared a table at the College Inn. It is a terrible thing, to die so suddenly, but also merciful not to suffer. Do you know what happened to her?''

''The police think it was an accident, that she fell down the stairs.'' I explained about her sleeping in my stairwell. Mr. Patel watched me carefully as I spoke, as if his eyes were reading my words. ''Do you know where else she might have been living?''

''No, we did not speak about where she spent her nights, only about a dream she was having recently, a man watching her while she slept. In my country, they would tell you she was dreaming her death. Perhaps that is why she did not sleep in the same place every night? But you see, changing where you sleep does not change your fate.''

The interpretation of dreams varies from culture to culture, but we all do it.

''I am a rational man. I think this dream came from her subconscious, from her feelings of guilt, perhaps.''

''What makes you say that?''

''She spoke about a son, a child who came to harm. And her husband, she spoke of with bitterness. I think they are dead, both husband and son. Perhaps the man in her dream is her desire to join them?'' Mr. Patel closed his eyes. When he spoke again, his voice came from somewhere far away. ''There is something else I have on my conscience. Mrs. Raines was asking me about a young woman who lives on the fourth floor.''

''A woman on the fourth floor? What about her?''

He opened his eyes. ''Ah, Anita, this young woman pretends to help the old people but really she causes trouble. Of course, if someone works for you, you must pay. But you see, sometimes a bit of money or a piece of jewelry couldn't be found after the woman was there. Old people, we forget things, yes, we lose things, but this was happening very often.''

''And they thought she was stealing?'' It's an old story, aides stealing from ill or addled clients; 99 percent of the time, the missing items turn out to have been misplaced.

''Mrs. Spivik, on eleven, was the first to complain, but no

one believed her." Mr. Patel smiled. "It's not the first time, you know, she has cried wolf."

Just because you're paranoid, it doesn't mean someone isn't stealing from you.

"But others also connected their losses with the young woman. One or two, they told her they would complain to Mr. Frank. She told them, go ahead, and he will evict you."

"Why would he do that?"

"Ah, Anita, he would do whatever she asks him to. We know also that our rooms can be rented for more money than we pay. New tenants mean more money for the owner! Like all of us, Mr. Frank and Mrs. Edna are not getting younger, and I think they are worrying about their job."

"They can't evict anyone without due process. Everyone who lives here is protected by rent control, and the Spragues know it. Let me talk to them. It isn't good to have that kind of thing going on in the building."

"No, you must not do that. You will not stop it, anyway. It is going on all the time. Now he is older, Mr. Frank has to work harder to keep her happy." Mr. Patel winked.

The obvious dawned on me. I could just see it, and this probably wasn't the first time a female tenant had paid her rent that way. Good grief.

"I think I should not have told you, Anita. Now you will be making trouble."

"No, no, Mr. Patel, I'm glad you did. I wish I'd known sooner. If I can't talk to the Spragues, then the police—"

"No, Anita. That is what we do not want. The police—if they come back and see my room, they will be making me leave, and where shall I go? The ladies too, they have perhaps a hot plate, a refrigerator. We do not want the police! Now they know how she is, no one lets her in."

"If Lillian Raines didn't live here, why was she asking about this woman?"

"That is what I do not know. She asked me if I knew this woman, if she could be trusted. The young woman, she cuts the hair, paints the nails." Mr. Patel tried, ruefully, to stretch his fingers out in a display of female vanity. He winced at the effort. "Then she is in the room, she can steal. This is what I told my friend Mrs. Raines."

I remembered Lillian's painted toes. "Do you know her name? What she looks like?"

"Her name is Hilton, I think. Like the hotel. Mrs. Roberts calls her the 'Hotel Queen.' She is skinny and not very pretty. Not like you!"

I let it go, as I did all Mr. Patel's personal remarks.

"I know we should be good citizens and speak up. But we are not so brave, we geezers." He smiled and the sun came out. "And if you tell the police, how will they prove it? No one sees her do it; there is only the word of forgetful old women."

Mr. Patel scratched a signature on the letter of authorization I'd brought, made sure I had the phone number of his emergency contact, Sylvia Chase, who I noticed also lived on the fourth floor, and I said my good-byes.

No one was in the manager's office when I stopped on the way out. I had intended to ask the Spragues about Virginia Hilton. She was helping some of my clients; I could play innocent and say I wanted to thank her in person. It would be counterproductive to antagonize Frank or Edna by confronting them, but with this Virginia—I've had to speak to private-pay home health aides about their treatment of the people in their care before. It's a dicey situation since I have no authority with the aides, but I'm obligated to speak up if I see someone taking advantage of a vulnerable person who can't advocate for herself. Protecting people from abuse, verbal, physical, or financial, is an integral part of my job. Virginia was a slightly different situation, but if she knew I was on to her maybe it would put a stop to what she was doing. It was worth a try.

I had a pang of conscience about not believing Naomi; I owed it to her to take her allegations seriously. When I went to the police station in the morning, I'd make an official complaint on Naomi's behalf. And I'd keep an eye out around the

Bike Building for the Hotel Queen, make an attempt to prevent her from taking further advantage of my clients.

I wondered why Lillian had been asking about Virginia Hilton. It had to be about more than a pedicure, but what could they possibly have to do with each other? The mystery of the lady of the landing deepened. Edna had the idea that she was wealthy, and she'd been able to pay the agency's full fees. The police thought she'd fallen down the stairs, but what was she doing up by the roof?

I thought about how easy it would have been for someone to follow her into my building, knock her down, and steal her money. The scene on the landing—Lillian's bare shoulder, the pile of clothes maybe, or the blood on her cheek…it felt wrong. No purse had been found with her body, that was something else off about the picture. If someone deliberately—what if Lillian had called for help and no one heard her? I couldn't bear to think I'd been so close, and not known.

I paused in front of the cathedral and considered going in for a moment of quiet contemplation. There was a scattering of panhandlers on the steps. I didn't have the heart to dole out my quarters and make eye contact with each of them. I headed for the driveway, giving my entire pocketful of change to a black woman with a paper cup held out in one hand, a book open in the other. She was reading *Great Expectations*. It got me thinking about the situations children could find themselves in when the grown-ups responsible for them were busy elsewhere.

What if I'd sent Clea to get the elevator while I was still in the kitchen, and she'd gone up herself to see what was wrong with the lady of the landing? What if the death wasn't an accident, and—I couldn't go there, not with Clea attached to the thought. My family was entirely too close to where Lillian had died. More even than about Naomi and my other clients, I was worried about Clea.

FIVE

I WORKED LATE that Monday, determined to bring all my case files up to date. I had no chance to talk with Emma; while I was at the Bike Building she'd come and gone, taking Debbie to a presentation on depression in the elderly.

There's more recordkeeping than you might think, in social work. Every phone call has to be noted on the monthly statistic sheet; every contact with client, relative, or other service provider should be recorded in the progress notes. A morning's work can be summarized in two lines: "Ms. X called for escort to Dr. app't. 5/2. Confirmed time with Dr., arranged for Ms. Z to accompany her." The problem is, there's hardly enough time to make the visits and calls, let alone write down what you've done. Which is a reason, but it's no excuse.

I left the office a little past 6:00. I have to admit, the one benefit of daylight savings time is leaving work while it's still light. The driveway can be spooky after dark, with the stone bulk of the cathedral on one side and tree shadows flickering in the lamplight. A luminous crescent moon hung low over the buildings west of Broadway, on its way down into an orange horizon. The air was still warm, promising the start of a spring heat wave. This is my favorite time of day, twilight, when the sky turns a deeper shade of blue and the first stars twink on.

I walked slowly, savoring the light, anxious about entering my building.

As I came down the block, I saw a few of my neighbors hanging out on the front stoop. I consider this to be one of New York City's major amenities, with all the advantages of a front porch plus a better show than any suburb can offer. A few blocks over, in Spanish Harlem, people put out lawn chairs and spend the summer on the sidewalk. It beats an apartment with no air-conditioning.

Our stoop isn't much—four steps leading up to a concrete slab. The outer doors are heavy glass French-style panels with decorative ironwork around the edges. For eight months of the year, Barbara Baker kept the stone planters flanking the stoop full of things that bloom. Right then it was miniature daffodils and thick stalks of purple, pink, and white hyacinths. The air was sweet with their scent.

The presence of Howard Orton indicated a suspension of business as usual. A former city employee, stickler for rules of all sorts, Howard made a crusade of breaking up any cluster in front of the building. "The front stoop shall not be used by the Tenants for lounging or other recreational purposes," it says in our proprietary lease. Clea and I ignore him, incurring his wrath by eating Italian ices on the stoop while we wait for Benno to come home. What could he do, evict us? That's the advantage of being shareholders in a co-op rather than renters.

The people with him were a familiar evening trio: Geoff Tate, dressed for the occasion in a pale yellow polo shirt and chinos, complete with bare feet in battered topsiders; the redhead, in tight jeans and a striped tank top that showcased her assets; Larry Turner, our resident yuppie MBA, a handsome blond with a ponytail and a pearl-gray suit.

Geoff often comes out in the early evening to meet Larry on his way in from work. They hang out and talk Wall Street shop until Howard chases them in, then they retire to Geoff's apartment for drinks.

Extending his suspension of the rules, Howard addressed me. "Good evening, Anita. How are you feeling after your grisly discovery this morning?"

"Tired, actually," I hedged. "Were the police here very long?"

"All morning. They did a very thorough job of asking everyone in the building if they saw or heard anything. They wanted to know how she got in." Howard turned to me. "As to that, I have my suspicions. There are some in this building with soft hearts."

He'd once accused me point-blank of giving Lillian a key, and I was able then as now to deny it with a clear conscience.

"No, Howard, I know you think it was me, but it wasn't. That would be a breach of security." I could be pompous too.

"I've seen you opening the door for her," Larry countered. He leaned one arm against a planter. A miniature daffodil rested its head on his sleeve.

"Did they say anything about how she died?" I sidestepped.

"Naturally, they couldn't say right away," Howard answered. "I did, however, get the impression that her death was not, in their opinion, caused by a heart attack or a stroke. I believe they think it was the result of a head injury."

"Did she fall, or did someone get smart and give her a little push?" Larry raised his eyebrows.

"Pain in the neck," Geoff said. "Smelly old woman, lurking in corners."

"Absolutely," Larry said. "I never approved of her presence in the building. And this incident will definitely have a negative effect on our equity in the building. If a potential buyer hears—"

"Woke me up this morning, all that noise in the hall." Geoff's affability seemed to have made an afternoon turn to belligerence. "And for what? Who cares about some smelly old hag, sleeping on the stairs?"

Geoff sat on the top step, the redhead between his knees on a lower step. He lit a cigarette. His hands shook, and his knees would have too if girlfriend hadn't had her elbows hooked over them. He waved the match out, grazing her hair in the process.

She glared in Larry's direction. "A woman died here, and all you can think about is property values!"

My sentiments exactly, I thought, surprised to find myself agreeing with her. I expected Larry not to see past the tip of his selfish nose, but his and Geoff's attitudes were downright callous. You don't have to like someone to feel pity when she dies.

I looked girlfriend over more carefully. Her hair was loose, held back by a black velvet bandeau. She wore silver rings on all her fingers, a coiled snake with a red eye, turquoise and onyx, a puzzle ring. Her nails were perfect ovals, a burgundy Janis would have died for.

"Yeah, it's a good thing it wasn't somebody who lives here who got pushed down the stairs, or you'd be sued for not providing better security!" She aimed this burst of illogic at Howard.

"Pushed! I'm sure the police didn't say she was pushed. I have, of course, notified the managing agent and our lawyer. I have always been concerned that we might be liable if anything happened to her. I wonder if the insurance—?"

Geoff lurched to his feet, stubbed his cigarette out in the planter. Howard pursed his lips and kept them closed.

"Crazy old lady," Geoff said. "Got what she deserved. C'mon, babe, let's go upstairs. We've got things to do."

Howard removed the butt from the planter and tossed it into the gutter. I lingered, giving them time to go up in the elevator before I went in myself. It was almost dark, and I'd told Benno I'd be home by 7:00.

Larry loosened his tie. "I heard she was filthy rich."

"I suspect that's simply a version of the urban myth about the homeless millionaire who chooses to eat out of garbage cans." Howard chuckled, uncomfortably it seemed to me, but I had to agree with him.

"It gives people an out. If homelessness is a 'lifestyle choice,' they don't have to feel guilty about not giving up their spare change," I said.

"So you don't think our lady's going to turn out to be one of the lost Hapsburgs or Anastasia or something?" Larry said.

I laughed, but that made it three times Lillian's supposed wealth had come up. And the police hadn't found any of her papers, or—I remembered her purse again, actually more like a kind of satchel, that she carried clutched to her chest. If it wasn't on the landing with her body, where was it?

I narrowed my eyes at Larry. "Who told you she had money?"

"I don't know, it was just one of those things you hear around. Yo, Mitzi!" A little dog tumbled up the street from Riverside Park, dragging a red leash. Larry patted down her delighted greeting.

Mitzi's a silky terrier, one of those tiny breeds Benno refers to as "kick dogs" because they make such tempting targets. Her owner struggled up the hill. Margery Clark, a white woman in her sixties, is living proof that at least a dog and a dog owner's hair can grow to resemble each other. Mitzi's coat, a wispy mix of gray, white, and black with tips of rust, does a good imitation of Margery's formerly hennaed shag cut.

Margery picked up the end of Mitzi's leash, with a guilty look in Howard's direction. "Wasn't it awful, what happened last night? I've heard all sorts of rumors, but I'm sure no one in the building would harm that poor woman. Did the police say what happened to her?"

"Who cares?" Larry said. "In my opinion, we're well rid of her."

Margery glared at him. "I know no one in the building liked her, but she was a pathetic old woman who never hurt anyone."

"No," Larry said, "she never hurt anyone, but her presence was definitely a liability. A lawsuit could ruin this building financially. Even when she was alive, who wants to buy an apartment with a homeless woman squatting in the stairwell?"

"I don't know how you can be so concerned about—"

I tuned out. Larry was as bad as Mr. Malinsky. "Just one of those things you hear around"? If the Hotel Queen knew about Lillian's supposed wealth... Did she fall or was she pushed? Now I was having suspicious, uncharitable thoughts about my neighbors, too. Enough was enough. I nodded at no one in particular and let myself into the building.

PERCHED IN THE top-front corner of the building, our apartment has the far-seeing ambiance of a crow's nest. From the time I first came to New York to take care of my mother's mother, it's been a safe harbor. I used to lie in bed, listen to my grandmother's raspy breathing, stare out over the Hudson, and imagine I could sail across the continent to California if I wanted.

Which I didn't. The city held me like flypaper; once I set foot here, I got stuck. I love the coffeeshops, the subway, sitting among strangers where white is only one option in a range of skin tones and ethnicities I can't even guess at. Here, people assume I'm anything from Hispanic to Hungarian, not just the mongrel American I am.

I lived with my grandmother for two years before she died and left me the apartment. Benno and I had known each other for barely six months when he gave up his rent-stabilized studio apartment in the Village—the New York equivalent of a long-term commitment—and moved in with me.

We were married a year later, when we needed to be legal in order to get Clea. At the time, there was what the nightly news referred to as the Boarder Baby Situation: healthy newborns whose mothers were addicted to drugs or otherwise unable to care for them were being boarded in hospitals because there was no place else for them to go. We applied to be foster parents, reasoning naively that it would be a good way to adopt.

In spite of its two bedrooms, great light, and river view, the apartment is less than 650 square feet. That we stayed here after getting Clea is due strictly to the realities of the Manhattan real estate market: we couldn't afford anything bigger.

Benno is an architectural woodworker, a skill in high demand in this town where people don't build new, they renovate. When he has time between paying jobs, he's slowly replacing my grandmother's ornate furniture with Deco-influenced built-ins made of bird's-eye maple, walnut, ash, mahogany. Even more now, the apartment is an island of calm above the city, with Benno my security, the roots that keep me safely anchored. Half Italian intellectual, half Polish peasant, all Jewish,

Benno's European sophistication balances what he calls my flights of California liberal kookiness.

Getting out of the elevator on the twelfth floor, I got a sick feeling in my stomach. A crisscross of yellow tape blocked the stairs going up, a pointed reminder that coming home might not be so safe anymore.

The smell of Benno's cooking reached out to comfort me. I identified the aroma: stir-fry. I cook to feed; Benno cooks with flair, and every pan in the kitchen. One of his culinary shortcuts is adding an order of Chinese roast pork from the Wok Inn to vegetables and black bean sauce.

"Mama, Mama, Mama! Mama's home!" Clea chanted. She cannonballed into me and wrapped herself around my legs, giving me the greeting usually reserved for Benno—the parent she hadn't seen all day.

"Okay, okay, let me put my purse down!" I picked her up, which was getting to be not such an easy thing to do. She weighs about fifty pounds, most of it legs and squirm. She weighed just under seven pounds when we got her, delivered to our door by a social worker in a taxi when she was six days old.

Clea's birth mother is mentally ill; no one thinks she'll ever be able to take care of Clea, but the laws are stacked in favor of the property rights of biological parents rather than the best interests of the child. Five years later, we're still caught in the nightmare bureaucracy of Family Court and the foster care system.

Clea's African-American, skin the color of chocolate chips, the apple of our eyes. With his olive skin, Benno could more easily pass for one of Clea's biological parents than I can, although my hair is more like hers—black, thick, the kind of curly that's torture to brush.

"Did you have fun at the shop with Daddy?"

"Come see my castle!" She pulled me into her room.

Benno's method of keeping Clea busy is to deposit her on a big worktable with the contents of his scrap barrel and a bottle of yellow glue. Her elaborate constructions were usually too big to bring home. This one was no exception; Benno must have been in a good mood, to have schlepped it on the subway. It sat on the floor, a square of plywood with blocks of various hardwoods piled into walls and towers. Winnie-the-Pooh, Piglet, and Eeyore were already in residence, along with two rubber sharks and a whale. I nodded and admired, but my thoughts were elsewhere, distracted and uneasy.

THE MORNING'S EVENTS didn't come up until I tucked Clea into bed. She sleeps in a Benno design—a reverse loft desk/bed, with the desk and a bolted-down swivel chair enclosed by a low railing of bookshelves on a platform above the foot of the bed. As Benno says, in New York you can't build out so you have to build up.

I turned off the light, sat beside her, started our bedtime ritual of "telling the day."

We're a modern family—in the absence of a unifying tradition, we've made our own. Although Benno's mother kept a kosher household, he gave up religion long before his parents died; he describes himself as a spiritual atheist. My lapsed-Catholic mother raised me without input from organized religion. As a teenager I shopped around in Eastern beliefs. Nothing took, but my spiritual expression tends toward alternative, holistic, earth-and-goddess worship.

Between us, Clea's upbringing is eclectic to say the least. Jewish and Italian culture from Benno; a dose of Episcopal doctrine at school; and me, I make it up as I go along. I invented "telling the day" when she started preschool, as a way for us to touch base after a day apart.

"This morning we woke up late so we had to hurry. You noticed something was wrong with the lady of the landing. I called an ambulance while you watched 'Mr. Rogers.' Then you went to the shop with Dad and made a big construction and brought it home. Dad cooked supper and I came home and we ate. You brushed your teeth and put on your nightie and now we're telling the day and it's time to go to sleep." I kissed her forehead and got up to go. No such luck.

Clea's arms snaked around my neck. "Mama, is the lady in the hospital?"

"No, the lady was very sick and she died." I didn't want to scare Clea, but I don't believe in lying to children. Misinformation is worse than no information. I could feel her trying to figure out what question to ask next, so I added, "Now they'll have a service for her, you remember, like when we went to the temple after Dad's cousin Marvin died?"

"I didn't like that place. Do we have to go?"

"You were kind of bored, weren't you? No, we won't go to the lady's service, that's only for family. I love you." I kissed her again and this time it worked.

BENNO HAD CLEARED AWAY the remains of dinner and done the dishes. For this kind of treatment, I could be tempted to find a dead body every day. We sat on the couch, had a second glass of wine, did our own version of telling the day.

"Did Clea seem upset about what happened this morning?" I asked.

"No, not really. You know our girl, out of sight, out of mind."

"I told her Lillian was dead. She took it in, but I think we should open her bedroom door a crack tonight in case she has a bad dream."

"We got a lecture about closing the outer door downstairs from the mayor of 111th Street when we came home." Benno gave Howard Orton his unofficial title.

"Did he write you up in the dread red notebook?"

"Probably. 'Mr. Servi came in with the little girl at six p.m. and told me to shove it up my ass.'"

"You didn't!"

"No, but it was an effort. Howard should have been a blackmailer—or the next best thing, a Park Avenue doorman."

Howard lives in the front apartment and he knows everything that happens on the block as well as in the building. He makes a hobby of monitoring mail and going through the recycling bins to find out who drinks what and how much. We thought his curiosity was a harmless alternative to daytime television until Benno found a spiral notebook in the laundry room.

Normally, Benno's fastidious about other people's privacy but when he saw it belonged to Howard some imp of curiosity bit him. He was shocked and appalled to find a surveillance log, complete with date, time, and commentary on all our comings and goings. In my opinion, it bordered on the obsessive.

"He's probably recovering from writer's cramp after all the action this morning," I said.

"Malinsky was out there with him, going on about the indignities he'd suffered from the police, muttering about 'that woman,' and 'certain elements in the building.' I think he was referring to people like us, the Clarks, the Wilcoxes—you know, the bleeding hearts." Benno lowered his voice in imitation of Malinsky. " 'Those policemen were very rude. I told them if I'd known she was here last night I would have escorted her off the premises personally. She posed a serious fire hazard, blocking the stairs to the roof. For many of us, those stairs are the only access to the fire escapes…' "

I snickered. Being a retired fireman, Malinsky delights in lecturing on the dire consequences of living in a building where every apartment doesn't have a fire escape. The fact that he lives on the second floor does nothing to quench his enthusiasm for scaring everyone else. Benno had his spiel down perfectly.

"Then Howard started in about how he did his best to keep Lillian from sleeping here, but you know he was too much of a wimp to confront anyone. I don't understand why they got so hot and bothered—bunch of control freaks, retired fussbudgets with nothing better to do than police their neighbors and give our female Super a hard time. Remind me not to get like that when I retire."

"As if you'd ever retire from woodworking!" I sometimes wonder who Benno is more attached to, me or his hand tools. "I just wish I'd been able to help her."

"You did what you could, Anita. She didn't want your help any more than she wanted your leftovers or your soup. I told you, it was a waste of good food."

"I know, but I kept hoping she'd accept *some*thing." In the first months after Lillian appeared on the stairs, part of my outreach efforts included leaving food for her. As far as I could tell, she never touched a mouthful.

"I wonder if the police found out why she slept here," Benno said.

"All day, I've been hearing rumors that she was rich." I was thinking out loud. "According to Howard, the police said it was an accident, but I'm not so sure. Did you see her body? Her skull was dented like a hard-boiled egg hit with a spoon."

"Anita. You're a social worker, not a doctor or a cop. Leave it to the professionals to figure out what happened to her."

I was getting a husband look, the one that says "You're cute, but you don't know shit from shineola about the real world."

I made a strategic retreat. "Margery Clark said she couldn't imagine anyone hurting the poor woman."

"What do you expect from a former missionary with a kick dog? Margery sees the good in everyone." Benno bumped me out of his lap and went to brush his teeth.

I followed him to the bathroom. "I've always wondered why the sisters took care of her. Do you think maybe they knew each other from the past?"

"I suppose it's possible, but don't you think they would've said?"

I held out my toothbrush for Benno to squeeze paste on it. "I don't like it, her dying here. What if she called for help and we didn't hear her?"

"Brush your teeth and come to bed, Anita of my heart. Some things are out of anyone's control. The lady of the landing wasn't your responsibility, and in any case the police are dealing with her now." Benno spat and rinsed. "The way you need to take care of everyone, I'm sure you've got a Jewish mother nesting somewhere in your family tree."

Actually, I suspected it was a Jewish father, although my mother would never tell me anything about him other than that he'd died before I was born and she'd loved him very much.

My looks are Semitic, and as Benno says, my personality has a superstitious Eastern European aspect to it. I rinsed those thoughts out of my mouth and tried to decide how I felt toward Lillian Raines.

The task of the old is to sum up their lives, come to terms. In the course of my job, I've had to accept the obligations imposed by the dead on the living. I'd cleaned out apartments, sorted through the mementos of a lifetime—a set of Limoges with faded gold filigree, wooden abacuses from China, hand-painted lacquer trays from Poland, a tarnished silver tea service, a collection of African cloth dolls with cowrie shells in their hair.

That's the part of my job I love, getting to know people, drawing out the stories attached to each object, finding pattern and meaning at the end of long lives. Lillian's life, however, had been closed to me. I'd been content to leave it that way, until I stood over her fragile body and felt the pull of the dead: Remember Me. Her death seemed to have opened a door and drawn me in. I couldn't stop thinking about her.

I was afraid I'd have trouble falling asleep, but Benno reached for me in the dark. His hands under the covers stroked away the image of Lillian lying alone on the landing and transformed Thanatos into Eros.

SIX

Crud Report 315 from Crusading Crud-Buster
To: All Shareholders
Re: Intruders, Invaders, and Avoiders of Responsibility
Purportedly, the Bored Directors and the Mismanaging
Agent installed an additional intercom system for the ex-
press purpose of keeping intruders out of the building. As
I have previously pointed out, an intercom system alone
is not adequate. Unfortunately several residents, whom I
am forced to call my fellow shareholders, continued to
allow an invader to have access to the building. The Bored
Directors and Mismanaging Agent remained unconcerned
about the dangers of having a Crud Creator take up residence in our common area. This invader, in addition to
depositing her crud on our stairs, presented a serious obstacle to accessing the roof as a means of exit in the event
of a fire. Now that this obstacle has been removed, I re-
spectfully request a written response detailing what those
charged with safeguarding our premises intend to do to
ensure that no further invasions occur.

IT WAS VINTAGE Malinsky, the memo slid under everyone's
doors in the early hours. Usually I didn't bother to read his
venom. In the wake of Lillian's death, however, it had a sinister
tone. What if Malinsky had taken matters into his own hands
during one of his night-owl perambulations? I didn't like sus-

pecting my neighbors and not feeling safe in my own building. I put the memo in my purse to show to the detective.

IT WAS A GORGEOUS DAY, supposed to be in the eighties later. We dropped Clea at school and caught the M11 northbound on Amsterdam. I put my head on Benno's shoulder, closed my eyes, and actually slept for the ten-minute bus ride to the Twenty-sixth Precinct. Expecting the usual delays of bureaucracy, we picked up coffee to go from EJ's Luncheonette on 125th.

The precinct house looks exactly like what it is, a bunker built in the sixties, two stories of yellow brick with arrow-slit windows. Inside the front door, a white satin banner with tarnished gold fringe says Welcome to the 26th Precinct. At 8:30 there were already two people in line ahead of us at the information window. A young black woman with a baby in one arm and a toddler in a stroller was complaining, loudly, about how was she supposed to get her mail if the mailboxes in the building had no doors and people stole it? The officer at the window, a slender blonde who looked too young for the job, told her to have a seat.

"Bureaucracy in action," Benno said. "Sit and wait, we'll get to you whenever we damn well please, preferably tomorrow."

We got lucky; Inez walked by. "Anita, Benno, *ay,* I tried to telephone, but you must have left already. At least you were smart enough to bring your own coffee. Come on in back."

It wasn't exactly a warm welcome.

We followed her into a room with a row of molded plastic chairs bolted to the floor in front of a long, battered table. A philodendron reached for the sky in a far corner. Inez gestured us to the chairs, then disappeared down a corridor.

"I knew it," Benno said. "The long arm of the law doesn't know what its left hand is doing, and we came up here for nothing."

"You're jumping to conclusions as well as mixing metaphors," I told him.

In the corner opposite the philodendron, which on closer inspection turned out to be plastic, stood the only items that didn't look like they lived in a war zone: three shiny vending machines. We drank our coffee while a rainbow coalition of men and women in blue uniforms fed dollars into the machines and went off with juice, coffee, candy bars, cinnamon rolls. A healthy, well-rounded diet.

Benno nudged me. "Notice how the cops here reflect the community?"

"So, no one's denying that there are black and Hispanic cops. This is Harlem, remember? The Midtown and Upper East Side precincts probably reflect their neighborhoods just as well—all white."

"And in Chinatown, a majority of the cops are probably Asian. Isn't that the point, that the cops should represent the community?"

"No, the point is that the white residents of Park Avenue can be served just as well by an African-American cop as by a WASP."

It's an old debate with us. I believe in taking a color-blind approach; Benno thinks there's nothing wrong with emphasizing one's ethnic heritage. Given our family constellation, it's a moot point. We each use Clea's fondness for marinara sauce to bolster our arguments.

Inez broke it up. She put a manila folder on the table and took out two typewritten sheets. "It appears that Ms. Raines' death was accidental after all. I tried to catch you—" She raised one shoulder in a shrug. "Since you're here, please read these over carefully and sign at the bottom."

"An accident?" I said. "That dent in her skull was an accident?" Benno kicked me. I ignored him. "Could someone have hit her? I mean, what if someone followed her into the building, or—there were people who didn't like her sleeping there—look at this." I pulled out Malinsky's screed.

Inez read it over. "Look Anita, I know you're upset. You found the body, you feel responsible for not doing more to help her while she was alive. This guy sounds like a harmless kook, but if you want I'll pass it on to Neville.''

I calmed down. ''If he's here, do you think I could see him? There's something else I want to talk to him about.''

''I can't promise anything, but let me ask.'' She went off again.

Benno wagged a finger in my face. ''Anita, you are out of your little mind. If the police think it's an accident, who are you to question their findings?''

That finger always gets my dander up. Benno knew it, too. ''Do what you want, but I'm not sticking around to back you up. Or bail you out when they lock you up for lunacy!'' He kissed my cheek and split.

''Ah, yes, Mrs. Servi?'' Detective Neville came in with hand outstretched. It was a large, firm hand, with skin as soft as the lilt of island accent in his voice. He looked to be in his late fifties, a dark-brown man with a neat mustache and the build I think of as typical cop, tall and broad.

''Thank you, thank you for coming in. I have, ah, I have read your statement about the events of yesterday morning. I understand you asked to speak with me? Please, come this way.''

He ushered me into a room with cinder-block walls painted the color Pepto-Bismol would be if it were green. It was enough to make even the innocent confess. He offered me a seat at a gray metal table, and a jelly doughnut to go with what was left of my coffee. I flashed on Persephone in the under-world, seduced by food.

Living in the People's Republic of Berkeley, I spent my early adolescence throwing rocks at cops, dodging nightsticks and tear gas. In those days, cops were pigs. A primal unease at being in the belly of the beast rose in me. A bumper sticker from the sixties swam into my head: ''Next Time You Get Mugged, Call a Hippie.'' I wouldn't go so far as to say some of my best friends were cops now, but I reminded myself that the times had changed. I took a bite.

"I was wondering if you found out any more about what happened to Lillian Raines, or located her family?" I asked.

Neville's eyes smiled at me but his mouth stayed serious. "As Officer Collazo has said, at this point we believe Lillian Raines' death was accidental, caused by a fall from the top of the stairs to the landing where she was found. What with her, ah, her general condition, her previous history of falling..."

Bureaucrat-ese for "I did my job, why are you civilians bothering me?"

"Excuse me, Mrs. Servi, but what is your interest in this person?"

Benno's point exactly. I tried to explain it, as much to myself as to Neville. "It's not every day that a former client of my agency dies practically on my doorstep, and in mysterious circumstances."

Neville cleared his throat. "'Mysterious circumstances'? I appreciate your concern, Mrs. Servi, but I must caution you against forming hasty conclusions. We don't know what state of mind Ms. Raines was in at the time of the incident. She may have been agitated, behaving in an unusual manner."

"Did you find her purse?"

"Purse? No, no such item was found. Perhaps you could describe it for me?"

Neville made notes on the back of the Crud Report while I told him about Lillian's satchel, black leather, square, with buckles and a long strap.

"Thank you, Mrs. Servi. We will look into the matter of a bag. It could, of course, be helpful in locating her family, if she had one. As to the nature of her death, as I said, until the complete autopsy results are in we won't be certain. Thus far, however, we have found nothing which would lead us to suppose her death was anything other than an unfortunate accident." Neville flipped the Crud Report over and waved it at me. "There are certainly some odd characters in your building. 'Bored Directors,' I like that. But surely you don't read it as a confession?" Neville's mouth joined his amused eyes.

First Benno, now Neville. I don't like not being taken seriously. I took a sip of cold coffee, put the lid back on the cup, and pushed it away from me.

"Was there something in particular you wanted me to know about this Mr. Malinsky?" Neville surprised me by soliciting my opinion.

I took a deep breath. "There was an incident last fall. I came in late and Mr. Malinsky was by the mailboxes, kicking at something and sneering 'Get out of there, you filth!' I thought he'd cornered a water bug. When he saw me, he backed off, and Lillian stood up. I put my hand on her arm to see if she was all right. She screeched at me like I was the one who'd kicked her, then she scooted off down the hall. I figured she was okay, but I told Mr. Malinsky if he ever touched her again I'd report him to the police. I called Protective Services, but they didn't do anything."

"Yes, I understand your concern, Mrs. Servi, but the incident you refer to was some time ago and as it was not repeated…" Neville paused. "Was there anyone else who had strong, ah, strong feelings about Ms. Raines' presence in the building?"

"Howard Orton, the board president, wanted whoever saw Lillian to call the police every time she showed up. It was mostly us on the twelfth floor who knew she was there. We're basically a live-and-let-live floor, and no one bothered. Lillian wasn't obnoxious or dirty; we all had warm beds, why shouldn't she? It seemed like the least we could do, so many people sleeping on the street. It was sort of like she was the building's contribution to helping the homeless."

"Ah, yes, the homeless." Neville turned his palms down, rested them on the table. A thin gold band bit into the flesh of his ring finger. "I, ah, I spoke with Ms. Emma Franklin and I understand that Ms. Raines had a history of mental, shall we say, mental instability. I must say, Mrs. Servi, I find it odd that you seem more concerned about Ms. Raines now that she is deceased than you were while she was alive." Neville said it gently enough, but he hit my sore spot.

"People think social workers have the power to force people

to do what's good for them, but this is a free country, people have rights. Lillian Raines valued her independence. If it led her to sleep in a doorway or a stairwell, she was—well, she was dignified about it." My eyes were starting to vibrate with the color of the walls. "What I'm worried about is, what if Mr. Malinsky or someone in the building had an argument with Lillian? I don't think anyone would intentionally hurt her, but what if it got out of hand?"

"Surely there were other ways to handle the situation?"

"Yeah, right, the building could have pressed charges on her for trespassing, which would have done nothing but run up the lawyers' fees." I glared at Neville, but it wasn't his fault. "In retrospect, yes, I should have tried harder, but it was a judgment call. I felt she was entitled to her privacy."

"Privacy? A stairwell is hardly what I would think of as private, Mrs. Servi."

You can question authority, but arguing with it is futile. I remembered the main reason I'd wanted to see him. "I did some home visits in the Bike Building yesterday—"

"That would be the Maramay, where Ms. Raines formerly had her room?"

"Yes, but that wasn't why I was there." Well, not exactly. "Two of the residents told me about a problem they've been having in the building." I passed on Naomi Spivik's complaint and what Mr. Patel had told me about Virginia Hilton. I left out the part about her affair with Frank Sprague. Infidelity may be immoral but it's not illegal.

The public-relations smile on Detective Neville's face never wavered. We could have been discussing the glorious spring weather. In response to Naomi's complaint, he said, "Yes, these elderly ladies who accuse their aides of theft. Spivik, Naomi Spivik, the name is familiar. Perhaps I've spoken with her concerning a previous incident. You must understand, without witnesses it is almost impossible to prove that a theft occurred. I will, however, I will have Officer Collazo and Officer Dougherty make inquiries."

Which was pretty much exactly what I'd expected the official response would be. I didn't say anything.

"We will, of course, we will do what we can. I simply caution you that we may not be able to entirely solve the problem."

In other words, as with Lillian, Naomi was a crazy, unstable old lady: case dismissed. It's how our society often reacts to the concerns of older people. I'd done it myself.

He sat up like it was getting to be time to go.

It was, indeed, for me. "And what about Lillian Raines?" I matched the coolness of his tone.

"The case will remain open until we have the final autopsy results. It may take a few days, it may take a week or more. For people who die without family as Lillian Raines did, as you have perhaps experienced in your line of work, the Medical Examiner is not in a hurry."

WAITING FOR THE BUS in the warm April morning without some superior male there to mock me, I thought it over. Who knew what motivated Lillian? Maybe she went to the top of the stairs—to hide her purse? to undress in private?—and lost her balance, plunged down to the landing. Then draped her coat over her own body like that, crosswise, instead of pulling it up? And what *had* happened to her purse?

Well, Lillian's death wasn't a closed case yet. While the police were waiting for the autopsy results, I could pursue her family. I'd done it before, tracked down a distant relative for a client. Of course, I'd had a little more to go on, but…I hadn't had a chance to talk to Emma yet; she might well know more than she'd written in the file. Or maybe Edna Sprague would recall something else about Lillian, or I'd find someone else in the Bike Building who knew her background.

As for Virginia Hilton preying on the old people—in the real world, equal treatment under the law is a relative concept. Despite the best of intentions, the poor, the elderly, people of color, people without power, are not treated with the same consideration extended to white, wealthy, connected people. At least Inez and Michael would be looking into the matter of the Hotel Queen, which was a relief. I didn't necessarily want to confront her myself, especially if she'd had anything to do with what had happened to Lillian Raines.

And I was free to see if I could turn up some additional information to help the police along. I'd have a better shot at convincing someone among Virginia's victims to report her than the police would. I'd failed Lillian; I was determined not to fail Naomi.

I got on the bus, dipped my MetroCard, took a seat, and considered my neighbors. Could one of them have harmed Lillian? The mere possibility worried me. Lillian wasn't the only perceived nuisance in the building. Clea's not exactly the world's quietest child, especially when she skips rope in the hall on rainy days. And the Wilcox sisters, they put birdseed out on the ledge. Pigeon poop was also a recurrent theme in Malinsky's Crud Reports. What if he finally decided to get rid of such annoyances himself? I had to be sure that my family, my daughter, were safe in our own building.

I got off the 104 on Broadway at 112th so I could stop by Mama Joy's to pick up lunch. I had my mind set on a roast beef wedge—a hero stuffed with rare meat, onions, lettuce, sweet pepper slaw, oil, vinegar, salt, pepper, the kitchen sink. It's two day's worth of lunch, and I felt I'd earned it.

TUESDAY IS Anne's weight-lifting day at the Columbia gym. She made no bones about being glad to see me when I got to work. "Good thing you're back, Ms. I'll-be-in-by-ten. The phones have been ringing all morning, and I didn't want to leave Emma to handle things by herself." She handed me a stack of pink slips.

"Good morning to you, too. I got held up at the precinct. Is Emma here?"

"They giving out brains at the Twenty-sixth today? How could I leave her by herself if she wasn't here? I'll be back by two, myself." She was gone in a swish of lavender.

If you ask me, the only advantage Emma's job has over mine

is her office. Her salary isn't much bigger, and she's got all the headaches of administration and fund-raising along with carrying a caseload. Her office, on the other hand, is a wonderful room with wood-paneled walls, a stone ceiling, a door that closes.

The casement window has a long stone sill protected by a spiky, twisted hedge of crown of thorns, its gray branches studded with flowers red as cautionary drops of blood. An Easter cactus in a wrought-iron stand was putting on its annual show of long white blooms with magenta tongues. It's almost enough to make me believe in the Resurrection.

I poked my head in her open door.

"Come in, Anita, sit." Emma gestured to the chair beside her rolltop desk. The desk has belonged to the cathedral for generations and looks it, but I covet the slots and drawers that keep her organized. "How are you holding up?"

"I'm okay." As soon as I said it, I realized I wasn't. Emma had the professional caregiver's genuine concern in her voice, and it reminded me of my mother, a private-duty nurse. Between lack of sleep, a corpse, and the police station, okay was really not the word for how I felt. I wanted to lay my head on her shoulder and weep.

Instead, I asked, "Do you have time to eat lunch with me?"

"Of course, you poor kid. Put the kettle on and I'll be right there."

We sat at the little table opposite the counter. Emma took her glasses off and held them up to the light. "Either I'm getting cataracts or these glasses are filthy."

It's an occupational tic of working with the elderly, worrying about the symptoms of aging yourself. Memory lapses can be a symptom of CRS—Can't Remember Shit. Emma, however, is in her sixties. When she says she's having a "Senior Moment," she is.

I took her glasses and looked through the lenses myself. "Let me wash them."

"No, no, don't baby me. Sit, Anita, tell me what's bothering you."

I gave her a brief synopsis of my morning at the police station.

"Well, I must say I think the detective is taking the sensible approach. People are always in a hurry to think the worst when someone dies suddenly. I'm sure she just lost her balance and tumbled down the stairs, and that's what I told him."

Emma's sympathetic blue eyes made me wish I agreed with them. "I know I'm an amateur, but Emma, if you'd seen her head, and the blood…"

"Yes, death can be messy, and head wounds do produce quite a lot of blood. In any case, Anita, it's useless to speculate." Emma gave me one of her trademark searching looks. "Are you blaming yourself? Thinking that if you'd found her sooner, you might have saved her?"

Tears caught in the back of my eyes. I bent my head so Emma wouldn't see.

"Come now, guilt is an absolutely useless emotion. Even if she had recovered, think what her life would have been like after a severe head injury."

People are always talking about "quality of life" for the elderly, as if it could be measured and quantified from the outside. To me it's a subjective state, determined only by the person whose life it is. I watched my grandmother struggle for breath, saw how much she hated the portable oxygen tanks, but she didn't intend to miss a minute of the life she was granted. I raised my head. Emma met my gaze. We've debated this issue before.

I changed the subject. "What was Lillian Raines like, as a person?"

Emma sighed. "She was rather aloof. I never felt I made contact with her."

"I didn't either. She radiated an aura of invisibility—except I saw her go off once, when the cops came to take her away. She called them Nazis." I put my sandwich down. "Emma, do you know if she was Jewish?"

Emma did the same double-take and pause as I had when Michael asked me the same question. "No, I don't think she was. She came from North Carolina, I believe, and somehow one doesn't think of southerners as being Jewish. Really, Anita, what a question."

Emma actually blushed. I wasn't the only one who'd unconsciously stereotyped Lillian.

"The case file mentioned a son. Do you know anything about him?"

"Yes." Emma took her glasses off again, rubbed the bridge of her nose. "I mean, no. I believe he died as a child, possibly as the result of negligence on Lillian's part. It wouldn't be possible today, but in the forties and fifties, heavy drinking was a way of life rather than a disease, the way we view it now. If she were from a wealthy family and she'd accidentally hurt her child, they might well have been able to confine her in a sanitarium in order to hush up what would have been regarded as a family tragedy, not a criminal matter."

"I thought there might be something you didn't write down, about her family or her finances. I heard a rumor that she was well off. The police didn't find any bank information, or an address book or any identification."

"Didn't they? Well, I suppose she'll be buried in Potter's Field." Emma's a devout pragmatist; once it's over, it's over. She got up to wash her glasses.

"They didn't do any more than go through the motions. She was a nobody, it was an accident, and that's the end of that."

"Anita," Emma put her glasses on, turned her blue eyes my way. "That's the guilt talking. You are not responsible for Lillian Raines' death any more than you were responsible for her when she was alive. We do what we can, but ultimately the client determines her own destiny."

"I know. I just thought if I could locate her family, maybe I could understand why she lived the way she did." I'd expected Emma to be more concerned.

"Anita, really, you need to let it go." Emma gave me an amused, tolerant version of the smile I'd gotten from Benno and Neville. "Now, I've got a funding proposal to finish so I can keep the wolf from the door."

She left her lunch things on the table for me to clean up. I threw the napkins in the trash, washed the plates, made another cup of coffee, and took it into my cube. I still had the day's work to do.

SEVEN

TUESDAY AFTER LUNCH, the least cosmic time of the week. Nothing memorable has ever happened on a Tuesday afternoon after lunch, according to my mother, and if it ever did no one would notice. I use Tuesday afternoons for home visits; it gets me out of the office.

Some social workers hate visiting. They're afraid of the neighborhoods; they don't like intruding on people. I enjoy it. You learn infinitely more about how a person manages when you see where she lives, what she eats. A client can sit in your office and tell you she had a bowl of cereal with a banana for breakfast, but if you look in the fridge and find only a stick of butter and a container of orange juice with a six-week-old expiration date, you get a better picture. People know how to say what social workers want to hear; dust and clutter tell the real story.

Home visits also give me the chance to see some great places. I have clients who live in three-bedroom, prewar apartments, rent-stabilized at such low rates it's cheaper to stay put than move. That is, if any of them had the energy to pack.

Another of my mother's axioms is that people expand to fill however much space they have. Condensing a large apartment's worth of stuff to fit into a studio is more than most people can face, let alone people in their eighties, understandably reluctant to dredge up memories stored in the back closets of a lifetime.

I chose to work for Senior Services because it's a community-based organization in my own neighborhood. Benno teases me about my greater metropolitan area being bounded by 108th and 116th, Riverside Park and Amsterdam Avenue. It's true; everything I need can be bought or found right here, with an occasional excursion to Pearl Paint on Canal Street for watercolor supplies.

The Senior Services catchment area extends from 96th to 125th, Riverside Drive to Morningside Drive, so I do travel beyond my borders. There are some dicey blocks in the area, especially the crack corners in the low 100s between Amsterdam and Columbus, but I refuse to be afraid. I make my visits during the day and I take the usual precautions: no handbag; no jewelry; a quick, purposeful stride.

Benno worries more than I do. If we could get by on what he earns—well, for an evolved male, Benno has the vestiges of some old-fashioned attitudes. I stayed home with Clea until she was two, by which time I was more than ready to rejoin the working world. Besides, I have a sweet deal with my job. Clea's school is right next door, and even more important, because I work for the cathedral, we get a break on her tuition.

But today I wasn't planning to go any further than the Bike Building. From what Mr. Patel had told me, I had a good idea of who to talk to. Like any predator, the Hotel Queen would choose the sick or weak. Homebound people like company; it took me four phone calls to arrange four visits.

I stuck a notepad in my bag and stopped at Anne's desk. "I'm going on home visits in the Bike Building. I'll be back by five, in time for Clea."

"Hey, Clea's no problem. She's a big help around here, unlike some people." She glared at Debbie's cubicle. "Are you going to see Mrs. Lord?"

My Monday afternoon regular; I'd put her off yesterday. "Honestly, Anne, it's CRS, but I just can't do it today." I was helping Mrs. Lord sort through mounds of bills, bank statements, beggar's letters. It was a slow process and a missed week wouldn't hurt. "Would you mind calling her and rescheduling for Monday at two? You're an ace."

"Yeah, you can't remember shit, and I'm a sucker for flattery," Anne said. She flipped through her Rolodex and picked up the phone.

ONLY TWO of the women I visited had been victims of the Hotel Queen. What I learned from them, after promising not to give their names to the police, was:

1. Ms. Hilton's first name was Regina, not Virginia.
2. She stole moderate amounts of money, $20, $50, at a time, as well as jewelry. Ruth Goldfarb was missing an antique watch and diamond earrings; Alberta Lu thought the woman had taken a strand of real pearls.
3. Regina Hilton was a short, bouncy brunette with a friendly manner; a stylish dresser who liked short skirts and bright colors.
4. She did reasonably priced manicures and pedicures in the comfort and privacy of their own apartments.

"You know, dear," Ruth Goldfarb confided, "the hairdressers don't do manicures anymore, and these nail places are all run by Koreans. I have nothing against the Korean people, but their English isn't very good, and you do want to talk to the person who's doing your nails. Regina, she kept up a good conversation."

Alberta Lu, in fact, still used her services. Her nails were a flawless coral. "My pearls are gone, and they're not coming back. A good manicurist is hard to find."

Neither of them had known Lillian Raines.

Ruth Goldfarb had confronted Regina, who denied taking her watch and made it clear that if Ruth complained to the Spragues, Regina would have her put out on the street. Regina had reminded Ruth how valuable her room would be, vacant, and bragged that she'd gotten Frank to evict a boyfriend who made trouble for her.

So naturally, neither Ruth nor Alberta had ever spoken to

anyone in a position to do anything. Nor were they, in spite of their openness with me, willing to file an official complaint. I warned them that I'd already told the police about Regina, and they'd probably be questioned as a routine matter.

Ruth set her jaw and said, "If the police come to me, I'll tell them what I'm missing. That's all. I won't risk my security. You don't understand the politics in this building, young woman, or the economics." She followed this with a lecture on the realities of the housing situation.

There used to be dozens of residential hotels like the Maramay on the Upper West Side. As the area yuppified, they became valuable properties, their occupants a nuisance. New owners convert vacant rooms to upscale co-op and condo units that can be sold for astronomical prices. Methods of getting tenants to leave range from legal action to subtle manipulation.

Evictions are threatened; financial incentives offered. Then they start in with major renovations: elevators upgraded, windows replaced, new plumbing and electric lines installed, boilers modernized—which means hallways blocked with dust and debris, days with no water or electricity or heat, weeks when elderly residents have to walk up and down stairs. It's a legal form of harassment that pushes still more tenants out.

In the area north of 110th, Columbia University is continually buying up buildings to feed its growing need for affordable staff and graduate student housing. According to Ruth, the Maramay is on the university's short list, adding substance to her insecurities.

While the women were aware of Regina's relationship with Frank, they were reluctant to talk about it. Both of them made me promise not to enlighten Edna. Ruth distracted me with tales of Regina's other boyfriends, a different one every week to hear her tell it.

Alberta implied that her reticence about Regina and Frank's affair arose out of consideration for Edna. It struck me as an odd brand of sisterhood, protecting the wife of a man who cheated. Not to mention the fact that keeping Frank's secret meant allowing his mistress to get away with stealing from them.

But Ruth and Alberta had said all they were going to. I had to be content to leave it at that for the time being.

WHEN I GOT BACK to the office, I found Clea at Anne's desk, swollen with responsibility. "Hi, Mama! I'm the secretary." She wiggled with excitement but didn't desert her post. "Anne's in Emma's office with a policeman and she said I'm in charge!"

"Looks like you're doing a good job, too. Are you too busy for a hug?" I bent down so she could put her arms around my neck. "What policeman, Bopster?"

"Police person," she corrected herself, my child of the nineties. "The one who was in our building. He didn't bring my badge."

"He probably didn't know you'd be here, since this isn't your usual place of employment. Any messages for me?" I looked over Anne's desk for pink slips.

"I put them on your desk. Anne told me to."

"How long have you been here, Bops?" Clea was supposed to go to the after-school program on Tuesdays. "Didn't you have ceramics today?"

"Jennifer was sick so we played outside and then they said I could come here because I didn't want to go in the gym."

Clea followed me into my cubicle, where there was ample evidence she'd been busy. All the colored markers were out; three new drawings had been pinned to the wall behind my chair. She's in a fairy-tale phase, so all the women had pointy caps with streamers flying from them. They were running away from a dragon shooting red and orange fire.

"Wow! These are beautiful, Clea. They go perfectly in this dungeon office."

Clea beamed. She plans to be an artist and a doctor when she grows up.

"Put the markers away now, please, and the paper. I'm going to tell Emma we're leaving."

"But Mama, Anne said to stay at her desk until she got back!" Clea protested.

"And where are you now? Besides, I'm your mother and that makes me a bigger boss than Anne is."

I KNOCKED ON Emma's door and opened it a few inches. Anne stood protectively behind Emma's chair. Michael's gun seemed large and out of place in a room crowded with women and flowers.

Surrounded by standing people, Emma seemed small and frail. "Come in, Anita, the officer is just leaving." She handed Michael a piece of paper. I recognized a statement form like the one I'd signed earlier. We had to trek up to 126th Street, but Emma got delivery service? The perks of power—or did it have more to do with Michael's interest in Anne?

Anne moved toward the door. "I'd better go relieve my relief. You saw I put your daughter to work?"

"Yes, thanks, Anne. Has she been good?"

"Always!" Anne slid out.

Michael shook hands with Emma. "We appreciate your co-operation, Ms. Franklin. Detective Neville will call you if he has any more questions."

"I've told you everything that I'm allowed to, Officer," she said. Michael followed Anne out of the office. Emma aimed her sharp eyes at me. "Anita, from now on, please refer all requests for information on Lillian Raines directly to me."

I didn't think I'd done anything wrong, but there are times Emma needs to remind me she's the boss. I put it down to that and nodded my obedience while she lectured me on the importance of confidentiality.

CLEA WAS GIVING Michael a tour of my cube—that is, of her art on the walls. Anne fussed with things on her desk, stalling, it seemed to me, in hopes of walking out with Michael. I gathered up my purse and Clea's backpack. The four of us left together.

Clea claimed Anne's hand and scampered ahead. I managed a private word with Michael.

"So did you spend your afternoon in the Bike Building, too?" I asked. Edna had been on the phone both times I'd walked by the manager's office, or I'd have heard if any cops were in the building.

"What?" Michael had his attention on the sway of Anne's long silvery raincoat.

"The Bike Building? The woman who's been stealing things from the old people? Detective Neville said he'd have you and Inez look into it."

"Yeah, we talked to the old lady with the rotten teeth, got a name, and ran it through the computer. Nothing came up."

"Well, I went over there and asked around—"

Michael stopped. "What do you mean 'asked around'? You think I didn't do my job?"

"No, I didn't mean that." The last thing I needed was to antagonize Michael. "I'm a trained interviewer too, you know, and I thought—"

"You thought you'd play cop?"

"I thought people who know me might be more willing to talk to me than to the police. And for your information, Naomi Spivik got the woman's name wrong. It's Regina Hilton, not Virginia. So put that in your computer and smoke it!"

"Okay, so it wasn't our top priority. I'll admit it, I don't like that building too well. And as much as those people don't want us going in there, that's how much we don't want to bother them either. It's like uncovering a cockroach nest, you gotta be prepared to deal with what you find." He tapped a warning on my shoulder. "You be careful what you say around there, Social Worker. The Spragues know more than you think about what goes on. This *is* a police matter."

Yeah, right, I thought, like you're taking it seriously. "Did you talk to Frank and Edna?"

"Of course I talked to them, what do you think? I got a pair of indignant denials, along with, 'Don't you have better things to do than chase after the delusions of a paranoid old woman?' Which, I have to say, I do. The abuse the police take…" Michael started walking again. "Without a credible victim willing to file a complaint, there isn't much we can do. Credible being the operative word here."

No one, me included, trusted cops these days. Inez and Michael were, in my opinion, exceptions, but they weren't going to do much, either. A bunch of *bubbes* complaining about petty, hard-to-prove larceny. I already knew more about it than they did. Unlike the police, however, I wasn't about to let it rest.

We caught up to Clea and Anne by the fountain.

"Nice seeing you again, Social Worker," Michael said. He turned to Anne. "Ma'am, if you'll consent to being seen in public with a man in uniform, would you care to join me for a sweet thing to eat?" He gestured at the Hungarian Pastry Shop.

Anne actually blushed. "No, really, thank you, I should get home. Maybe some other time? Maybe lunch?"

"Woman after my own heart. Why settle for cake when you can have pastrami? How about tomorrow?"

We headed off in our three separate directions.

"Mom, how come Anne talks funny to that policeman?" Clea asked.

"Talks funny?"

"You know. Like she's whispering."

"It's called flirting, what her voice does. People do it when they like each other."

That gave Clea pause to think, and allowed me to shift gears. I never worry about dinner until I'm on my way home. Small New York apartments have small kitchens with small refrigerators, which means daily trips to the store.

Benno had cooked last night; thank god for leftovers. We could get by with a detour to Mama Joy's for bialys, a plain bagel, sliced ham for Clea's lunch. I was hoping for an early night to catch up on that lost hour of sleep. My internal clock was still behind the time, and no amount of daylight was going to make up for it.

WE BUMPED INTO Barbara Baker on her way out of the hardware store. She was in jeans and a T-shirt instead of the regulation Super's green coverall Howard tries to get her to wear, but even in plainclothes Barbara's something to see. She's medium tall, medium brown, medium heavy; her graying hair, augmented by matching extensions, is done in hundreds of shoulder-length braids.

"Hey, how's my girl?" she said to Clea.

"Fine, thanks, and you?" I answered, prompting Clea. It's a wonder children ever learn manners.

"You're getting good with those cornrows, Anita, you got some unique diagonals going on there. If I ever get tired of extensions, I'll get you to do me!" Barbara shook her gray braids.

"Then I'll know I've really graduated!" People always ask Clea who did her hair. Her response is an indignant "My mom!" Then I get astonished praise, as if being white implies an inability to braid hair. We're cultural ambassadors to both races, Clea and I.

Barbara exchanged fractional nods with a street regular, an emaciated white guy with a long, pointy gray beard.

"You know that man?" I'd never seen him pay the slightest attention to anyone before.

"Yeah, Miriam Katz on the third floor, that's her son, Sam."

"I didn't know Miriam had a son." You live in a place for years, you never really know your neighbors. Same with the street people, you pass them every day but you never learn their stories. I'd seen Sam a hundred times, in his frayed brown bell-bottoms with duct tape patches on the knees, and never known he was related to Miriam. Sam Katz had an intense look, like he could go off on you. In typical New York fashion I figured if I didn't notice him, he wouldn't notice me.

"He lives over in the Bike Building," Barbara explained. "He's a little off, mentally—shell shock or traumatic stress, whatever they call it. Slinks in late at night sometimes to get a meal off his mother and pick a fight with her. He must've broke every one of her dishes, because I saw she just bought a set of plastic."

"Does he hit her?" Great, I thought, another potentially dangerous person with access to our building.

"Just throws things, far as I know."

We stopped in front of the building and put down our shopping bags. Barbara lit a cigarette and my craving woke up. "You got another one of those?"

"You smoking in front of the baby?"

"Smoking is bad for your health," Clea pitched in.

"She's not such a baby," I said. And this wouldn't be her first experience with that old parental standby, "Do what I say not what I do."

Clea started to root around in my purse, looking for the keys so she could get the mail, her new big-girl thing to do. There was no way I was going to let her enter the building by herself after what had happened, so I distracted her with a piece of gum. Clea plunked herself down at the other end of the stoop, opened her backpack, and took out a doll baby.

Barbara handed me her pack of Winstons. I quit smoking years ago, but I hang on to a bumming habit for times of stress or alcohol. The cigarette tasted foul but necessary.

"That detective from the islands was here again today. He's got some kind of nerve, making nice with the Wilcoxes then giving me six kinds of a hard time. I don't know who he thinks he is, Mr. Detective Neville! Those two gave that woman a key, but did I say anything? No, not even when the board was after me about it. But that one, he got the sisters *blaming* me for her being here. Trying to protect their own selves, is what." Barbara lowered her voice. "He was back to see Howard, too. Somebody must have told him about that book he keeps." She scrutinized my face.

I must not have looked blank enough because she said, "Oho, it was you! I knew you were the one! Social workers, they know everything. Howard keeps pretty tight to that book."

"Actually, it was Benno who found out about it," I said, in defense of my profession.

"Another thing I don't understand—detective said it was an accident, so how come he's poking around?" Barbara asked.

"I'm not so sure it was an accident." I stubbed out my cigarette and flipped it toward the street.

"No Anita, not you too! I got half the building after me, worried about security. People are saying Mr. Malinsky's got a point, and when he starts looking sensible..." There was no need for her to finish the sentence.

"Detective was real interested in that leather bag thing she used to carry. Said it hadn't turned up." She put her cigarette out against the side of the planter and tossed the butt into the gutter. "I hear our homeless lady had a million dollars in the bank. Do you believe it?"

Barbara, too? I was definitely beginning to credit the stories. Rumors, like stereotypes, are often built around a grain of truth. Plenty of old people have small fortunes stashed away, and you'd never know it to look at them. Take Naomi Spivik, for instance.

"I don't know about money, but I heard she used to live in the Bike Building."

"Did she? So how come the police aren't going after them all over there instead of hassling us?" Barbara shifted gears abruptly. "Did you know John Clark has a mistress lives there?"

I blinked. "A mistress?" John Clark, husband of Margery, owner of Mitzi, always on the side of the underdog in building disputes? Good grief. It was my day for being shocked by the sexual carryings-on of older men.

Clea was braiding her doll's hair and paying no attention to the adult conversation going on over her head. I hoped.

"I guess John got tired of all that Methodist black Margery wears, because girlfriend is a dresser. Must be in her seventies, but she's got a shape like an hourglass. About ten years ago, I worked in the God Box, you know, the Interchurch Center, New York headquarters of all Protestants? She was a secretary for the Mission Society. Her name's Sylvia Chase."

Sylvia Chase? Mr. Patel's emergency contact?

"Sheesh, Barbara, you talk about social workers, but you're wicked. How do you know this stuff?"

"You'd be surprised what I see. People come down to do laundry, they got all sorts of things to say. I'm just the Super, hey, I'd be invisible even if I wasn't black. Last fall, Margery was away at her sister's in Chicago. I'm getting my mail and in comes John with girlfriend on his arm, in a red suit with a fox fur collar. 'Course, I had to recognize her. You know me, foot in mouth, I said hello. John turned red as her jacket and Sylvia looked past me like we hadn't ever worked together. It wasn't hard to figure out, so I shut my mouth."

The outfit sounded like the Sylvia Chase I knew. Peyton Place meets the Upper West Side. Clea finished with the doll's hair and rocked her in her arms. One thing about Clea, she can amuse herself.

A door slammed in the hall. Howard Orton headed for the stoop. We watched him tape a sheet of paper to the inside of the inner door.

"Look out, we're about to get caught loitering." I nudged Barbara. She shut me down with a look. We used to call Howard Casper the Unfriendly Ghost because of his shape, the way he wears his pants belted high up around his waist, and the bureaucratic pallor of his skin—but that was before he represented job security to Barbara.

"Mrs. Baker, Mrs. Servi, good evening." Howard gave us his tight version of a smile. "I'm putting up a notice about building protocol."

It was a densely typed reminder to make sure both doors were locked, to come down for deliveries rather than buzzing delivery people in, etc. A person could get mugged, standing out here long enough to read the whole thing.

Barbara nodded at it. "That'll help, I'm sure," she said. "I've got to get these groceries inside." She went down the outside stairs to the Super's basement apartment.

Her ironic tone breezed right by Howard.

Before he could say a word about the contents of Clea's backpack being spread out on the bottom step, I gathered it all up. We said good evening and went inside.

A Dalmatian puppy burst out of the elevator, almost knocking Clea over. She stood her ground and let him lick her face. For some reason unknown to me, Clea and Benno both love dogs. I'm a cat person; I hate to be slobbered on.

"Luigi, down! Are you okay, honey?" Tabitha, the puppy's owner, was never far behind.

Clea hugged the wiggling dog. Tabitha, a business administration student at Columbia, is Clea's idol, with her pencil-thin, waist-length dreadlocks.

Tabitha looked down the hall toward the door. "Uh-oh, the mayor's on the stoop. Better get this leash on! Do you believe what happened? I'm glad I've got Luigi for protection. I saw Larry Turner this morning, and all that creep could think about was his equity!"

"Well, everyone has their own priorities."

"I'll tell you his other priority! Men like that make me want to be a feminist."

"Men like what?" I asked. I knew better than to point out to Tabitha that whether she liked the label or not, she owed her future career to feminism.

"Men who talk to your chest instead of your face. You never noticed that?"

Maybe I'm too old, or too married, but I hadn't. I reached for the elevator, but it had gone up.

"He does it to Geoff's girlfriend, too. I mean, this is the twentieth century. Larry knows a lot about Wall Street, but the way he acts—Down, I said, down, Luigi!" She let the dog drag her toward the front door.

I gave Clea the mailbox key. She's barely tall enough to reach our box in the second row; it was crammed full, and two magazines landed on her head. I bent to pick them up.

When I stood, I noticed Mr. Malinsky lurking on the stairs. We stared at each other for a second. The back of my neck prickled with apprehension. I definitely did not like that man.

I hustled Clea toward the elevator. The door opened from inside and I held it while Miriam Katz made her exit.

"Thank you, dear," she nodded. "It's a lovely day, isn't it?"

I smiled back at her. She tottered off down the hall, a small woman with her hair twisted up in an untidy gray nest.

MY WISH FOR more sleep was granted, but it wasn't restful. I zonked out in front of the TV in the middle of *NYPD Blue*. Benno covered me with a blanket and left me on the couch.

Sometime after midnight, a noise woke me. It sounded like someone was turning our doorknob. While I watched, I could have sworn the knob moved a half turn, then back.

I went for the peephole. The hall, of course, was empty.

But what if someone were crouched down out of sight in front of the door?

I checked to make sure the deadbolt was locked. It was.

I tiptoed into the bedroom and got the baseball bat Benno keeps in the closet. It's not much as far as protection goes, but it's a lot more comforting to have a Louisville Slugger around the house than a Glock.

I tapped the bat against the bottom of the door from the inside. If someone was there, I thought I'd flush whoever it was out into the hall. I looked out the peephole again. No one went running. I unlocked the door and jerked it open.

The silent hall stared back at me.

Feeling like a paranoid fool, I took my clothes off and crawled into bed. What I love even more than Benno's cooking is his butt, and sleeping curled around it.

IN THE MORNING I was groggy with dreams, a dark warren of rooms, people whispering things to me. It didn't take Freud to see that Lillian's death was having an effect. I hadn't mentioned anything about the Hotel Queen to Benno. I don't always feel good about it, but there are times when silence is better than a fight.

The spell of hot weather was holding, so I had to scrounge for something that wasn't wool to wear. Another by-product of small apartments is small closets; my summer clothes were still in deep storage. I found a pair of gray silk pants, miraculously already ironed, and topped them with a teal-green tunic.

It looked like Clea got up on the wrong side of the bed. She had her shirt on inside out, for starters. Then she decided to make herself a bowl of cereal—except the milk hit the counter instead of the bowl. She started howling before I could yell at her. Benno calls it her "best defense is a good offense" wail; how can you be mad at a child who needs to be comforted?

So she had a bagel to eat, toasted with nothing on it, while we walked. It was a gorgeous morning, white clouds blowing across blue sky, daffodils bright as the sun in new grass. We swung our hands together as we walked. From her first steps, I insisted that Clea hold my hand on the street; her little paw in mine always makes me feel good.

Sometimes our life seems enchanted, for New York City. We may live month to month in a tiny apartment, but we have a slice of river view. Benno's commute is only half an hour. My job and Clea's school are on the grounds of the largest Gothic cathedral in the world, where a flock of fancy chickens and four peacocks make their homes amid the herbs in the Biblical Garden. A peacock was preening on the lawn, tail spread in an iridescent fan. Surrounded by bricks and cement, our days are laced with magical visions.

I kissed Clea at the door and sent her frolicking off with her classmates. The peacock had folded his tail when I went by again. He looked small, ordinary, despite his feathery crown.

Going in to work jolted me back to the mundane. Anne, in magenta with a splash of silver earrings, held the phone out to me.

"No one is here!" Naomi accused. "You said you would find someone to take me to the doctor today!"

What was she talking about? I had no memory of her asking for an escort. Okay, I have on occasion forgotten something, but once reminded I've never not remembered. If this was CRS, it was a serious case.

"Naomi. What time is your appointment?" I asked.

"Eleven o'clock, I have to be there! I've been waiting over half an hour!"

That gave her a good two hours to get downstairs, get in a cab, and make the twenty-minute ride to Amsterdam and 68th. Even at the speed Naomi moves, it was more than ample. I, stupidly, pointed this out to her, but she was adamant: if I didn't send someone over *right now,* she would cancel her appointment. I could hear her blood pressure rising.

Interns don't usually do escorts, but Debbie was willing. Naomi, however, seemed put out at having her request filled so promptly and hung up without a word of thanks.

Social work graduate students spend three days a week working in the field. It's a good idea, in theory at least. The students get experience; the agencies get free help. In practice, it's a kind of roulette, and students often take more energy from paid staff than they give back. With Debbie, we break a little better than even.

She's a corn-fed blonde from Ames, Iowa, with wide eyes and freckles. The old people adore her. It's a good thing; any other population would eat her alive. I don't know how much social work she gets done, but she has a gift for getting the seniors to talk. It would be a treat for Naomi.

Having vowed to write up my visits while they were still fresh in my mind, I got Alberta Lu's and Ruth Goldfarb's case files from the closet. I'd just made myself a cup of coffee when the phone rang. Anne was on the other line, so I answered it.

"I knocked and knocked, and she won't answer her door! They don't have the key, and I don't know what to do. Can you come?" It was Debbie, on the edge of hysteria.

"Did you call nine-one-one?" It's the standard instruction we give the interns—when in doubt, it's better to call and not need the ambulance than not call and need it.

Debbie gulped. "Yes, I did, but I—"

"Okay, you did the right thing. Just hang on, I'll be right there." I closed Alberta's file, grabbed my purse, and told Anne where I was going.

She rolled her eyes. As far as Anne's concerned, Debbie's more trouble than she's worth.

I went out into the sunny world with my fingers crossed, devoutly hoping Anne was right—that Naomi was in the bathroom, say, and Debbie had panicked for no reason.

EIGHT

WHEN I GOT TO the corner of 112th, there were two police cars and an ambulance in front of the Bike Building. Another similarity between social workers and cops is that both professions rely on intuition more than either likes to admit. Some people call it experience; whatever it was, I had a feeling Naomi Spivik wasn't going to need that ambulance.

Sam Katz was part of the clump of residents at the far end of the stoop. Now that I knew who he was I could see his resemblance to Miriam, the narrow face dominated by spiky eyebrows, the angular cheekbones. I wouldn't have guessed he'd been in the military; to me he looked like a poet or a philosopher, with his inward-seeing eyes.

Geoff Tate's girlfriend was there, too, which struck me as odd. Sam Katz was hovering at her shoulder. "What's going on?" I asked her.

"Something with one of the old people." Her hair was back in a ponytail again. It gave her a foxy look, emphasizing the point of her chin. She shrugged. "I think they're waiting for a locksmith or something."

As she spoke, Sam's arm came up behind her. He grazed her shoulder delicately with the tips of his fingers, a small petting motion. Then, as if he'd surprised himself by making contact, he clasped his hands together behind his back and bowed his head. Ponytail ignored him, but I thought her eyes softened when he touched her. Seeing them together made me uncomfortable. I wondered if Geoff knew he had a rival. Just what I needed, more secrets and infidelities.

Ponytail took a key ring out of her jeans pocket, stepped forward, and used it to unlock the door for me.

"Do you live here?" I was startled. Another person with ties to both buildings?

"Sometimes." She grinned. "You going in, or you want me to stand here and hold the door all day for you?"

EDNA WAS IN the hall outside the office, hands in the pockets of her housedress. "Good thing it's you, Anita. That little girl you got working for you has everyone all upset about Mrs. Spivik."

"What happened?" Being right in this situation did not please me.

"That Debbie came down here, asking did I see Naomi Spivik go out? Puh! She never goes out by herself. Debbie gives us a story about taking her to the doctor but Spivik's not answering the door, am I sure? Sure I'm sure! You can't miss Spivik. Moves like a turtle on Jell-O!" Edna laughed at the image. It wasn't bad.

"So?"

"So Frank goes up with her. Spivik always leaves her door unlocked, but no, Debbie says it's locked. I was surprised she had the wit to try, but you never know, do you?" She shook her head. Edna could go on. I wished she would.

"Don't you have her keys?"

"That's the thing. No keys on her hook. We're supposed to have everybody's keys, that's the rule, only some people get extra locks and don't give us a key. We got some paranoids in here, you know? Anyways, Frank leaves Debbie up there banging on the door and comes back to look for them keys again. Next thing you know, we got cops and EMS. So Frank found the keys and went up with 'em. Lucky for you!" Edna pointed her finger at me. "Senior Services woulda paid for the door, otherwise."

There's nothing worse than entering an apartment with reason to think the occupant's dead or unconscious. A person who's fallen and can't get up is scared, disoriented. Paramedics are good with bodily injury, but they're too busy to pay much attention to the soul. A hand to hold can mean as much as an IV and a stretcher. I headed for the elevators.

DEBBIE AND FRANK were in the hall outside Naomi's room, along with two uniforms. Frank scowled down at one of the cops, a heavyset white guy with a mustache. Debbie was talking to the other one, a crew-cut blond. I could see her making an effort to be calm.

"Here's Anita," she said. "She'll be able to tell you about Ms. Spivik. Oh, I'm so glad you're here!" Debbie launched herself at me. I put my arms around her, patted her on the back. What else could I do?

"Okay, okay. Tell me what happened."

To her credit, Debbie backed away and stood up straight. She gave her side of what Edna had already said, with glances at Frank for confirmation. He nodded, shook his head, kept his mouth twisted shut. When she got to the missing key, he interrupted.

"Yeah, I told you we got a key for her, it just landed on somebody else's hook. If you'd held on a minute, I'da found it the first time. Now look what we got here." He waved a hand at 11D.

Naomi Spivik lay on the floor, surrounded by white jackets. The paramedics had an IV started. One worked a bag-and-tube contraption to force air into her lungs while another did CPR. A bag of clear liquid lay on the floor, attached by a tube to the IV in Naomi's arm. They'd cut through her dress and her bra. Her breasts sagged on either side of her chest, nipples dark as dates. It was a miracle that the paramedic pushing on her chest hadn't ripped her rice-paper skin.

Her skirt had gotten twisted around while they were working on her. She wore stockings and a girdle, but no panties. Her pubic hair, whiter and thinner than the undyed roots on her scalp, barely covered the wrinkled lips of her vulva. There was a huge pool of urine around her that everyone managed to avoid by concentrating on her upper body. Revulsion gave way to the thought that if she wasn't already dead, awareness of her present state would have killed her.

Out of respect, I averted my eyes. On the far side of the room were two more pairs of NYPD blue legs.

"Yo, Social Worker, don't you think it's time we stopped meeting like this?"

Dougherty, who else? It wasn't funny, but I smiled.

"Hello, Anita. This woman is your client?" Inez asked.

"Was," Michael said. "Must've happened quick, like a heart attack. There were no vital signs when we got here, but EMS has their protocol. Your intern over there said you spoke with her a little after nine? So they get here within a half hour, body's still warm, they gotta go for it."

He looked at his watch; I looked at mine. 9:45. Naomi on the phone had been annoyed, but that was nothing unusual for Naomi. She hadn't been short of breath, and surely a doctor's appointment wouldn't agitate her enough to bring on a heart attack.

Had something else happened to upset her? Scare her enough to lock her door? I looked around the room. It appeared to be in its normal disheveled state, with a little extra chaos added by the activities of EMS. If there was any evidence of foul play, no one would recognize it for what it was.

"They'll stop soon," Inez said. "The intern said you'd know her next of kin?"

I found Naomi's frayed red leather address book in a pile of papers on the card table. I called the great-nephew at work, got his voice mail, and left an urgent message. I tried his home number in Riverdale and reached his wife, a woman with a sensible voice who said they'd been expecting this for years, she'd come as soon as she packed up the two-year-old.

By the time I got off the phone, EMS had called it quits. Torn wrappers from sterile equipment littered the room. Someone put towels on the floor to soak up the urine. They'd left the breathing apparatus taped in Naomi's mouth. Her eyes were open, bulging with the indignity of it all. Everyone stepped around the body, careful not to touch her now that she was officially dead.

I took the flowered comforter off the daybed and draped it over her. It didn't seem right to cover her face with the tube still in her mouth, but those eyes were more than I could take.

While I was bent over her body, I glanced around the floor, under the bed. It occurred to me to wonder if she'd tried to take her medication and dropped the bottle. All I saw was dust and stray envelopes covered in Naomi's wavery script.

I pulled the spread up and covered her head. Everyone stopped to watch me. The smell in the room was choking.

"DON'T GIVE ME that look, Social Worker." Michael scowled at me. "I checked the records this morning. Seems Ms. Spivik made seven complaints in the past year, all about missing items presumably stolen by housekeepers. Not exactly what I'd call credible."

"So, she's like the boy who cried wolf," I argued. "This time it was true."

"And you think someone offed her because she made complaint number eight?" Michael said. "Get real. In the twenty minutes between when you talked to her and the intern got here?"

"Naomi never locked her door. If it had been open, Debbie might have been able to get help in time to save her. And what about the extra key?"

"Well, she locked her door this morning, and the key wasn't missing. Frank found it."

"Not soon enough to do her any good, though, was it?"

"Excuse me, you two," Inez broke in. She had a prescription pill bottle in her hand.

"Where did you get that?" I asked, my voice sharp.

"From the tray by her bed. Why?" Inez frowned at me.

"I just wondered if she'd taken her medication or—"

"Or what?" Michael cut me off. "Give it a rest, Anita. Old people die! How come every time you lose a client lately, you're calling it murder?"

Inez glared at us like we were quarreling children. "Based on her condition and the medications she was taking, the paramedics think it was a heart attack. Do you have her doctor's name and number, Anita?"

"Yeah, I've got it." I found the page and handed her Naomi's address book. "Wouldn't an autopsy show if she'd taken her pills?"

Inez lost her patience. "Look, if the doctor agrees with EMS, there won't be an autopsy. If the doctor says he'll sign a death certificate then she doesn't have to make a trip to the morgue and all our jobs are a lot easier."

Michael gave me an I-told-you-so look. "Look, if it'll make you happy, we have to have a superior sign off on this. I'll ask for Neville, see if he finds anything suspicious, although with the mess EMS made..." Michael waved his hand at the room. "How soon will the family member be here?"

"Should be by noon," I said. "You worrying about your lunch date?"

"I might just make it. We were first on the scene, we have to stay until the body gets picked up. Jesus, Mary, and Joseph, what a job—no wonder cops don't have lives. After this, who could eat?" His voice was bleak, but I found it hard to imagine Michael without an appetite.

"Sometimes they really get to you, don't they?" I felt tears starting up. I stared out the window over the roof of the building below, taken aback by the realization that what I felt was not guilt but sadness. You don't get up into your nineties without a strong personality. For all she made me want to tear my hair out, I had admired Naomi Spivik.

"Anita? Are you still here?" Debbie called from outside the door.

Damn. I wiped my eyes on my sleeve and went out to the hall to talk to her.

"I'm sorry, Naomi," I whispered to the flowered mound on the floor.

Debbie put her hand on my shoulder. The tears came back.

I let them. Debbie found a tissue in her purse and handed it to me.

"Oh Anita, I'm so sorry, I should have known right away when she didn't answer. I thought it was just taking her a long time and then those people…" She looked down the corridor to be sure Frank wasn't there.

I blew my nose and told her she did the right thing, for a person Naomi's age a few minutes wouldn't have made a difference, it was a blessing to go quickly in her own home, she didn't suffer—trotted out all the clichés, and they worked. For both of us.

THE GREAT-NEPHEW'S WIFE came, took a brief look, needed neither condolences nor counseling. The paramedic gave her the word from Naomi's doctor: based on her history, death was due to a massive heart attack. The doctor would be happy to sign a death certificate to that effect, so no morgue and no autopsy.

I could read the writing on the wall. A thief was preying on elderly women in the Bike Building. Naomi had reported her to the police; Naomi was dead. Lillian Raines, who'd been asking about the thief, was dead. The police didn't see anything suspicious in either death. Detective Neville would come, they'd all have a good giggle at my suspicions, and that would be that.

But it wasn't, not for me. I could hear Naomi's querulous voice, "No one listens to me!"

FRANK SPRAGUE WAS in the manager's office. Maybe it was my new awareness of his private affairs, but it seemed to me that he leered at us through the yellowed Plexiglas. Even if I hadn't been with Debbie, that smirk would have stopped me from asking him about Regina Hilton.

I was hoping to catch Geoff Tate's girlfriend if she was still on the stoop. I figured if she lived here "sometimes" she probably knew Regina. Approaching Regina through a friend might get me further than coming on like the indignant social worker I was.

So much for luck; the stoop was deserted. I took Debbie out for a cup of coffee and a little grief counseling. Dealing with her first direct experience with death helped me get a grip on my own emotions. Education, I reminded myself; it's all about education.

BACK AT THE AGENCY, I spent the rest of the morning firming up the arrangements for next week's bus trip to the Dogwood Festival in Connecticut. When Anne left for her lunch date, I took her place at the receptionist's desk. The phone was quiet. I ate the second half of yesterday's hero for lunch and caught up on my progress notes.

I took out a pad and wrote down what I knew about Regina Hilton. The more I thought about the whole situation, the less satisfied I was. I doodled a garland of feathers in the margin and wished for a cigarette. I pulled Naomi's file to make a final entry.

Maybe I could get Michael to reconsider. If I convinced him figuring it out would advance his career...

Think of the devil. Anne and Michael blew in on a gust of balmy air. I had to admit they were handsome together, tall and laughing, navy blue and hot pink.

"Hey, Social Worker, they got you answering phones now?" Michael winked.

"I'm glad one of us is in a better mood. Where'd you guys eat?"

"Mama's Place," Anne answered.

The perfect compromise. Michael may have been a pastrami eater, but Anne was a devout vegetarian. Mama's makes the best quiche in the neighborhood as well as a Reuben guaranteed to clog your arteries at three bites.

I vacated Anne's desk. "So did Detective Neville agree that Naomi Spivik died of natural causes?"

"Yeah, and he had a good word for you, too. Seems the ME was having a slow week and the autopsy report on the lady who died in your building came in this morning. It confirmed that cause of death was a head injury resulting from a fall. No bruising on her arms, nothing to indicate she was pushed." Michael tipped his hat. "All in a day's work, ladies, keeping the crime statistics down and the mayor happy."

"Isn't that just typical of how the world works," Anne said. "Something happens to an elderly person and no one cares. They lie in hospital beds and the nurses ignore them, they die in stairwells and the police can't be bothered, they—"

"Hey, no fair!" Michael objected. "We put in a couple days on this. We found absolutely nothing, zero, nada, zip. Okay, if it happened on the Upper East Side, maybe they'd've put more people on it, fingerprinted the whole building, whatever. But this is the real world. Resources are limited. Anyway, no East Side matron sleeps in a stair well!"

"So now you're saying she deserved what she got?" Anne's face flushed. "She was in the wrong place, so what do you expect?"

I could see a beautiful lunch going down the tubes. Anne was making my argument for me on emotional grounds. Unfortunately it would take facts to sway Michael. I kept out of it for the moment.

I went to replace the case files I'd worked on. When I opened the Closed Cases drawer to add Naomi's file, I thought I'd pull Lillian's file. I wanted to read it again and see if I could pick up on some overlooked thread that might lead to Lillian's people. I went through all the drawers twice, but her file was nowhere in the closet.

A missing case file is a serious matter. The information they contain is personal, sensitive, private. Maintaining client confidentiality is a sacred responsibility, even after a client is deceased.

I shuffled through the piles on my desk and emptied my drawers. Neither Anne nor Debbie had seen it. Emma wasn't there to ask, so I checked her office. No file.

Case files *never* leave the agency; it had to be somewhere. But it wasn't.

NINE

SINCE IT WAS such a nice day, I took Clea to the playground in Riverside Park after school. I needed to fill my lungs with fresh air, watch the squirrels go about their business, give my brain a rest. Clea's recently mastered the monkey bars; she climbed up to the top circle and crowed. I worked on mastering proud rather than terrified by watching the cars go down Riverside Drive while keeping the corner of one eye glued to her capering figure.

Harriet Briggs, a nonagenarian resident of the Bike Building, accompanied by a walker and a home health aide carrying a plaid blanket, made her way across the drive. The aide, a young black woman in turquoise sweats, settled her on a bench. Harriet closed her eyes, tilted her head up to the sun, and fell immediately to sleep.

That's the thing about working in the community where you live—you can't get away from the people you serve because you run into them on the street, the bus, in the park. Seeing clients outside of working hours, however, does have some advantages. I made the most of this one. I waved at Clea to make sure she saw where I was going, and went over to sit with the aide.

"Hi," I said. "Looks like the walk tired Mrs. Briggs out."

"It don't take much. She's good, though. Likes to get out in the air, not like some of them, sit in their rooms with the shades down all day." The woman wasn't as young as she looked; the pompom of hair on top of her head was laced with gray.

She was a private aide, paid directly by the client, part of the informal network operating in the neighborhood.

"I'm Anita Servi, the social worker from the cathedral. I'm sorry, but I don't remember your name?" I stuck my hand out.

She took it. "Yeah, I know who you are. I'm Mar-Lee Hymers."

"You work for other people in the Bike Building besides Mrs. Briggs, don't you?"

She nodded.

"Do you know someone named Regina Hilton, sometimes does manicures for people?"

Mar-Lee laughed. "Yeah, I know her. You been asking around about her."

"How do you know that?" I didn't have any sense of threat coming from her, but you never knew.

She stuck her chin out. "I seen you over there, one. Two, I do Mrs. Briggs' wash. I hear the ladies talking in the laundry room. I could tell you something maybe you don't know, but what's in it for me?"

Always a catch, but at least she came straight out and asked. "What do you want?"

"I want work. Mrs. Briggs, she's only afternoons. You put in a good word for me, I could pick up some more hours."

It was against Senior Services policy to recommend private-pay aides; we make referrals to home-care agencies. That way there's recourse if the aide quits, calls in sick, runs up the phone bill. Unofficially, however, we do occasionally suggest aides we know to be reliable. That Mar-Lee was willing to go to the trouble of taking Mrs. Briggs out spoke well for her; most aides don't bother to do more than the minimum.

"Okay," I agreed. "I'll let you know if anything comes up."

"Yeah, that's what I want. I don't like that bitch, and that's a fact. I was brought up to respect my elders, and what she been doing, worse than taking candy from a baby. Almost as easy, too!" Mar-Lee's smile flashed a gold front tooth with a heart cutout. "Besides, she give us all a bad name. Old people, they quick to accuse us of stealing. Regina, she really do. The lady who died this morning? Regina took her to the hairdresser and the lady only give her a dollar. Regina took money out of her purse to get even.''

Score two for Naomi. ''Regina told you that?''

''She always bragging. You never stole nothing? That's half the payoff, somebody else knows you got away with it. No, don't start on me about no po-*lice*. I stay away from them, they stay away from me.''

''I heard Regina has a thing going with Frank Sprague.''

Mar-Lee hooted. ''You know what she did? She first come to the building, she moved in on Marky Mark. Then she figured out what side her bread was buttered on, took up with Frank and had Mark put out of his own place. Yeah, she got that fat old man wrapped right around her finger!''

''Marky Mark? The guy on the bus ads?'' I didn't get it.

''No man, we call him Marky Mark because his name Mark!'' She looked at me, not without reason, like I was stupid.

''What's his last name? Do you know where he moved to?''

''He didn't move nowhere. He's big, he sleeps all around here.'' Mar-Lee flapped her hand, indicating the lower levels of the park. ''Marky Mark, he know what Regina did with what she stole.''

''What's he look like?''

''You know Mark by his gold jacket, got the name of a football team on it. Forty-nine, some number. You tell him you know me, and he talk to you.''

I rifled through my mental file of the regulars on the street, didn't come up with anyone in a 'Niners jacket. If I'd ever seen him, I would've remembered—as long as I've lived in New York, the San Francisco 49ers are still my team.

''Did you know a woman used to live on the fourteenth floor, Lillian Raines?''

''Little old lady in a black coat, look like she afraid of her shadow? Regina after her, too, she said that little bitty lady was the richer than Trump. All I know is, she definitely had some secrets. You ever hear her talk to herself?''

"Every second person in New York talks to herself!"

"Yeah, but that lady told a story. You could tell it made some kind of sense—'and then this happened, and then that happened,' like that."

"What was it about?"

"You kidding? I don't go around listening to no crazy people! You know what else? She used to sit by the grave of that baby, do her knitting, tell her story to that stone thing."

"The grave of the Amiable Child?"

"Uh-huh."

Clea had left the monkey bars. I located her on the swinging bridge. The Wilcoxes had also mentioned Lillian sitting by the Amiable Child. Maybe we'd take ourselves a walk up to Grant's Tomb. Clea loved to climb on the mosaic benches, and I could check out the grave.

Clea the curious came over and stood between my knees, thumb in mouth, eyes on Mar-Lee. I could tell she was worried; I was talking to a woman she didn't recognize. It's one of the first things we teach our children about the world, don't talk to strangers.

"That your child?" Mar-Lee asked.

"My one and only. Clea, say hello to Mar-Lee."

We taught Clea to be polite and respectful to people, even the panhandlers—to say "you're welcome" if they say "thank you" when we gave them money. The regulars all know her by name. I see it as a safety net, those invisible eyes watching out for her.

"Hello. Do you want to watch me climb the monkey bars?" Clea asked.

"Yes, baby, I'd like to see that." Clea ran off. Mar-Lee cocked her head. "You make her?" she asked me.

People always wonder when they see us together. I appreciated the direct approach. "No, Clea's adopted."

"Yeah, if you made her, she have more milk in her." Mar-Lee waved at Clea on the jungle gym. "That girl can climb! So you got something to write my phone number?"

Harriet Briggs let out a snore and woke herself up. I chatted for a minute, but I was itching to move.

BY THE TIME I WENT to collect Clea, she'd taken root in the sandbox with her friend Eve and a pile of plastic sand toys. Clea and Eve were best buddies in day care. Now they go to different schools; I didn't have the heart to tear Clea away, and besides, Eve's mother waved me over.

My friendship with Sarah is totally kid-centered. Our circles of friends don't overlap; Sarah lives on 92nd Street, a world away by New York standards.

"I see Eve's still into braids." I joined Sarah on the bench. Eve has long, thick, blond hair but she envied Clea's beads. She pestered her baby-sitter, Aisha, a City College student, into braiding her hair in an approximation of cornrows.

"Two of the girls in her class at P.S. Seventy-five have cornrows," Sarah shrugged. "I think what she really likes is the barrettes Aisha uses. It's a lot easier than brushing it every day, but it gets pretty ratty by the end of the week. So, how's it going with the adoption?"

"Dead in the water, at the moment. We're still waiting on the court to move on the termination of parental rights." The proceedings in Family Court moved like molasses in Antarctica—not at all. They were waiting for a Mental Hygiene Study of Clea's biological mother, who's been institutionalized in a state psychiatric hospital for the past year.

Needless to say, I didn't make it up to the Amiable Child that afternoon.

ON THE WAY HOME, I remembered flowers. We stopped in at the florist on 112th and I let Clea choose. She went for a pot of tulips—purple, her favorite color. They cost more than I'd planned to spend, but I figured I'd save the bulbs for Barbara to put in the planter boxes. The florist, a woman much too grouchy for someone who worked with blooming things, wrapped the pot in pink foil. Clea carried it home, tulips painting yellow pollen on her chin. Maybe a memorial would prevent Lillian's spirit from becoming a vengeful ghost, haunting the building in death as she had in life.

A cab pulled up in front of the building and the opera singer from our floor climbed out. She wasn't exactly what I'd call a fat lady, but she was big in all directions—tall and broad, with a deep speaking voice. Although she'd owned her apartment for over a year, we'd never said more than a hello in the hall.

We crowded into the elevator and the opera singer smiled down at Clea. She was wearing baggy brown corduroy pants and a black cotton sweater, hardly glamorous. Her pale face had traces of heavy theatrical makeup, black smudges above her eyes. Clea, of course, stared.

"Do I look like a raccoon?" she asked. Clea nodded.

"I'm an actress and I wear makeup for my job. I've just finished a matinee."

She held the elevator door open for us on the twelfth floor, then stopped, keys in hand, and said, "That poor woman! It's so tragic, isn't it, when someone like that dies? You don't know what to feel. Do you know, the police think I was among the last to see her alive."

"You saw her Sunday night?"

"Sunday afternoon. I thought it was odd, because I'd never seen her in the middle of the day before." She lowered her voice. "I was leaving for a Sunday matinee, but a woman came out of that apartment"—she nodded toward Geoff's door—"and I didn't want to ride down in the elevator with her. It's not very charitable of me, but I didn't want to be in that small space with her smelling of cigarettes, so I pretended I forgot something and went back inside. When I came out, the homeless woman was hovering at the foot of the stairs. I said hello, but she ignored me. I was a little hurt, because after all we do allow her to sleep here. I thought she might be looking for a handout, but when I opened my purse she turned her back on me and went up the steps. The elevator came and that was the last I saw of her." She lowered her voice to a stage whisper, accompanied by wide eyes and raised eyebrows. "Do you think someone killed her? The man in Twelve B, he's always muttering about her, or—''

I had to laugh; she did look like a raccoon, a melodramatic raccoon.

She laughed with me. "I know, it's my theatrical nature, he probably wouldn't harm a cockroach!"

The Wilcoxes' door opened. Catherine stepped into the hall. "Oh, hello, hello," she said. "We heard your voice, Anita. Sister would like you to come inside if you have a moment, please, if you would?"

"Of course," I said. Clea headed for the parakeets. I took the pot of tulips out of her hands. "Let me just put these on the landing."

"Flowers for the departed! What a sweet idea!" the opera singer trilled. "I have a vase of roses, I'll put them there too— yes, that will make me feel better." She disappeared into her apartment.

I climbed up the first section of stairs and put the tulips against the wall under the window. The marble floor smelled faintly of Clorox, and there was a pale blotch where Lillian's head had lain. I went the rest of the way up to the area in front of the roof door.

The floor here is the only exposed patch of original tile in the building, small white squares bordered in a pattern of black and dark orange. It had been mopped recently, probably Barbara cleaning up after the crime scene tape was removed. So much for detective work; if there'd ever been any sign of Lillian's presence on this upper landing, it was gone now.

I watched, unseen from above, as the opera singer set a cut-glass vase of yellow roses next to our tulips. Then she lit a votive candle in a dark red cup, crossed herself, and murmured a prayer that sounded like "Hail Mary, Mother Goddess, Pray for us now and at the hour of our death, Amen." Feminism joins the Catholic Church? I'm all for it.

AT THE WILCOXES', Clea was perched in a corner of the sofa with a plate of saltines. Catherine hovered over her, cooing to the birds while Clea alternately ate crackers and poked them through the bars. The only parakeet I could tell by name was Charlie, because he (or she, as the case may have been) was green; Bird and Parker were blue.

Elizabeth was in her power spot, next to the table where the sisters ate their meals and conducted their business. The table's cabriole legs presented their ankles under a purple linen cloth. Plastic lace place mats held permanent positions on top, along with a lazy Susan loaded with sugar, salt, pepper, jam, honey, mustard, Louisiana hot sauce, and a half dozen vitamin bottles. An unsteady pile of magazines and bills, two checkbooks, the TV remote control, black glass rosary beads, a leather cup of miscellaneous pens and pencils, various spools of thread with needles stuck in them, a pincushion, a box of bird seed, and god knows what else, were held at bay by Elizabeth's elbow.

An antique wooden chair with padded arms and a mound of pillows was Elizabeth's throne. She had an afghan of black granny squares with purple, violet, and lavender centers spread across her lap, a cordial glass like a scepter in her right hand.

"Catherine!" Elizabeth thumped her cane. "Pour Anita a glass of sherry."

Sherry meant serious business. Elizabeth waited for me to have a sip before she spoke. The Wilcoxes favor amontillado, and it went a fair way toward easing the memory of Naomi Spivik's body.

"Anita, we are in trouble. Following your advice, when the gentleman from the police department came calling, we made a clean breast of things."

I bet they did. Elizabeth had managed Catherine's career and protected her from more than a few unsuitable suitors, which unfortunately didn't mean either one of them was immune to good manners and subtle flattery. If Neville had gotten them talking about the people in their wall of photographs, there wasn't much they would have held back.

"Detective Neville, yes, a very nice man," Catherine added from the couch. She put a hand to her hair, dyed the jet black of youth partly from vanity but more to annoy Elizabeth with the way it highlights her café au lait skin. You're never too old to flirt.

"So we thought," Elizabeth said, "but I fear we were taken in by good manners and a refined accent. I will say, it was a relief to have the truth about the key out in the open. He gave us his word he would not report us to the cooperative's Board of Directors. However, we have just had a visit from Mr. Orton."

Catherine abandoned Clea. She refilled her own glass, added a drop to mine. "He threatened us!" she said. "He said he knew it was we who gave her the key, and if her heirs sued the building, he would hold us personally responsible!"

I took rather more than a sip of sherry and explained, first, they were not in any way responsible for Lillian's death, even if they'd given her a key, and second—"What heirs, Miss Catherine? Did the police locate her family?"

"No, no, no." Elizabeth tapped her foot for emphasis. "Mr. Orton was speaking hypothetically. The problem is that we have a responsibility to the deceased which we do not know how to fulfill." She stared across the table at Catherine, who got up, went into the bedroom, and shut the door.

I raised my eyebrows in a question. Elizabeth sipped sherry and ignored my look. I took another sip myself, then asked her how well they'd known Lillian Raines. It seemed like an unlikely friendship, on the surface.

"We first saw her while we were feeding the birds. If this nice weather holds, I'll go with Catherine tomorrow. It seems like years I've been shut up in this apartment." Elizabeth poked her finger at a bag of shredded bread on the table. "Of course Catherine couldn't leave the poor thing in peace but had to start a conversation, and then what do you know, she's sleeping in our doorway."

Elizabeth plucked at the afghan in her lap. "She made this for us. Left it on Christmas Eve, with a card. She had a beautiful penmanship. Young people today, the handwriting is not what it was." She rooted around in the pile of envelopes.

Catherine came out, a black leather satchel held like a platter in her two hands. She presented it to me.

The bag was about sixteen inches by twelve inches, maybe three or four inches thick. It had a leather handle and was held closed by two straps with metal buckles. I set it upright in my lap.

"Mrs. Raines left this with us the week before her unfortunate demise."

"And you didn't turn it over to the police?"

My sharp tone activated the sixth sense children have tuned to their parents' voices. Clea hooked her chin over my shoulder, asked, "What's that?"

"Something that belonged to the lady of the landing," I answered.

"Here, child, give this to the birds, and let me talk to your mother." Elizabeth held out a stalk of millet seed. Clea went reluctantly back to the cage. From the chirps and warbles, the birds were delighted.

"Mrs. Raines gave this to us for safekeeping. We promised not to let the police have it, not under any circumstances." Elizabeth scowled as if I'd accused her of breaking a sacred trust. "After her death, Catherine was of the opinion that we should turn it over to the authorities. I might have given it to the detective, but I have learned that where men are concerned first impressions are not enough to form an accurate picture. And you see I was right! He did not keep our confidence. Her family should have it, they and no one else."

"But the information the police need to find them might be in here!" It was catch-22 all over again.

Elizabeth leaned toward me. The sherry and the anxiety on her breath were so strong I had to turn my head. "You had better open it."

Which was exactly what I'd been dying to do. I undid the buckles, lifted the flap over the handle. The black had rubbed off along the seams and bottom edges, and on one side a rectangular object had left an impression in the smooth leather.

"It's been quite a burden to us." Elizabeth folded her hands in her lap.

I took each item out and put it on the table. A plastic shopping bag with yarn and crochet hooks; a stale, half-eaten blueberry muffin wrapped in a napkin; a package of peppermint Lifesavers; a zippered makeup bag, clear plastic gone yellow and stiff with age, with the usual—comb, hairpins, nail file, compact, two lipsticks; a square blue velvet jewel box with most of the plush worn off, and a rectangular red leather box bordered with a geometric pattern in faded gold leaf.

The blue box held several rings—a square-cut emerald set between diamond baguettes; a wedding set, two plain platinum bands and a third band encircled by diamonds; a fire opal surrounded by tiny pearls—and an emerald solitaire pendant and earrings.

In the red case were a man's Patek Philippe watch with a worn leather band; a tie pin and pair of cufflinks in red gold with an engraved *T;* a man's pinkie ring in the shape of a mermaid curled around a rather large ruby; a double strand of pearls with a broken clasp.

The family jewels. The only time I'd seen anything like it was when we got our wedding rings at David Webb, the Madison Avenue jewelers where one of Benno's hundreds of cousins works.

"Put it back," Elizabeth whispered, with a nod at Catherine and Clea.

The opal winked an invitation to slip it on. I shivered with temptation. I lay the boxes aside and felt around in the bottom of the satchel. I came up with two holy medals on a safety pin, several stray cough drops, a silver chain with a square silver locket etched with a pattern of dogwood flowers. The left side of the locket was empty. The right side held a picture of a little boy in a sailor suit.

Elizabeth picked up the medals and turned them over in her arthritic hands. "Saint Nicholas and Saint Anthony. Patron saint of children and patron saint of lost things."

I handed her the locket. She located a magnifying glass in

the clutter and examined the photograph. "Mrs. Raines once told us she had a son who drowned accidentally at the age of four. On another occasion, she said her ex-husband brought the boy to New York City, and she'd come here to find him."

"Did she?"

"As I said, Mrs. Raines was not quite right in her mind. I did not credit her story. You may not be aware of it, but the Amiable Child 'drowned in the fifth year of his age.' Of course, that was in 1797. I thought she went there to mourn the loss of her child, but perhaps..." Elizabeth handed the locket back to me. "When she knocked on our door with this bag, she appeared quite happy. We had never seen her smile and Catherine remarked on it. Mrs. Raines asked if we would safeguard this until her affairs were settled."

"Miss Elizabeth, you have to give this stuff to the police. Maybe they can trace Mrs. Raines through the jewelry. It could have something to do with her death."

"Is there a jeweler's name in the boxes?" Elizabeth asked.

I credited her astuteness, but there was nothing, not even a logo, to identify store or maker. "Do you know what she meant by 'until her affairs were settled'? Did she say anything about seeing a lawyer, something like that?"

"She didn't like to discuss such things, and we never pried. We gave her what help she would accept. I must say, Anita, she didn't always welcome your approaches. She complained about 'interfering social workers,' which I thought was rather uncharitable of her since you had the best of intentions." Elizabeth drained her glass, sat back, and gave me a self-righteous smirk.

The road to hell; damned if you do, damned if you don't. Well, I knew how it felt to be on the receiving end of meddling foster care workers who asked intrusive questions on their monthly visits. It was part of why I'd finally let Lillian be. If she wanted it, Elizabeth could have the credit for being more effective in helping Lillian. At least she'd provided the blanket that kept her warm at night. Nevertheless—I put everything back in the satchel and buckled the straps. I held the bag on my lap and tried to convince Elizabeth to turn it over to the police.

"Perhaps the watch," she finally conceded. "There might be a serial number they could trace. But not the stones, absolutely not. The police are no better than bandits. Things have a way of disappearing once they get into their custody. We gave Mrs. Raines our word to take care of her things, and I don't see how these pieces can be of use in locating her family. That's enough, now, Anita. I will call the detective in the morning."

Our low-voiced argument attracted a curious Clea and Catherine. Elizabeth thumped her cane and glared at Catherine. She got the message, plucked the bag out of my lap, and spirited it off to the bedroom.

With children, speed is the better part of discretion. I carried Clea home, long legs dangling, before she could ask any awkward questions.

TEN

I WAS ALREADY AWAKE, gemstones dancing in my brain, when the alarm went off at 6:30. I snuggled under Benno's arm and put my head on his chest. He's got just the right amount of chest hair—enough to run your fingers through but not so much that you can't touch skin. With a few silver strands, a slight cushion of middle-aged flesh, it makes a great pillow.

Benno ran a hand up my thigh. "You were talking in your sleep again," he informed me.

"What did I say then?" No one had ever told me I talked in my sleep before Benno, and I refused to believe it.

"Something about Girl Scout cookies? When I tried to order thin mints, you told me to shush."

"Girl Scout cookies?" I raised up on an elbow to look at him.

"Don't believe me then. I'm going back to sleep. I don't have to be at the architect's until nine-thirty." He slid out from under me and rolled over, so I got out of bed.

Clea was awake already too, barricaded in her bed with a pile of books. "I'm not going to school," she announced. "I'm staying in bed and reading all day."

Child after my own heart. Not that Clea can read words yet, but she knows the stories that go with the pictures. Our favorite days are gray and wet, when we stay in our nightgowns till supper. This, unfortunately, was a school day. "Not today, Bopster. It's Thursday. Come on now, get up and brush your teeth."

The early start gave me time to take a shower, make oatmeal

for breakfast, and compensate for Clea's uncooperative mood. She complained about the oatmeal because it wasn't winter; she didn't want to bring Benno his cup of coffee in bed because his mouth smelled bad. I surrendered—gave her the usual plain bagel and brought the coffee myself.

Then she wouldn't walk down the hall to push for the elevator. I shooed her out ahead of me so I could close and lock the door.

"Look, Mama, Miss Catherine dropped her sweater." Clea picked up a lavender cardigan from the floor in front of the Wilcoxes' door. "It smells funny."

I sniffed. What that sweater smelled like was gas. Now I noticed it, so did the hall.

I pushed Clea back inside our apartment and closed the door very, very slowly behind us. With gas leaks, the risk of an explosion is the biggest danger. New York apartments have metal fire doors; the metal on metal click of a latch can easily make a spark.

"Here, Clea, in my bedroom." I opened the closet door and tucked Clea in with the laundry. The tone in my voice put her past questions and into whimpering. I gave her a hug. "It's okay, Bops, I'm not mad at you. Just stay here for a minute. I'll be right back."

The Wilcoxes' spare keys were easy to identify in the jumble by the phone. I grabbed for the clear plastic high-heeled shoe filled with sequins and pearls that was attached to their ring.

Benno came out of the bathroom with a towel around his waist.

I handed him the cordless phone and nudged him into the bedroom. "There's gas coming from the Wilcoxes'. I put Clea in the closet, just to be safe. Close the door and call nine-one-one. Tell them we need an ambulance and oxygen, fast. I'm going over there."

Benno grabbed my arm. "No, you're not!"

"I know what I'm doing, Benno, I've done this before. I just have to turn off the stove."

The towel around his waist came loose. I took advantage of

the distraction to get out of the bedroom and close the door behind me. With two doors and brick walls, Clea and Benno were as protected as possible—besides, I wasn't going to set off an explosion.

I HAD TO BE QUICK, and given how strong the smell was, extremely careful. I turned the handle of the sisters' door, gently, and pushed. It was, of course, locked.

I put the Medeco key in the top lock, turning it as slowly as I could. It clicked over to the right. I tried the doorknob again. No luck.

I slid the Medeco out, put the other key in the bottom lock. It wouldn't turn.

Damn. I backed the key out a hair, gave it a delicate jiggle, tried again. Nothing. I pushed the key all the way in, pressed firmly to the right; no movement. Left, and the lock turned over. I opened the door.

The gas was almost palpable, a cloud that stung my eyes. I held my nostrils closed with one hand so I wouldn't inhale any of it and went for the stove. The two front burners were hissing. I shut them off.

Still holding my breath, I went through the open door to the sisters' shared bedroom. Catherine, in the twin bed to my left, lay curled on her side, facing into the room, sheets pulled up to her chin. Elizabeth was on her knees, half out of bed, blankets twisted around her waist.

I let go of my nose to touch her forehead. It was cool and clammy. I took an involuntary breath—a big mistake. I was instantly nauseous.

I aimed for the window between the beds. Good thing they still had the old wooden frames; no chance of them sparking. My stomach heaved up with the window. I sprayed a stream of coffee and oatmeal across the front of the building.

I took a couple deep breaths. Somehow Benno was coughing next to me in the open window.

"I think they're alive," he rasped. "You okay? Let's get them out of here."

My head was light, detached. Benno, bare-chested but wearing jeans, picked Elizabeth up like a baby, blankets and all.

I rolled her royal purple comforter around Catherine, turning her into a caterpillar in a protective cocoon. Her body was limp.

I wrapped my arms across her chest and pulled her off the bed. I overbalanced, fell back on my butt, and landed with Catherine in my lap. Her head flopped back against my shoulder. Benno took her away from me, using the covers like a sled to pull her along.

My stomach rose, but I was too dizzy to stand. I crawled back to the window and stuck my head out. There was nothing left to come up. The back of my throat tasted like gas. Sirens wailed. A police car slammed to a stop in the street below, followed by a fire truck and two ambulances.

Benno came in again, put his arm around my waist, and led me out of the apartment. I sank to the floor next to Catherine, with my head between my knees. The nausea ebbed. I slid a hand under Catherine's neck, feeling for a pulse. Her skin was warm. I found the faint beat of her blood.

Glass crashed on the upper landing, followed by the rare sound of Benno cursing. So much for the opera singer's vase. The stairwell window screeched up.

Firemen in rubber suits and gas masks poured out of the elevator and collided with Benno. The situation degenerated from there, with too many bodies in too much gear trying to figure out what was going on. Mercifully the EMS people ignored the big picture and went for the obvious victims: Elizabeth and Catherine.

My throat burned. My stomach revolted every time I raised my head. I was quite happy just to sit on the floor. The gas was off, the windows were open, the sisters were getting medical attention. I kept my head between my knees.

Then I remembered Clea. I had to get her out of the closet. I lifted my head and tried to push myself upright.

But she hadn't waited for me. Clea was crouched by the door of our apartment, thumb in mouth, eyes big. I opened my arms. Clea crawled into them. I held her tight. Guilt mixed with relief, anger, worry about what she'd gone through, alone in the dark.

"It's okay, it's okay, everything's okay now," I soothed and patted.

Clea curled into a ball like a threatened porcupine, but it didn't last long. She poked her head up and thumped my chest with her fists. "Why did you put me in the closet?" she demanded.

Good, indignation was good. I apologized, explained about gas leaks, praised her for picking up the sweater. I kept her turned away from the chaos in the hall but Clea the curious peeked over my shoulder and took it all in.

"Are they very sick?" she asked. Her voice held a child's scientific interest, not an adult's dread. I sighed with relief. Nightmares grow from the unknown; curiosity expressed can be satisfied.

"They're going to be okay, honey," I said. When it comes to Clea, the answers I give are always rosy. I rocked her back and forth, closed my eyes, and prayed for it to be true.

Benno's voice explaining the situation had reached a level of impatience approaching contempt for the denseness of the person he was talking to. In a minute I'd get up. Clea was quiet in my arms. My mind floated off.

"Where did this blood come from?" A loud voice brought me back.

There must have been a dozen people standing around, not to mention the Wilcox sisters, Clea, me, and the paramedics on the floor. The sisters had been unrolled from their blankets and lay in positions that would have caused them profound embarrassment if they'd been conscious.

Everyone standing took a step back, as if the voice had choreographed them. A crimson path led across the black and gray linoleum and up the stairs.

"Someone is bleeding," the voice announced. Everyone looked at their feet.

The trail ended at Benno. He lifted his right foot. Blood spurted.

"Daaaaddy!" Clea wailed. She struggled to get out of my lap. I held on. "It was the vase," I said, as if knowing its cause would stop the bleeding.

Benno turned his palms up and looked at his hands. He swayed forward, his knees buckling. Not one of the professional rescue personnel cluttering up the hall summoned the presence of mind to catch him.

Clea howled. It started me on a wrenching coughing fit. I doubled over, involuntarily shoving her out of my lap. She grabbed frantically at my hair and switched from "Daddy, Daddy," to "Mommy, Mommy."

Just as I managed to detach Clea from my head and get a comforting arm around her waist, we attracted the attention of a paramedic, who tried to lift Clea away from me. She resumed her death grip on my hair. My yell stopped the coughing, I'll say that, and the EMS guy backed off.

Clea let go. I sat up and she crawled back into my lap. My head hurt like fire. Tears ran down my cheeks. The paramedic, god bless him, held out an oxygen mask. "Would you like to try some oxygen, ma'am?"

He sounded like a person offering free samples in a grocery store. What I really wanted was to deck him, somebody, anybody, whoever I could reach. My throat was so tight I couldn't swallow. My head throbbed where Clea had pulled. I accepted the mask, nuzzled at it like a baby, and got a whiff of cool, moist clarity.

I wouldn't have believed air could taste so good. I breathed, in and out, in and out. The world inside me settled down to a single anxiety: Benno. The situation in the hallway resembled a Heironymous Bosch painting. I could see Benno on the floor but I couldn't tell what the paramedic bent over his foot was doing.

I lifted the mask. "Is my husband okay?" I asked.

"Keep the mask on, please, ma'am, and I'll check," Mr. Politeness said.

A door opened. A man's voice said, "What is going on out here? It sounds like someone's being murdered!"

I turned my head to the left. I was eye level with a sagging scrotum and a limp, uncircumcised penis: Geoffrey Tate, thank you very much, providing a surreal coup de grâce to the situation. I choked into the oxygen mask and gave up on following the action. At least Clea's face was buried in my neck.

I closed my eyes and didn't open them until the paramedic came back to report that the Wilcoxes seemed to be okay but in view of their ages were being taken to St. Luke's "just to be sure everything checks out okay."

I took the mask off. "My husband? The man with the bloody foot?" My tone of voice went right by him.

"I, uh, I'll go check." The man looked like he was about fifteen, with smooth cheeks and a blond mustache that would have benefited from a bit of mascara.

I heard Geoff grumbling about police at ungodly hours of the morning and old ladies dying in the hallway. I risked another glimpse. He'd put on a pair of ratty sweatpants and a gray T-shirt.

I relaxed my hold on Clea. She squirmed free and started for Benno. I grabbed a hand, distracting her with the oxygen mask. "Here, Bopster. Try some of this air." I held the plastic cone out to her.

She poked her nose in for a tentative sniff, then jerked back. "It's cold!"

"Yes, but doesn't it taste good?"

"Air doesn't have a taste." It was a good imitation of my what-are-you,-stupid? voice. She whispered in my ear, "Is he drunk, Mama? He's talking and no one's there." An observant child in an apartment building learns a lot at an early age.

"No, he's what's called hungover. It's how people feel the morning after they're drunk. Here, try the air again. It makes the inside of your brain feel clean." She allowed me to put the mask back over her nose and mouth.

"Hey, is the little girl all right?" Geoff squatted next to us. "I'm sorry I scared you. I heard screaming and I opened the door, I forgot I wasn't wearing any pajamas. Do you know what happened? No one will tell me anything."

Saved by the cavalry. The elevator door opened. Michael Dougherty and Inez Collazo stepped out.

"Yo, Social Worker, you people always party in the hall-way?"

Geoff tapped Michael's chest with his index finger. "Hey, Officer, maybe you can tell me what the hell's going on. Old ladies are dying like flies around here, and you people—" he lurched from friendly to aggrieved with undertones of outrage.

Michael picked Geoff's hand off his chest like it was a ta-rantula. He spoke with extreme courtesy, using his body to back Geoff toward his own apartment.

Inez knelt next to me. "We heard there was a gas leak. It wasn't our call, but the address— Are you all right?"

Clea took the mask off and put her thumb in her mouth. She bumped her head against my chest, twice, a gesture I inter-preted to mean "What about my badge?" Talk about a one-track mind. Clea was fine.

"Not a leak, Inez. The two front burners of the stove were turned full on." Memory kicked in, and I saw the apartment as it was when I entered. "The door to the bedroom was open. I know I didn't turn the knob, because I was so aware of not doing anything to cause a spark. The door should have been closed, so no draft would— Oh shit, the parakeets!"

"Charlie Bird Parker!" Clea scrambled out of my lap. I started up after her but my feet wouldn't obey my brain.

In any case, there was a firefighter standing guard at the Wilcoxes' door. He turned Clea away and she made a beeline for Benno.

"I'll find out what's happening. You stay put." Inez aban-doned me.

The EMS guy, Hotkowski was the name on his badge, took her place. "He's fine, ma'am, just a little cut on his foot. It hit a minor artery is why there was so much blood, but they got it stopped. They'll take him over to St. Luke's for a few stitches. No problem, only the little girl wants to come too."

Hotkowski frowned. It made him look about fifteen and a half. "I guess it's okay though, seeing as there's nothing serious with your husband."

I tried to stand. Hotkowski put a hand under my elbow to help me balance. My legs tingled with needles and threads, as Clea calls them. I hobbled over to Benno. They had him in a wheelchair, a blanket around his shoulders and Clea firmly ensconced on his lap. I'd never seen his face so pale.

"Looks like our girl is going to get her wish to ride in an ambulance," he said. "Wanna come?"

No such luck. Hotkowski sat me down on the stairs to see if I merited further medical attention. He took my blood pressure and my pulse, listened to my heart, asked me what day it was, and decided that Inez and Michael could keep me. Someone, it seemed, had to give a coherent account of the morning. I was the only one left standing.

Benno insisted it was no big deal, and anyway he'd rather have Clea in the Emergency Room with him than me. I have a horror of cutting; the combination of surgical steel with the flesh and blood of my loved ones makes me faint. Clea, on the other hand, was in her glory, ready to roll. I kissed them both and told Benno I'd join them at St. Luke's as soon as I could.

I invited Michael and Inez into my apartment and offered to make coffee while I called in late to work again.

"No thank you, Anita. Go make your call, then come over to the other apartment and show us what you did, please, we need to get going." Inez, all business, headed for the Wilcoxes'.

While I was on the phone with Anne, I picked up shoes and a shirt for Benno. By the time I left, the hall was clear. Michael and Inez were in the Wilcoxes' living room.

Michael made me go over the part about unlocking the door. "It seems pretty clear. One of them, probably the one who was half out of bed, got up to answer nature's call. The stove's in a convenient location for her to put a hand out for balance. So she hit one burner on the way to the can, the other on the way back. Happens all the time with these elderly people."

I knew that was what he'd say. In spite of my promise to let Elizabeth talk to Detective Neville herself, I felt I had to say something about Lillian's satchel. I don't believe in coincidences.

"Not to question your judgment, but I'm not so sure what happened was an accident. The Wilcoxes have a bag that belonged to Lillian Raines, with some fairly valuable jewelry—emeralds, pearls. They showed it to me last night, and Elizabeth was going to call Detective Neville this morning. Maybe I should just make sure it's still here?"

"Why didn't they tell us this to begin with?" Michael glared. "Is the bag right out in plain sight? No? Then no one's going through this apartment without the occupants' permission or a warrant."

I suggested that Lillian's jewelry might give someone a motive for killing her and attacking the sisters.

"What is your problem with admitting that old people fall down the stairs and have heart attacks and leave unlit gas burners on by accident? If I didn't know you, Social Worker, I'd say you're getting paranoid!" Michael slapped his notebook closed, shoved it in his back pocket. "I'm out of here."

Inez tried reason. "Did anyone other than you and the Wilcoxes know about this stuff? Did anyone else know who had it? There's no sign of forcible entry, and you're positive both locks were locked. Besides, how much could that stuff be worth to a fence? It's just not credible, Anita."

"I don't know." But I had to admit she'd raised some good questions, not least of them whether the jewelry was worth killing for.

"Look, Anita, our official report will state this as an accident. You're not happy with that, then you ask the sisters where the stash is and bring it down to the station. Then we'll see. Can we go, please?" Michael said.

I didn't push it any further. Now I was the girl who cried wolf, with about as much credibility in the eyes of the law as Naomi Spivik.

As for Charlie, Bird, and Parker, whether it was the draft

from the open bedroom door or the gas that did them in would take an autopsy to determine.

"And I'm sorry to disappoint you, but New York's finest do not investigate the deaths of parakeets!" Michael was not even amused. He locked the Wilcox apartment and gave me the keys. I put the plastic slipper in my purse.

They did, however, condescend to give me a ride to St. Luke's.

On the way out of the building, we passed Mr. Malinsky lurking by the mailboxes. "Pardon me." His eyebrows bushed out over gold-rimmed bifocals. With his ramrod posture, he was taller than Michael. "Officer, would you please be so kind as to inform me what exactly is going on here?"

Howard Orton opened his door with the same question. This did not bode well for my getting to the hospital in a hurry, but I waited while Michael explained the situation. Malinsky scowled I-told-you-so at Howard.

"Tell me, Officer Dougherty, will these women be fined for creating a fire hazard?" Mr. Malinsky asked. I could see him working up his next Crud Report.

Michael tried to put an end to the conversation. "I'm sorry, sir, but we don't write summonses for this kind of thing. Now, if you'll excuse us?"

"Just one moment, Officer. I'm sure the insurers will want to know that some action has been taken," Howard chimed in.

"I think this is a matter for social services, not the police department," Michael said, smoothly passing the buck in my direction.

He was right, but I was furious with him for putting me on the spot like that. The two elderly men turned to me. Before either of them could get his mouth open, I handed Howard a Senior Services card. "My agency will be working with the Wilcox sisters to ensure that there's no further cause for concern," I said, somewhat snappishly, I have to admit.

Mr. Malinsky snorted.

"Thank you, Anita, we'll be in touch." Howard stepped back and gestured Malinsky into his apartment.

I was totally taken aback. Malinsky's Crud Reports were so critical of the board, it was hard to imagine him as a welcome guest of the board president's. But Malinsky went right in, as if this were a prearranged meeting. For all I knew, it could be a Machiavellian twist on building politics—Howard using Malinsky as a lever to shift the board toward more rules and regulations. Or the two of them plotting to rid the building of problem shareholders? I shuddered.

I SAT IN THE BACK of the cruiser and brooded. Michael was right, accidents and heart attacks did happen to older people. I'd made enough of a fool of myself with unsupported theories and suspicions. If the police didn't believe me, well, I'd keep quiet until I had something that would convince them. There were still a couple of things I wanted to check out. Like talking to Marky Mark about the business with Regina Hilton.

And I had worries of my own. Benno's voice when he was wheeled away had been warm and reassuring, but I knew there was going to be hell to pay for my conduct this morning. Now that it was over, I realized what a chance I'd taken—I'd done the best I could to protect my child, but I'd rushed in with no thought for the danger I might be in myself. Benno would be well within his rights to chew me out for it.

Social work is not what you would call a risky occupation, except of course for those who work in prisons, mental institutions, emergency rooms; with juvenile delinquents, drug addicts, abusers of all stripes. Not to mention disaster relief—hurricane, tornado, mass suicide, rampaging teenager with a rifle—when they send the social workers in on the heels of the National Guard.

The elderly are a fairly safe population, if you discount the occasional violent Alzheimer's patient prone to attacking aides with a cane, but the problems they present often involve issues of life and death. Working with senior citizens living in the community rather than a nursing home has meant learning to handle all sorts of medical emergencies. The Wilcoxes was the worst case of gas I'd dealt with, but not the first.

Fortunately for my thought processes, it was a short ride.

St. Luke's is an old hospital, and no attempt has been made to brighten it up. The walls are a dingy cream, streaked and splotched with unidentifiable smears in colors that suggest the insides of human bodies. The ER waiting room has rows of orange molded plastic chairs, bolted to each other and to the floor, littered with human misery. The personnel aren't much better. No one looks up or smiles. No one answers any questions, let alone offers information. If you're not bleeding copiously or screaming hysterically, all you rate is "Have your insurance ready and stay seated until your name is called."

Patients move through the ER like elephants through a boa constrictor. The police escort got me behind the counter, into the warren of corridors and cubicles where those lucky enough to merit a bed are stored. I followed the sound of Clea's voice and found Benno.

The resident on duty had decided a row of butterfly bandages would work better than stitches, to Clea's disappointment. She's chosen her calling well, my daughter the future doctor. Benno put on the shirt I'd brought and managed to get his hurt foot into an untied running shoe.

I left him filling out forms that promised the hospital his next-born child if our insurance didn't cover everything, and went to hunt up the sisters. A Filipino nurse told me they would be admitted as soon as a double room became available and directed me to a pair of beds behind a striped curtain.

Catherine's eyes were closed, her skin blanched. She was still breathing oxygen from the EMS cone-type mask. Elizabeth had been switched to pale green tubes in her nose and had the situation well in hand. She was insisting, as loudly as her raspy throat would allow, that Michael tell her what had happened to her birds. "I may be feeble, young man, but I am not senile!" Her hand slapped the bed for emphasis.

"I was just telling Ms. Wilcox that we won't need to be bothering her right now and she should get some rest." Michael greeted me as if I were an angel of deliverance.

I held Elizabeth's wrinkled hand while I broke the news.

She took it like a trouper. I had to promise to put Charlie, Bird, and Parker in plastic bags—"A separate bag for each one"—and store them in the freezer so they could be buried in Riverside Park when she and Catherine were able to get out again.

I asked if there was anything else she needed.

"Yes, please, Anita, call Mrs. Clark and tell her we will be unable to care for Mitzi. The Clarks are going to Chicago this afternoon, and she will need to make other arrangements."

I agreed to that request also. At least Elizabeth's mind was clear. Catherine looked like an over-made-up corpse, with bright red splotches of color on her cheekbones. I stroked the hair back from her forehead. She opened her eyes, glanced at my face, and closed them again. Her breathing calmed.

"That young doctor says she'll be all right, but what he knows about it I don't know! Looks to me like he still needs his mother to comb his hair for him." Elizabeth, as tart as ever.

Inez ducked through the curtain with a cup of tea for Elizabeth. She was followed by a doctor who could have been Hotkowski's twin brother. He vetoed the tea, and we left him to deal with Elizabeth's protests.

Amazingly, it was only eleven o'clock in the morning. I felt like I'd lived through a week in the past few hours.

Benno was on the pay phone, rescheduling his morning meeting. Clea, for a change, was paying more attention to the assortment of minor casualties in the waiting room than to the omnipresent TV muttering in a corner, even though it was tuned to *Sesame Street*. An unshaven white man with a large belly and a half-smoked, unlit cigarette in his mouth was fascinated by Oscar the Grouch in his garbage can; Clea was fascinated by the hand cradled at an odd angle in the man's lap.

I decided to try for a normal day. Benno was anxious to catch the architect before lunch. Clea didn't seem to be suffering any ill effects from the closet; I figured a return to her routine would be the best way to minimize any lingering upset.

If she had any problems at school, they'd bring her over to me at work.

Inez and Michael gave us a ride in the squad car. They treated Clea to the works, from explaining why there are no door handles in the backseat—so prisoners can't escape—to siren and flashing lights. Clea was going to be queen of the kindergarten.

I HAD A WELCOME of a different sort when I straggled in to the office. The fact that Michael stopped by to see her did nothing to improve Anne's mood.

"Good morning, Anita. It's so nice of you to grace us with your presence." She swiveled her chair away from me. "You've got a welcoming committee in the conference room. They've been here almost an hour."

Spurred by Naomi's death, Ruth Goldfarb and Alberta Lu had decided to come forward and file a complaint about Regina Hilton. They wanted me to go with them to the Twenty-sixth Precinct to "swear out a warrant," as Ruth put it, with fine disregard for the distinction between the role of the courts and the role of the police.

Their timing couldn't have been better. With Inez and Michael right there, I was able to pull off something social workers rarely get to do: provide a service more immediately and more conveniently than anticipated.

I introduced Officers Dougherty and Collazo and let them run the show. Inez asked questions and took notes; the women directed their answers to Michael. It's a dynamic I've noticed before.

Many of the older women in this neighborhood are retired librarians, nurses, teachers, social workers, secretaries. They'd run offices and departments, been administrators at Columbia, Barnard, Jewish and Union Theological Seminaries. They were career women at a time when men held the prestige positions and the ostensible power. Ruth Goldfarb had been a secretary in the provost's office; Alberta Lu had been executive assistant to the dean of Asian Studies. These women had exercised considerable authority, but always in the name of their bosses, and they retained the habit of appearing to defer to the male sex.

Michael smiled and nodded sympathetically; the women smiled and complained. Inez kept them on track and managed to establish a few facts, all of which I already knew.

1. A woman named Regina Hilton, who lived in the Maramay, Apt. 4D, had stolen money and jewelry from them.
2. She then threatened them with eviction if they reported her.
3. The eviction would be carried out by Frank Sprague, the building manager, with whom Regina was having an affair.
4. Mr. Sprague had already evicted another of Regina's lovers, a man described as heavyset, black, with a mustache or beard.

Without revealing my source, I added Mar-Lee's information that the ex-lover's name was Mark something and he now slept in Riverside Park.

They made Inez promise not to name names when they talked to Frank. I still couldn't understand why the women were so worried about reprisals. Tenants, especially elderly tenants who pay their rent on time, are well protected in New York City. Apart from letting Regina's thievery go on unchecked, the Spragues generally looked out for the building's elderly occupants, calling in Senior Services if necessary. It was in their interests to keep stable tenants in place. Their salary was the same, regardless of whether the rent was paid with Section 8 vouchers or at rent-controlled rates.

Although if the Bike Building was sold, that could change. If the purchaser was Columbia, the Spragues were likely to lose their jobs so the university could put its own people in place.

Ruth and Alberta, however, had heard that a private developer was interested in the building. As Alberta put it, "Frank

Sprague is a full-service building manager. If the new owner wants vacant rooms, he'll be happy to oblige. He has no sense of loyalty to us long-term tenants who have overlooked his innumerable lapses in the past!''

In truth, I had no doubt that Frank had, over the years, resorted to extralegal methods to get rid of undesirable tenants. It wasn't difficult; you take someone who's behind in his rent, put his belongings in the street and a new lock on his door; it was probably how Frank had gotten rid of Marky Mark... But murder?

Ruth was convinced Naomi had been done away with for her room. ''We're nothing but old women. When the powers that be start to move, we're the pawns in their game and we get sacrificed!''

Although these were competent women who had resources and knew their rights, age breeds insecurity, especially in people who've grown up knowing the bottom can drop out at any time. Together they put up a strong front, but their individual lives were precarious. I knew from their charts that Alberta had been a widow for thirty years; Ruth had carried on a long-term affair with a married colleague, now a widower with Alzheimer's.

Which might explain why they didn't want Edna to know about Frank's extracurricular activities. Keeping secrets becomes a habit, along with protecting the wives. There's nothing more destabilizing to a long-running affair than a wife who's confronted with it. As long as dignity is maintained, things are fine; but back a wife into a corner—

Well, they'd given the police something to get started with, although they hadn't been able to provide exact dates of when things had gone missing. Michael made a little speech, reassuring and pompous, to acknowledge their courage in speaking up. They left the office fluttering with pride at their good citizenship.

MICHAEL LEANED OVER Anne's desk. She raised her voice in answer to whatever he'd asked her, and directed it at me.

"I already have a dinner date, thank you very much. Miss Clea has invited me to her school potluck tonight, and I've made my fabulous Greek salad."

"Potluck? Oh, shit." I'd forgotten about the Cathedral School's spring event.

"I'm very fond of children, you know," Michael persisted

"What do you think, Anita? Will Clea mind if I bring this lug too?"

Clea couldn't care less, I thought. She was generous with her invitations.

"Sure, why not?" I said, my mind elsewhere.

ELEVEN

NOT FOR THE FIRST TIME, I wished we had a couch in the office. What I really wanted was to lie down and sleep for a few days, wake up to find I'd dreamed the whole thing.

I called Benno instead. The potluck wasn't his kind of event, and I knew he'd try to get out of socializing with what he refers to as "yuppie parents who think the sun rises and sets with their kids." Not that we don't feel the same way about Clea, but we also believe grown-ups should have the final say.

It's not a popular attitude. Clea, however, is a pleasure to be around—unlike a notable few of the monsters she goes to school with, who whine, demand, interrupt, and run their parents ragged. They have televisions in their bedrooms and more toys than F.A.O. Schwartz; in Benno's opinion, the parents deserve what they get.

The meeting with the architect had gone well, and Benno said he'd knock off early. Not that he'd admit his foot was bothering him, but—he promised to join us at the picnic. About that, Clea would be delighted.

Anne turned out to be my saving grace. I accepted her peace offering of soup for lunch, along with the loan of her *Times* and permission to do the crossword puzzle. I took it over to the fountain, where I sat on the warm stone and let the negative ions from the spray do their work of reviving my spirits.

The Peace Fountain is actually quite a morbid piece of sculpture. Satan is getting thrown, decapitated head first, out of heaven by the Archangel Michael. A bronze disc in the center has the moon on one side, the sun on the other. A gentle giraffe drinks from a corner of the moon's lips, which is fine, but the figures stand on a huge crab with Satan's severed head dangling from one claw. The horned face hangs upside down, grimacing, still attached to its body by ropes of neck sinew.

The lion and the lamb lie down together in the sun. The angel's huge wings rise above the spray; his sword rests on the crab, which represents the instincts. The water issues from bronze mouths, flames of freedom spewing forth chaos to bathe a pedestal in the shape of DNA's double helix.

It's about opposing forces—good/evil, harmony/violence, life/death—reconciled in God's peace. I pondered the dual nature of the murderous angel and the victimized devil. It seemed more like contradiction than resolution. I gave it up and headed home for a picnic blanket.

I WALKED DOWN 111th, preparing to resist the siren call of my couch. When I first got the job at Senior Services, I went home for lunch. It didn't take long to realize there were better things to do with a lunch hour than breakfast dishes. Not to mention the temptation of taking a nap if I went home. My attempt at a mental inventory of my desk made it clear that regardless of how much I had to do at work, I was too tired to think. The lure of sleep was likely to triumph.

The transition from hot sun and street noise to dim hallway put me in a trance. The elevator smelled of vinegar and hot pepper—Barbara cooking pig feet. I leaned against the wall, closed my eyes, let myself be transported up. When I stepped out on the twelfth floor, I was more than halfway dreaming.

"Hell-*lo*." A woman's voice woke me.

My heart pounded in my throat, two sharp beats, before I realized who it was. The redhead smiled at me, hands on her hips. I could have sworn she'd just come out of the Wilcox apartment, but how could she have? I drew a blank.

"Are the sisters home?" I asked.

"No, and from the look of things, neither are you." She tilted her head and studied me. "Geoff thought he heard a noise, so I knocked and no one answered. It was terrible what happened, wasn't it?''

Her voice was high and perky, reeking of friendliness. Geoff's closed door stayed closed. Something was happening, but I didn't know what it was.

I stuck out my hand. "I don't think we've really met. I'm Anita Servi."

She put a cool, damp hand in mine. I noticed the rings were gone and her nails were an iridescent pearl. She met my eyes for a quick second. What I read in her face could have been amusement, caution, curiosity, contempt; what it wasn't was friendly.

"I didn't get your name?" I tried again.

"Regina."

She circled around behind me, opened Geoff's door, and stepped inside.

I turned with her, stuttering some nonsense about Regina being a pretty name, what was her last name? She closed the door in my face.

It had to be. She'd been on the Bike Building stoop when Naomi died. She had access to the building. I'd found Regina Hilton, Hotel Queen, thief, and—murderer? In the apartment right next to mine?

My need for sleep evaporated. I unlocked my apartment door, went inside, and locked it behind me, the ramifications of Regina's identity percolating through my brain.

I got the stepstool out and was rummaging for a blanket in the built-in cabinet above the door when I heard the squeak of hinges from the Wilcoxes.

A bag of Clea's baby clothes followed me down in my hurry to get to the peephole. I stepped on it, fell to one knee, and was too late to catch anyone in the hall.

The elevator dial was dark, which meant no one had just gone down or come up. I put the baby clothes away, got the blanket, folded the stepstool.

Remembering my duty to the parakeets, I knocked on the

sisters' door. No response. I tried the knob. It turned, and I pushed the door open.

This did not compute. Michael had locked up in the morning; I remembered him handing me the keys. That door should still have been locked.

I did what stupid heroines in books always do—went into the apartment. "Hello? Miss Catherine? Miss Elizabeth? Is anyone home?" I closed the door behind me but I didn't turn the lock.

In spite of the open windows, there was still a trace of gas smell. I kept up a running commentary as I walked around, trying to compensate for the silent birdcage—and to quiet my imagination. I noticed a layer of grime on the chairs, dust on the picture frames.

The half-closed bedroom door hit another wrong note. During the day it was always wide open, allowing light to filter into the tiny kitchen. I tiptoed into the bedroom. The bedcovers tossed on the floor, the curtains moving in and out the open window, spooked me. I wasn't comfortable even being there, let alone searching through the sisters' bedroom without permission, but I tossed the covers back onto the beds and looked underneath—nothing.

I checked the closets, under the sofa—no satchel. I couldn't bring myself to touch the dead birds with my bare hands so I used a paper towel to pick up their little bodies, stiff under the soft feathers. I put each one in its own plastic bag, as instructed, and put them in the freezer.

When I left, I made sure I locked both locks.

IT WAS A RELIEF to hit the hot street. Spring had become summer overnight. People carrying coats slung over their shoulders actually smiled at one another. Mama Joy's had the air-conditioning going full bore. I bought two liters each of Coke, Sprite, and seltzer. My cooking is not in the same league as the school's cadre of gourmet moms, but I've found it's impossible to be humiliated by beverages.

Sunlight shimmered in the trees along 112th. My thoughts

danced with the leaves. Regina Hilton and Geoff Tate's girl-friend were one and the same. That bit of knowledge tied everything together. She stole, she threatened, she killed Lillian Raines, she killed Naomi Spivik, she tried to kill the Wilcox sisters.

It was nice and neat. I'd tell Michael and she'd be arrested. Once the police had the connection, it would be easy for them to find evidence.

But *why* did she do all this? my inner devil's advocate asked. Okay, so Lillian had jewels, but why didn't Regina just steal them like she did with the others?

I don't know, I whined back. I just know she did. Then killed Naomi because Naomi threatened to expose her. She had to get the Wilcoxes out of the way to get the satchel—or maybe she thought they knew she'd killed Lillian for it?

And how did she get in all those locked doors? the devil's advocate mocked.

Oh, shut up, I told the voice, although I had to admit it had a point.

CLEA CAME IN from the after-school program promptly at five. Anne said she'd wait a bit for Michael and sent us across to the canon's lawn with her salad. Clea immediately joined a group of kids in a game involving three big beach balls. I picked a spot in the sun, off to the side by a feathery patch of yarrow, and lay the paisley bedspread on the grass.

I'd been looking forward to the spring event because it's held outside rather than in the school cafeteria, and because I'd figured out which parents to talk to—and which to avoid.

I laid out cups, napkins, plates, forks. It was good to be useful, to make small talk with the other mothers. Someone had brought wine. I poured myself a glass of red, got a plate of crackers, cheese, and grapes, and went back to my blanket.

I was staring off toward the unfinished dome of the cathedral when I caught sight of Anne and Michael strolling toward the tables of food under the trees. Anne was in red, from high-top Reeboks to burgundy crushed velvet skirt to crimson silk tunic.

Michael provided a sartorial surprise, in black jeans and a highly starched oxford shirt, light blue, unbuttoned at the neck, sleeves rolled up. He seemed almost slender without the waistload of equipment. Motorcycle boots added to his height.

"Who's the hunk?" I asked Anne.

"He cleans up pretty good, doesn't he?"

Michael blushed. "Hey, Social Worker, you got any old ladies in distress hiding under this rug or is it safe to sit down?"

Clea spotted Anne and dragged her off to referee the game. Michael helped himself to a cracker and a piece of cheese from my plate.

"Make yourself right at home," I said. "I've got some information that'll crack the case for you."

"What case?" Michael frowned. "There is no case, Anita."

"Yes there is." I told him first about Regina's identity, then that I hadn't found the satchel at the Wilcoxes', and added my conclusions.

He listened, working his way through my grapes, until I wound down. We watched Anne flashing like a red macaw among the children. Dead silence was not the reaction I'd expected.

Finally he faced me. "Look, Anita. I'm not a detective, but I'll tell you what any NYPD detective will tell you: we don't get paid to invent crimes. What we have here is two deaths. One was an accident. The other was natural causes. We have death certificates that say so. The department has no interest, zero, zip, nada, none, in increasing the annual total of homicides committed in this city."

Michael gazed across the lawn at Anne. I waited. He shook his head like he'd just come back to earth.

"Your neighbors didn't tell you where the bag was?"

I shook my head.

"So for all you know, it's tucked away safe and sound. Okay, let's play the rest of it out. What's your evidence? Regina may—remember innocent until proven guilty?—*may* be terrorizing a bunch of *bubbes* with more money than brains.

We're working on that. As for her knowing both victims, if that were all it took you'd be a prime suspect yourself."

I didn't say one word.

"How did Regina get into Spivik's locked apartment? You adding breaking and entering to her purported criminal activities?"

By then, I'd worked it out. "That's elementary. Regina's sleeping with Frank Sprague, so she had access to the office. Frank couldn't find Naomi's keys because Regina had them, and he covered up for her. Or maybe Frank did something to cause a heart attack and scare Naomi to death. Or—" I was going to bring up Sam Katz, but Michael cut me off.

"Yeah, that's the ticket. Those paranoid old ladies were right all along, Sprague's killing them off for their rooms. I suppose Donald Trump hired him to do it so he can turn the building into condos, that's it, and Edna's going to be the next victim. Then Frank and Regina will live happily ever after on his ill-gotten gains. That sound like a plausible scenario to you?" Michael radiated sarcasm.

So much for being taken seriously. I took a sideways tack and aimed at the behavior of Regina's that we knew was criminal. "Have you found anything more on the thefts?"

"As a matter of fact, Inez and I tried to locate your Ms. Hilton but she wasn't at home when we called."

"Obviously, since she was in my building this afternoon." I couldn't keep from needling.

Michael ignored it. "We'll try again tomorrow, the boyfriend's place too, now we know where else to find her. Your Marky Mark turns out to be one Mark Jenrette, main place of residence the New York Central railway tunnel, up near 120th. One of the community outreach guys knew him."

The train tracks under Riverside Park had been abandoned for decades until Amtrak recently started running trains up the west side again. The community of homeless people who'd taken up residence in the tunnel were mostly relocated by the city, but a few iconoclasts continued to use the northern end, up by 125th Street where there's easy access near the river.

Michael rooted around for another grape and came up empty. He threw me a bone instead. "I was just in your building. The weirdo on the first floor, with the notebook? Neville asked me to return it to him on my way over here. You didn't hear this from me—I read through it, and on Sunday night, according to Mr. Orton, the redhead left the building around eleven p.m. in the company of Geoff Tate and another man referred to as 'young Mr. Turner.' She came back in by herself, around six-thirty a.m. He had a few good lines about her tits, excuse me, breasts, comparing her to the Whore of Babylon. Favorably."

"What does that prove?"

Michael spaced his words like he was talking to a retard. "If Ms. Hilton left the building at eleven p.m. and returned at six-thirty a.m., it confirms her story of being out all night. No way was she bumping off the old lady in the stairwell sometime after midnight. Orton is strange, but I bet he don't miss much. Has a fish-eye peephole, you can turn in all directions."

"When did Larry and Geoff come back in? He missed that, didn't he?"

"They live there, Anita. Orton doesn't actually write down everything everyone does, just what he finds interesting. There's some cast of characters you got there—you didn't hear this from me either, but Tate's not the only one with a girlfriend in the Bike Building."

"I knew that." John Clark and Sylvia Chase. I could just imagine what Howard Orton had to say about poor Mr. Clark. I wondered who else knew about their affair, and how hard John tried to keep it a secret. It was a thought I didn't share with Michael.

People started lining up for food. Anne came laughing over to get us.

Michael grinned up at her. "See, it's true what they say, isn't it, Sun Risin'? Now you're delightful, but this morning it was sailors take warning!"

"What are you on about?" Anne favored him with a scowl.

"Sure, you know the old saying, 'Red sky at night, sailors'

delight. Red sky at morning, sailors take warning,'" he quoted. "And tonight you are a delight."

It was enough to make a married woman gag.

I WENT TO ROUND UP Clea. If I didn't make her eat, she wouldn't realize she was hungry until we got home. Benno limped in and I fixed him a plate, too. Clea played doctor, using her backpack as a pillow to elevate his foot. We left serious subjects aside and enjoyed the warm evening.

It was after nine when we left. Clea's motto is "Bop till you Drop"; she had to make the rounds and say good-bye to everyone. I drifted on ahead of her and Benno, and stopped by the guard booth to wait for them. There was a glow from the side window of the Senior Services office—Anne probably left a light on in the reception area.

The light went out. The door opened. A woman stepped out, with Emma right behind her. Emma turned to lock the door. Her companion moved aside, into the light from an all-night bulb over the door to the gym. It was Regina.

I faded behind the guard booth so they wouldn't see me. They spoke together in low voices. Benno came up, carrying Clea. We followed Emma and Regina toward Amsterdam.

"Emma puts in a long day, doesn't she?" Benno remarked.

"She's doing funding proposals," I said. Emma and Regina? I couldn't come up with a theory wild enough to explain what they were doing together.

Regina crossed the street. Emma hailed a cab. It was just pulling away when we got to the curb.

We tucked Clea into bed, unwashed, in her underwear. It was all I could do to brush my own teeth. We were all out like lights by ten.

I think there were trains in my dreams, but it could have been Benno snoring.

TWELVE

IT WOULD BE HARD to imagine a week that started with a corpse in a stairwell ending any worse than it had begun, but that one did. Clea thudded into my side of the bed just after dawn. She burrowed her way under the covers and started sucking on a strand of my hair. Kid saliva, the perfect conditioner.

Once I was awake, I couldn't get back to sleep. The red eye of the rising sun reflected off a window in the building between us and the river, filling the bedroom with an orange light. I thought about the grave of the Amiable Child on its bluff overlooking the Hudson, and the train tracks running underneath. I wondered if Mark Jenrette was an early riser.

I elbowed Benno. "I'm getting up. Will you take Clea to school? I want to go down to the park before work."

He grunted, opened one eye. I took it for a yes and started to get out of bed. Benno reached an arm out and pulled me back down.

"No, you don't. I get first shot at the bathroom."

New York apartments. Our bathroom has the floor space of a phone booth. At night when we crowd in together to brush our teeth, we elbow and push, spit rinse water at each other, have a good old time. Mornings, however, are serious business. Benno's at the top of the pecking order; I let him go first.

Clea eggbeatered the covers into a knot, leaving me cold and exposed. I got up to pee, unfortunately for Benno's privacy.

I'm quite partial to the view of Benno in the shower, his penis in profile with water dripping off the upturned ridge—

my own personal Priapus. It's a brief pleasure, though; I got out fast when he turned the shower off.

I'm not a morning person. On the rare occasions I find myself wide awake at dawn I like to get out and about. It's as if I've been given an empty space in the day, a piece of time to spend as I like. The trees in Riverside Park beckon me down the hill; my legs want to move. When I walk, my body takes over and my unquiet mind shuts up. It's meditation in action.

I don't jog, and I'm not into fancy workout clothes. Thanks to another of Benno's hundred cousins, I have a slightly used pair of state-of-the-art sneakers. I pulled on a faded magenta sweatshirt and an ancient pair of gray sweats with a hole in one knee from a roller-blading incident. A fashion statement it's not, as Benno tactfully puts it.

I used the stairs to do some leg stretches while I waited for the elevator. Barbara had mopped up Benno's bloodstains and put the roses in a plastic vase. I realized with surprise that not once in the times I'd been in and out yesterday had I glanced up at the landing or thought about Lillian's body lying there. Nothing like fresh troubles to take your mind off old ones. The window was still open. I hoped her spirit had found its way out.

I got on the elevator and managed two quick knee bends before it stopped at 11. Just who I wanted to see: John Clark, with Mitzi like a dust mop on a leash.

I made the third knee bend a deep one, avoiding his eyes. Mitzi bounced around me, sniffing my face, delighted to have someone down on her level. Her one redeeming feature is she never barks—not when she greets you in the hall, not when she's left alone in the apartment, not at pigeons on the windowsill.

"Mitzi, *Mitzi!* That's enough! Sorry she's so excited," John said.

I stood up, shrugged, smiled vaguely in his direction.

On an ordinary morning, we would have left it at that. Elevator etiquette, especially at an early hour, requires no more than a nod. Speaking to people who may not have had their coffee yet is considered extremely rude. Recent events, unfortunately, seemed to have broken down more than one social boundary.

"Thank you very much, Anita, for taking the time to call and let us know about the Wilcox sisters' accident yesterday," John said.

"I'm sorry you had to cancel your trip."

"Oh, no, not at all. Margery went anyway. It's her sister, you see, and it was actually somewhat of a relief to me not to have to go along."

You heel, I thought. Nice to have your wife out of town so you can fool around. But I said a polite thank you when he held the elevator door open for me.

It was a gorgeous morning, not a trace of winter left in the air.

"You're going to the park?" John asked. "Do you mind if I join you?"

"Don't you take Mitzi to the dog run? I'm heading the other way." I made a stab at salvaging my solitary stroll.

"No, there are too many big dogs in the run at this hour and Mitzi is easily intimidated. I like to walk north myself. It's quieter in that direction."

Just my luck, and I'd already indicated where I was going. We crossed the Drive. In the early morning, Riverside Park belongs to dogs and runners. The dog people like the middle level, where the leash laws aren't enforced until after 9:00 a.m. I'm happy to leave it to them and stay up top. Between the urine smell and the confetti of crack vials in the corners, the stairs are not particularly appealing.

The low, early-morning sun glittered in the air. The trees blushed green with spring. It takes a plant with a hardy nature to bloom here, and the ability to flourish in spite of neglect. Tiny grape hyacinths and wood violets rose to the challenge. Tasting nasty helps, too—even squirrels won't eat daffodil bulbs. A profusion of yellow dotted the slope down to the Women's Grove.

Mitzi zigged and zagged, snuffling through last year's leaves.

"Do you know about the Grave of the Amiable Child?" I asked.

"Yes, the little boy who died back in the seventeen hundreds. It's just north of Grant's Tomb, isn't it? Is that your destination?"

"Uh-huh. You don't have to come all the way, if you'd rather not."

"No, no, on the contrary, I expect I'd better come along. That area has a slightly sinister feel to it, don't you think?" John Clark set his shoulders like he was ready to be my bodyguard if it became necessary. He's a thin man, with wire-rim glasses and an advanced case of male-pattern baldness. I figured I'd be doing the protecting, if push came to shove.

North of 120th Street, the park is not at all well maintained. Just south of the Amiable Child, on the west side of Riverside Drive, is a scenic overlook—a roofed pavilion with low walls and columns. At the turn of the century, people sat and watched the boats on the Hudson and enjoyed the breeze. Now it's a summer camp for homeless people, a derelict, melancholy place. The fluted Doric columns are girdled with graffiti. Loose boards hang from the coffered ceiling. Sections of the ornamental wall have been inelegantly patched with cinder blocks

A pile of old leaves, soggy from snow melt and rain, huddled in a protected corner. There was a blackened area in the center of the stone floor where someone must have built a fire to keep warm.

As we got to the long, open side of the pavilion facing Riverside Drive, Mitzi went ballistic. She lunged forward, yanking the leash out of John's hand, and ran to the pile of leaves in the corner. Her bark—well, it was more like a cross between a growl and a howl than a real bark—startled both of us. Then she reared up on her hind legs and danced backward, her front paws shadow-boxing in the air like Muhammad Ali in training.

It was the weirdest thing I've ever seen a dog do. She dropped down to all fours, ran to the leaves, and started digging with frantic terrier intensity.

John shook his head. "I forget she's a dog, with an animal's sense of smell—the last time she got this excited, it was over a dead rat. Mitzi! Let's go!''

She pranced backward on her hind legs again, her teeth bared, daring all comers. John reached for the leash and reeled her in.

''I hope it's not another rat,'' I said. We've had a problem this year, since Columbia knocked down the former student center. Mitzi's discovery was something small, paler than the brown oak leaves that had been covering it. I was looking around for a stick to prod it with when my brain registered the shape.

I backed into John Clark and almost knocked him over. We both recoiled from the contact.

''Is that a hand?'' John asked.

The piled leaves were not a slick, compacted mass like you'd expect after a winter of exposure; they had been redistributed to form a mound the length and shape of a human body.

I nodded. I was shocked speechless, but Mitzi had found her voice. She trembled and howled in John's arms. It was all dog, a sound nothing in her life had ever required her to make before. John carried Mitzi out of the pavilion but it didn't calm her down.

I knelt on the damp floor. The hand appeared to belong to a woman; its ringless fingers were manicured with French tips painted a frosty pearl. The skin was a metallic bluish white. I pulled the sleeve of my sweatshirt over my hand and brushed leaves aside in the area where my primal brain thought a head should be.

Her hair was the same reddish-brown as the leaves. I exposed an ear, a gold hoop earring. Mitzi had found a woman's body. I stumbled backward again. I had to get away from it.

''Oh god, I've got to get away from here.'' John voiced my thoughts. He was paler than the hand, and on the edge of howling himself. ''I've got to get Mitzi away from this.''

''Yeah, okay.'' I took a few breaths. ''Why don't you call the police, and I'll stay here, in case—go on, go. I'll be all right, you take care of your dog!''

Mitzi's need to free herself from John's grip was deep and desperate. Her bark made the hair on my arms stand up. John headed toward Riverside Church for a phone.

THE SUN WAS WARM on my face. The pavilion wasn't really a secluded spot, but the southbound traffic speeding down Riverside Drive made me realize how alone I was. There were no joggers; no one waited at the bus stop. It was still too early for any of the God Box employees to be parking their cars.

I remembered I'd wanted to find Marky Mark. Now I hoped to hell he was nowhere around.

I stared into the pavilion. The body was completely covered, except where Mitzi and I had scraped the leaves away. I told myself I didn't have to touch her, she was dead, there was nothing I could do. But what if it was hypothermia? Every minute counted. And I had an urgent need to see her whole face, to make sure of who she was.

I went back into the pavilion and looked over the far wall. There are boarded-up rest rooms down below that someone could be living in. I didn't see or hear any signs of human habitation.

The woman lay on her stomach, her head facing toward me. The exposed hand rested by her cheek. I had a sense of déjà vu, as if I'd come across a corpse in the woods at some other time or place in my life. It felt familiar in a way that finding Lillian hadn't, which was odd, because that was an experience I'd actually had before.

I wrapped the sleeve of my sweatshirt around my left hand again and slid it under her wrist. The arm stuck out of a brown leather sleeve. It was stiff, resistant to being lifted. I noticed the nailbeds were a dark blue under the iridescent polish. I felt for a pulse with the fingertips of my right hand. As soon as I touched bare skin, I knew I was touching death.

I put the arm down gently. I pulled the sleeve of my sweatshirt over my other hand, stroked the hair and leaves away. Regina.

I WAS STANDING with my back against a column in the opposite corner of the pavilion when the sirens wailed up. I didn't open my eyes until I felt a hand on my shoulder and heard Michael Dougherty say, "Yo, Social Worker, we *really* have to stop meeting like this."

No snappy response came to me. Michael put an arm across my shoulders and squeezed. "That bad, huh? Hey, come sit in the car. I just got coffee when the call came in. Since you're my favorite social worker, you can have the first sip."

It was hot and sweet, just what I needed. Michael pulled his notebook out of his back pocket and squatted next to me. I sat sideways in the car, my feet out the open door. "Just tell me what happened, Anita," he said.

I lowered my gaze to the blue paper cup in my hands. Its Greek chorus said, We Are Happy to Serve You.

"Michael. It's Geoff Tate's girlfriend, Regina, the woman I think is the same as Regina Hilton? Did you tell Inez?"

He patted my knee. "Hey, give me a chance. You're the first thing that happened this morning. What makes you think it's Regina Hilton?"

I sipped the coffee, spoke slowly to keep control of my voice. I watched Michael's hands as he wrote. He had long, fine black hairs between his knuckles and a college ring with a blue stone on the ring finger of his right hand.

When I got to the part about feeling for a pulse, Inez interrupted. "Was that all you did, besides clear her face? Touch her wrist?"

I nodded and gulped more coffee. The warmth spread around my ribs. I felt like I was hovering over the scene, a dispassionate observer. The sugar brought me back.

"She may have been strangled," Inez said. "There's a scarf wrapped around her throat."

I closed my eyes and the scene reappeared. Regina's face, like her hand, was a faint metallic blue, her hair the dead colors of autumn. Her open eye was oblivious of the leaf debris clouding its vision.

"Congratulations, Social Worker. It looks like you might've actually stumbled on a real homicide this time."

Inez nodded. "Looks like it. Here's Detective Neville."

Michael and Inez deserted me to fill him in on the situation. I finished the coffee, added the cup to the mess on the floor, and leaned back against the seat. Sunspots danced red behind my closed eyes.

Marky Mark, Geoff Tate, Sam Katz, Frank Sprague. The men in Regina's life struggled with each other. Lillian and Naomi raised their heads and asked, What about us? Edna leered at me from behind her Plexiglas partition. Mar-Lee dished dirt on Regina. Regina as murder victim rather than murderer short-circuited all my theories.

I stood up, stretched. *Go know* Benno's Aunt Rose added to the chorus. It wasn't even nine o'clock. I wished my mind was as clear as the blue morning sky.

Inez came over with a Polaroid of the dead woman and the good news that she and Michael would take me home. While they were at it, they'd show the photo to Geoff and ask him to confirm my ID. After that, they were assigned to go by the Bike Building to see if the Spragues could also identify the dead woman as Regina Hilton.

We rode the twelve blocks crammed into the front seat. I was grateful to be between them, their solid human warmth a bulwark against Regina's fate. Michael groused about the coffee I'd finished. The caffeine, amplified by three sugars, buzzed in my fingers. I wished I'd saved him some too, but I knew better than to complain.

I left them pounding on Geoff Tate's door and went to take a quick shower. I had to change into something more professional and call work. It made four days out of five I'd been late, Anne pointed out, and wasn't it lucky I had such an understanding boss? It was.

WHEN I CAME OUT of my apartment twenty minutes later, Inez and Michael were still in the hall. Geoff leaned against the door frame, trying to focus on the snapshot he held in one shaky hand. He was wearing baggy jockey shorts and a Pearl Jam T-shirt—cooler than I would've credited. His hair stood up in clumps.

"Do you know this woman?" Michael asked, for about the fifteenth time, judging from the edge in his voice.

Geoff registered my presence. "Hi, Anita. These officers are showing me a picture." He waved the Polaroid at me. "You want to see?"

Inez signaled me to keep quiet. "Okay, Mr. Tate. Sorry to bother you." She held her hand out for the picture. Geoff ignored it.

"'Sno bother, I was only sleeping. Had a late night last night, had a fight with…" He gestured into the apartment.

"Is your girlfriend here with you, sir?" Michael asked.

Geoff peered into the gloom. "You never know. She split, but she might've come back. You know how women are, they—"

"Could I just take look?"

Michael edged around Geoff and disappeared into the apartment. Geoff ran a hand over his head, trying to focus on the picture again. "You know, it kinda resembles my lady friend. She looks about as bad as I feel."

Michael spoke from the bowels of Geoff's domain. "Nope, looks like you slept alone, bud. No women here."

"Yeah, I told you she wasn't here." He handed the picture to Inez.

Michael stepped around Geoff. "So what did you two fight about?"

"Shit if I remember. The usual, she wants to get married, I don't, something like that. Has a very high opinion of herself, does Regina. Regina Vagina, I call her." He sang it, soft and mocking. "Excuse me ladies. She got royally pissed last night and she walked out on me. I think it was last night, I don't know. Good riddance to royal rubbish, that's what I say."

"What's Regina's last name?" Michael persisted.

"Regina, Queenavagina Hilton. Like the hotel. Takes after Leona Helmsley, another bitch on wheels. What do you want from my life? We had a fight, it happens all the time. She complain to the cops?" His eyes narrowed at Inez.

"Did you hit her, sir?" Michael asked.

Geoff swayed backward. "Hit her? That what she said? Do I look like the kind of man hits women? Yeah, she provoked me all right, but I'll show you who did the hitting. Have a look at this."

He stuck his chin out, offering the stubbly underside of his neck. There were two short, deep scratches. "That's what she did to me, the lying bitch."

Inez spoke. "The woman in this photograph was found dead this morning, Mr. Tate. We need to know if you recognize her."

"You're putting me on, right? I just saw her last night, she was hot as a pistol." Geoff took another look at the picture and seemed to sober up. "Yeah, that could be Regina, uh-huh. What happened to her?"

"Her body was found less than an hour ago. Would you happen to know her address?" Inez said.

"She lives over on 112th, in the building with all the bikes in front. Uh, sorry, ladies, I gotta go, if you know what I mean." He cupped a hand over his jockeys, made a conspiratorial face at Michael, and closed the door on us.

"There's a nice display of grief for you," Michael said. "Show the man a picture of his dead lady friend, and what happens? He needs to urinate. Some neighbor you got there, Social Worker."

"Maybe he wanted to cry in private." I pushed for the elevator. "Or maybe he was embarrassed. How would you feel, swearing at someone, then finding out she was dead?" I almost felt sorry for Geoff. It wasn't the kind of news to face with a hangover.

"Well, his girlfriend's last name is Hilton," Inez said. "You were right about that, Anita. Didn't you say someone else used the same nickname, the Hotel Queen? I expect Neville will want us to bring Mr. Tate in for a conversation."

"Yeah, but we might as well let him sleep it off. He'll make more sense when he sobers up. He's not goin' anywhere right now anyway," Michael said.

"When he sobers up?" I laughed. "I look at him as the best lesson Clea could have in the dangers of demon rum."

"There is that," Michael agreed.

THIRTEEN

THERE ARE MOMENTS in New York when everything seems to go quiet. No horns, no jackhammers, no radios, no car alarms, no cars even. The whole city shifts into neutral at the same time, inhales, pauses to reflect. It doesn't last long, and the background grind starts up again. We stood on the front stoop, blinking in the bright, silent air.

"Seems like déjà vu all over again, don't it?" Michael took his hat off and scratched his head. "Didn't we start the week on this stoop?"

"Can I tag along when you talk to the Spragues?" I asked.

It was pushing my luck, and I knew it. There was no reason for me to be there, but I'd been on the edge of Regina's life all week and I felt I had a right to see the thing through. Find someone's dead body, you're responsible for her forever?

Inez and Michael looked at each other. Some silent communication passed between them, a partner thing I guess.

"This is a murder investigation," Inez said.

"It's a free country," Michael said. "We can't stop you."

It was better than nothing.

"We're lucky you knew who she was, Social Worker. Saved her from being a Jane Doe. Who knows how long it would've been before anyone came looking for her?"

Not so lucky for me, I thought, remembering Regina's staring eye.

We drove the three blocks to the Bike Building. The sugar rush had worn off. I felt old, weary, sick of life, afraid of death.

Three women had died; two others had come close. My safe world wasn't anymore.

IN A RARE BURST of ambition, Frank Sprague was out front hosing down the sidewalk. It's a morning ritual, Supers washing sidewalks. Out-of-towners think it's laziness, a waste of water—why don't they sweep? The natives know it's a sanitary necessity. What happens on New York sidewalks, from dog shit to vomit, requires more than a broom.

The sight of the patrol car appeared to cause Frank acute intestinal distress. He shut off the water, grimaced, turned his back on us, and threw the hose down the outside steps. The basement door scraped closed behind him.

"A warm welcome," Inez said to Michael. "It looks like you will have another opportunity to use your considerable charms on Mrs. Sprague."

"The lovely Edna, the charming Edna— Whoops. Anita, your neighbor has rubbed off on me. I'm feelin' lyrical."

"Hush." Inez frowned. A skinny white guy in a souvenir T-shirt from Montana with a grizzly bear on it opened the door on his way out. Frank and Edna were in the office.

There was no small talk this morning. The Spragues knew they had to put up with the police; the police knew the cooperation they'd get would be the minimum necessary. Inez slid the Polaroid across the counter.

Edna picked it up by one corner and snorted. "Huh. That's the hussy from the fourth floor. Hey, Frank, they got a picture of your girlfriend. She don't look too good!" Edna passed the picture to Frank.

"She have a name?" Michael winked at Edna.

She smiled back. "Regina Hilton. Four B. Something happen to her?" Edna was already looking for the key.

Michael told them. Watching Frank's face, I'd swear one of the emotions that crossed it was relief. Edna, on the other hand, had a glint of malice in her eye. No, there would be no shortage of suspects in Regina's death.

I waited in the manager's office while Michael and Inez went up. They took the elevator; even cops didn't want to risk interrupting a transaction on the stairs.

Edna offered me a cup of coffee, which I declined—although I could have done with the shot I was sure she'd add to hers. She went through the door into their apartment. I was alone with Frank.

"So is there any truth to the rumor Columbia's negotiating to buy this place?" Might as well jump right in.

"I don't know where you heard it, but the university's not interested in this building." Frank headed for the door and had another thought. "I like you, Anita, but you want to be careful. We don't need no nosy social workers asking questions and stirring things up with the tenants, you hear me?" He shook his finger in my face.

I was half a second away from biting it. I hate to be pointed at and told off.

Frank glared at me. I looked down. There was a malevolence in his eyes that I didn't need any more of.

Edna came through the manager's door. Frank shot her a warning look and split; she hauled a pack of Salems out of her pocket and offered me one. I took it even though it was menthol. Cigarettes are as good a way to establish rapport as any. I tried my line on her and got a nibble.

"Where'd you hear that? University sniffed around, but we got too many occupied rooms for them, it ain't good community relations if they start evicting."

"So the building is up for sale?"

"Did I say that?" Edna wriggled off the hook. "See how things get started? I do my job, I don't pay no attention to the men in suits unless they're talking to me. Why don't you go wait for your friends by the elevators, now?"

There's nothing New Yorkers love so much as discussing real estate; if neither Frank nor Edna was willing to gossip, something had to be up. The superstition is, you don't mention a pending sale. Anything can queer a deal.

I WAS DISAPPOINTED not to find anyone occupying the chairs by the elevator. Usually a few of the braver souls congregate here to exchange the news, watch who goes in and out, wait for the mail.

Sitting is a major recreational activity for older people. Some feed the birds and squirrels in Riverside Park; others prefer the bustle of Strauss Park on 107th. The most hotly contested turf, however, is the Broadway medians. The homeless people leave their stuff on the benches where they can watch it while they panhandle; the old people like to sit where the action is. Neither group wants to share, so it's first come, first served.

Broadway, the street, puts on as good a show as any theater on the Great White Way. One time, Catherine and I saw a tall black man gamboling around in nothing but a pair of red wool socks. Two cops chased after him, lumbering hippos to his graceful gazelle. It made both our days. Who needs TV talk shows?

The Bench Brigades are also an excellent source of rumor. The same people sit together, day after day, year after year, and keep up a running commentary on neighborhood affairs. I sometimes make the rounds, doing outreach. If I had time later, or maybe Saturday morning... There was bound to be information out there.

THE ELEVATOR DOOR opened. Michael was swinging a Ziploc bag of prescription bottles. "Looks like your dead girl knew how to party. Got your ups, downs, and sidewayses, every one from a different doctor. You know any of these people, Anita? Agnes Haley, Helen Rakov, Dorothy Jackson, Naomi Spivik?"

"All elderly women who live here. And you know Naomi Spivik, who died Wednesday?" The one I believe was murdered by Regina, I thought but didn't say.

"Looks like she did a little steal-and-deal. Haldol, Percocet, Valium, Xanax, Dexedrine, Zoloft, Prozac," Michael read. "A regular pharmacopoeia. You'd think people would've raised holy hell if these meds were missing—some of this shit is pretty addictive."

"Can I see it?"

"Yeah, just don't open the bag. Inez is talking to the neighbors, and I'm off to give Edna a receipt for the key."

It amazes me, what doctors prescribe for old people. Half the stuff in the bag was psychotropics, complete with side effects such as drowsiness, loss of balance, loss of appetite—not to mention hallucinations, if compliance and dosage weren't carefully monitored.

I had a client who was given Xanax after her husband of fifty-six years passed away. She walked around in a groggy haze until she stumbled and broke her hip. In the hospital, they switched her to Prozac for depression. The result was a different kind of stupor.

Yes, I've seen Haldol make Alzheimer's patients more tractable, but at the expense of alertness. We're not that far from the bad old days when nursing homes routinely sedated elderly patients for the staff's convenience. The difference now is, people are unnecessarily medicated in their own homes. It's still cheaper than getting them to a day program, or involved in activities where they could put their experiences and abilities to use.

It wasn't hard to imagine what Regina had been up to with the medications. She'd been in people's rooms; once she knew what they took, she could just call in a renewal—and pick it up without telling the person whose prescription it was. The pharmacist would assume she was doing someone a favor; I'd done it myself, for homebound clients. Whatever she paid would be a fraction of the street value.

Inez and I left Michael chatting up Edna in the office and went to wait out front.

He came out whistling. "Seems our Edna did know Frank was *schtupping* Regina. It's Yiddish for 'your place or mine,'" he said, in answer to Inez's look. "Frank liked the female tenants to show their appreciation for the privilege of living in his fine building. Seems he liked Regina so much, she wasn't paying rent."

"How did Edna feel about that?" I asked.

"The sex? As long as he kept his hands off her, she didn't

care who he stuck it to. The rent? She was pissed. Seems they had words about it just last night.'' Michael wiggled his eyebrows at us.

I offered to buy him a cup of coffee to replace the one I'd drunk. He and Inez did another partner consultation with their eyes and accepted. I figured I was already late for work; might as well be hung for a sheep as a lamb.

Inez locked the bag of evidence in the trunk. They left the car where it was, parked at a hydrant, and we walked to the Hungarian Pastry Shop. I wanted to get a table and talk.

''Yes, it's nice to sit in the sun, but I don't think you would enjoy the comments some of our tax-paying citizens address to cops in uniform when we eat in public,'' Inez said. ''As if we are not entitled to a break like everyone else!''

But then, as if she agreed with the public about a cop always working, Inez insisted they had to get back to the crime scene. So I bought Michael his coffee to go, and we all went to work.

''I THOUGHT YOU WERE going to be here in fifteen minutes, two hours ago?'' Sailors take warning: Anne was in red again, scarlet silk blouse with black skirt and vest. ''What's your excuse today? Another body in the hall?''

I hadn't told her about Regina when I called in late. Talking about it would have made it more real, and I wasn't ready for that yet. ''No, the body I found today was in Riverside Park.''

Anne's jaw dropping was such a rare sight, I told her the whole story. It appeased her, but not by much. Anne had left something out of our earlier conversation, herself—Emma wasn't coming in to work.

''She said she was here late last night and she woke up with a migraine, she just couldn't get out of bed. She wants us to go ahead with the tea anyway, you know how everyone looks forward to it. At least you remembered the cookies!'' Anne finished.

Friday afternoon at Senior Services means high tea, a small gathering of staff and clients, described by Emma as ''an opportunity for agency and community to interact in an informal situation in order to increase communication and build bonds of trust.'' It's a ritual she insists on, come high water or low budget. When we're flush, we have fruit platters from Mama Joy's. This close to the end of the fiscal year, funds are low and we all chip in.

I looked down at my hand. I was still holding the white bakery box with two pounds of butter cookies I'd splurged on at the Hungarian Pastry.

Emma worked late last night. Emma left the office accompanied by Regina Hilton. Regina was dead. My stomach did a sick lurch.

Anne plowed on. ''An Elizabeth Wilcox has been calling for you from St. Luke's every fifteen minutes since five minutes after nine this morning. They're keeping her sister for another night, and she refuses to be discharged. I paged Dr. Lorenzo at ten.''

I put the box of cookies on Anne's desk and retreated to my cubicle before she could read my face. What had Emma and Regina been doing together?

I stared at Clea's princesses, the dragon's fiery breath lapping at their gowns. What was going on? Too many questions. I picked up the pile of pink message slips, forcing myself into social worker mode. This, at least, was a situation I knew how to tackle.

The Wilcox story could be read chronologically from the messages. First Elizabeth, panicked because they wanted to send her home. Then the social worker from 9B, the floor they put the old people on, panicked because Elizabeth refused to be discharged. Elizabeth, twice more. A note from Anne saying she'd paged Dr. Lorenzo. Social worker again, could I verify Elizabeth was unable to return home unassisted—which meant rules were about to bend.

By the time I reached Elizabeth, Dr. Lorenzo had decreed that she needed another day of ''observation.'' Catherine would not be abandoned in the hospital. Half the time, if you do nothing, situations sort themselves out; clients are often capable of more than we give them credit for. This is the part of social work that keeps me humble.

Elizabeth requested that I pick them up the next day, told me what clothes they needed, and where to find everything. I didn't ask Elizabeth about Lillian's satchel. She was agitated enough already; it could wait until they were safely home.

But I kept seeing Regina in the hall outside their door. What-ifs and whys circled my brain. I tapped at the crystal prisms hanging in my window, sent rainbows rocketing around the room. Three women were dead.

To silence my thoughts, I called Benno for comfort and re-assurance. The dangers he imagines for me are so exaggerated, it makes the real risks of living in the city and working in poor neighborhoods seem manageable. Today's events, however, were beyond anything even Benno could have foreseen. I got his answering machine, chickened out, and left a nonurgent message about going out to dinner. Friday nights we try to have a nice meal, to wind up the week as a family. Tonight, there was no way I was going to cook.

ATTENDANCE AT the tea was by invitation. How people get on the guest list is known only to Emma, although Anne and I speculated endlessly on her criteria. Sometimes it's obvious—people who are withdrawn, depressed, in need of socializing, with a few cheerful ones thrown in for balance. Then there are the discourteous, argumentative whiners, people even Emma is unable to be civil to. Anne thinks they're her version of a hair shirt; I think she's trying to teach them manners and can't accept defeat.

Anne had put a copy of the guest list on my desk. Today's criteria were not hard to read: Ruth Goldfarb and Alberta Lu, being rewarded for blowing the whistle on Regina Hilton; Mr. Patel and Sylvia Chase at my request, so I could see them before his surgery next week. Helen Rakov, by coincidence one of the pill bottle ladies, was also invited—the token kvetch?

I drew doodles around the names, letting my thoughts float.

I'd never known Emma to miss a tea. I reached for the phone and dialed her home number. The answering machine picked up. I didn't leave a message. What could I say? "Hope you're feeling better soon, by the way, did you strangle Regina Hilton last night? Do you mind if I tell the police I saw the two of you together?"

AT 1:45, DEBBIE AND I set out chairs and card tables. Anne made two pots of tea, Earl Grey and Tension Tamer. The guests arrived promptly at 2:00.

The news of Regina Hilton's death seemed to suck the life out of the room. To have the burden lifted so suddenly, after they'd nerved themselves to defy her—only Mrs. Lu was gleeful, and made no bones about it. "I knew it! A person who takes advantage is taken advantage of! We thank you, Anita, but you see fate also has a hand. Very good!" She hummed with satisfaction.

"Oh dear no, it's not good at all!" Helen Rakov spoke in a whisper. "We're in danger, in serious danger. It's not just the young woman, it's three women dead. All from the Maramay, all—oh, dear!"

Ruth Goldfarb backed her up. "Obviously there is a serial killer at work, and what are the police doing to protect us? Nothing! Any one of us could be next!"

Anne broke the stunned silence by spouting the party line according to the police, along with a reassuring touch of Michael's pomposity. "Ms. Rakov, I know you're upset, but just think for a minute. The police have ascertained that Ms. Raines' death was an accident, and Naomi Spivik's doctor said she died of a heart attack. If Ms. Hilton was killed, you can be sure the police will make every effort to apprehend the perpetrator. You don't have anything to worry about."

"Nothing to worry about? Have you heard a word we said, young woman?" Ruth snapped a cookie in her hands. "If it's not a serial killer, it could be someone with more practical motives. There are powerful interests who have financial reasons to want elderly tenants out of the Maramay. The police are turning a blind eye. The building manager is a weak vessel. This would not be the first time senior citizens in New York were terrorized into leaving rent-controlled apartments!"

"Now, Ruth, surely you're not suggesting that Mr. Sprague—" Sylvia Chase took a turn at reasoning with her.

"There's not much I don't think Frank and Edna Sprague are capable of! They'd crush us like cockroaches if we were in their way. I've heard a private developer made an offer for the Maramay. The university is one thing. They'd let us coexist with the students, but a developer will wring obscene profits from the building. Those Spragues know which side their bread and butter comes from. Our rooms are worth ten times what we pay. We're in danger, and what are the police doing? Nothing!" This time Sylvia was on the receiving end of Ruth's wrath.

She took it on the chin. "This is not the East Side in the 1980s. No SRO in this neighborhood is worth killing for, even to a private developer."

"That's easy for you to say!" Ruth shot a glance at Mr. Patel, sitting silent by Sylvia's side. "I for one do not intend to be a sitting duck. I'm going to the hardware store for a new deadbolt, and I will *not* be leaving an extra key in the office. I don't care how risky it is, Anita, you can save your breath!" She stalked out, leaving a plate full of crumbled cookies.

"Wait, Ruth, I'm coming with you!" Helen Rakov gathered up her purse and cane and tottered off.

"Would anyone like more tea?" Debbie offered. There were no takers.

I HAD WANTED TO talk to Sylvia alone, but I couldn't figure out how to do it, tactfully, during the tea. I watched her walk down the driveway with Mr. Patel. At the corner, he crossed Amsterdam to 111th. She turned right, toward the cathedral. I caught up with her at the top of the stairs, outside the huge bronze doors.

A sculptor stood on a raised scaffold in the middle arch, carving the Portals of Paradise. His chisel and mallet tapped out the song of a solitary woodpecker. Six to a side, saints emerged from stone to usher the sinners in. I called Sylvia's name. She turned around, her hand on her heart, her face pale. "Oh, Anita. What is it?"

"Ms. Chase, do you have a minute? I wanted to ask you—"

"I was just going inside. After your news, I felt the need of quiet and contemplation. Come along, if you like. And please, call me Sylvia."

We passed into the dim hush of the cathedral, down the left-hand aisle. We settled at the side chapel devoted to a gigantic cluster of quartz crystals from a mine in Arkansas.

At seventy-two, Sylvia Chase is one of the younger old people and still what they used to call a "looker," with her hair colored a natural light blonde. Her suit, navy blue linen with gold buttons, was a Chanel she'd probably owned for twenty years. Granted, she had a serious foundation garment on underneath, but it fit her like a glove.

"You've been very thorough with the arrangements for Mr. Patel's operation. I can't think of anything we haven't already discussed?" Her tone was polite, her attention clearly on other things.

"I hope I'm not intruding, but—you're on the same floor as Regina, aren't you?"

She gave a small nod. I couldn't read her expression in the gloom. I spoke quickly, before I lost my nerve.

"Did you know Lillian Raines? I'm wondering if Regina, if they knew each other…" I noticed Sylvia's pained frown and shut up.

"You must have been sent by the powers that be." Sylvia gazed up into the vaulted reaches of the cathedral. "I came here to think things through on my own, but perhaps you'll be able to help me. I want to do what's right. I know I should talk to the police, but it's not possible for me." She twisted a gold ring on the middle finger of her right hand.

I waited. Sometimes silence works better than questions.

"I overheard something last night which may have a bearing

on Regina's death. I came in a little after midnight, and I heard voices—I listened. The way Regina was talking, it was terrible.''

Sylvia gave me a rueful smile. ''I liked her. She gave a good manicure''—Sylvia displayed her nails, short ovals of Raven Red—''and she never tried anything dishonest with me. We were neighbors, and she was always polite. Which is more than I can say for some—let me tell you, those women—yes, Regina entertained Frank Sprague, and he took care of her rent. It's an old arrangement.'' Her smile grew into an amused grin.

''You look shocked, but he was young once too, and handsome. Charming. You young women, you think sexual harassment was invented yesterday. We've all had bosses with 'Roman hands and Russian fingers.' More than one of those women, Ruth Goldfarb included, has had a month's rent 'overlooked' by Frank Sprague. I never held that against Regina. She took care of herself. She didn't judge people, and she had spunk.''

So did Sylvia Chase.

''Last night she was very angry. It's one thing you young women do that women of my generation were trained not to do—you speak your minds. Regina was giving whoever he was a rather large piece of hers. When she moved on to his sexual competence—I did catch a bon mot.'' Sylvia chuckled. '' 'If there's no will, there's no way.' Not a very tactful way to put it, but wickedly accurate, don't you think?''

It *was* a good line. Had it been thrown at Geoff Tate? He said he'd had a fight with Regina; if he hadn't been able to get it up, that could explain why he'd been home alone.

I did, of course, encourage her to tell the police.

''No, I've told you, Anita, and I feel better. If it becomes necessary, then you may tell them and I will confirm the story on strict guarantee of anonymity. I was not alone, and I cannot say anything that would involve my companion in any way. I tell you this only so you'll understand why I will not come forward.'' She stood up to leave.

I decided to try the direct approach. "Were you with John Clark?"

I caught her totally unprepared. Something like fear flickered in her eyes as she sank back in the chair.

She looked me in the eye and lied. "I don't know what you're talking about."

"Yes you do." I said it gently. "I live in the same building as Mr. Clark."

Sylvia exhaled. "Yes, I know. And Regina has been seeing his upstairs neighbor. I knew the coincidence would bring us trouble. Anita, you must understand that extramarital affairs have rules as strict as marriage vows. I will take the secret of mine with me to my grave. His wife does not know about us, and protecting her at all costs is part of our agreement. That is all I will say, now or ever."

To live outside the law, you must be honest?

But at least it put Geoff with Regina later than Emma.

I left Sylvia sitting, head bowed, in the cathedral.

FOURTEEN

BACK AT SENIOR SERVICES, I folded my arms on my desk, put my head down, and closed my eyes. A dream swirl of images spun me through a castle overlooking the Hudson. It was a dark afternoon, rain clouds threatening women in long full skirts who promenaded along stone parapets. I recognized Anne, Regina, Mar-Lee; John and Margery Clark strolled arm in arm while Sylvia Chase watched from a far corner. Lightning cracked behind a parapet wall.

"Mama! Mama, wake up!" Clea bumped her body against me. My chair rolled away from the desk. I came to with the sense of something waiting to happen. Clea was mad.

"Don't do that! You're not s'posed to sleep at work. I'll tell on you!"

"No, you won't," I grouched. She flounced off to report me to Anne anyway.

The phone rang. Since Clea was bending Anne's ear, I answered. It was Benno.

I gave him an abbreviated version of the morning. Sometimes I can't tell if he's angry or worried; this time he was both. He got fixated on why had I gone to that part of the park alone; when I explained I was with John Clark, he switched to why had Mr. Clark left me there with the body.

Clea came back in and I stopped him from further ranting by changing the subject to supper plans. Not that we never argue in front of her, but we make an effort to cork it when she's around. An unintended benefit of this policy is that it gives us a self-imposed cooling-off period. By evening, Benno would calm down enough to realize I hadn't done anything wrong, or stupid, or been in any danger myself.

We agreed to meet at the West End at 7:00. Thank the goddess for Fridays. It had been a long week, and I was pretty well wrung out.

The temperature was in the high eighties, the sky a baked blue. Summer, no doubt about it. New Yorkers are pessimists by nature, greeting an April heat wave not with relief after a dreary winter but as a dire reminder of how hot July will be. I was just grateful the humidity hadn't set in yet.

In the suburbs, summer means the Good Humor truck; in New York it's street vendors and Italian ices, or the Hispanic version, *helados,* shaved ice in a paper cone served with a squirt of syrup, in exotic flavors like guava and tamarindo. At 25 cents a scoop, iceys are the cheapest thrill in Manhattan. My current favorite is mango; Clea goes for cherry topped with rainbow. We took ours to the playground.

I kept my eyes peeled for Mar-Lee and Marky Mark, but no luck. I did notice more blue patrol cars than usual trolling up and down Riverside Drive and two pairs of cops on foot strolled past the playground. It was gratifying to see my tax dollars at work.

I squeezed my icey up out of its little paper cup and worried about Clea. She's sunny by nature, doesn't brood over things. From her behavior on the monkey bars, neither Lillian's death nor the gas attack on the Wilcoxes had slowed her down.

I was the one having a hard time with mortality. Being close to a death brings awareness of the thin barrier between the living and the dead. When you see how permeable the membrane is, you realize just how easy it is to get to the other side. After my grandmother died, I felt death beckoning me to cross over every time I stepped into the street, waited on a subway platform, drove a car. But now I had Benno and Clea to keep me firmly on the side of life. I sucked the last taste of mango and tossed the cup in the trash. It was enough with death already.

AT 6:30 WE HEADED over to the West End, with a nod for the bust of Samuel Tilden at the foot of 112th. When I moved here, I took him as a sign that I'd come to a good place. Tilden Park, in the Oakland hills, was the wilderness next door where my mother took me hiking. To me he's a Californian, for all that the plaque said he was governor of New York.

I forced my brain to focus on the street scene. Compartmentalization is an effective coping mechanism, but you can wall things off for only so long before the images seep out. If I didn't talk about my grisly discovery, every pile of leaves I ever saw would be growing hands, every stairwell would bloom with blood stains. This wasn't the time to be thinking about corpses. Until I had time to decompress, however, distraction would have to do.

Clea and I swung our hands together. A nun in full black habit with a white wimple, rosary beads at her waist and black suede Birkenstocks on her feet, glided down 113th to the brownstone convent.

Clea tugged my hand. "Mama, do nuns wear underwear?"

I couldn't answer, I was laughing so hard. Clea made for a pretty good coping mechanism, herself.

When we got to the corner, Miss Sharp-Eyes noticed Anne and Michael at an outside table. I would have gone in after a quick hello and given them some lovers' privacy, but discreet is not yet in Clea's vocabulary.

"Mama! Anne's eating with the policeman and he's not wearing any uniform."

Heads turned. I cracked up again. Michael was, in fact, dressed—jeans with a pale yellow oxford shirt this time.

Clea knew the looks and the laughter were for her, but she didn't get the joke. Her face crumpled into tears. Anne lifted her over the rail and took her off to the ladies' for some girl talk. Michael offered me a seat. There were two bottles of Dos Equis on the table.

"Anne was just telling me about the tea party. You know, those women might have a reason to be frightened. We filled Neville in on Regina Hilton's activities. He hasn't reopened the elderly women's cases, although he said to tell you he's keeping an eye out for any possible connection. The phrase *multiple murderer* is not being used, but when we did the door-to-door in the Bike Building, we told everyone to check their locks.''

"Do you know anything about a developer interested in buying it?"

"You still hung up on Donald Trump? Me, I'd prefer a serial killer on the loose to dealing with real estate interests. Serial killer's easier to stop!" Michael tipped his beer in my direction.

"I'm serious, Michael. I asked the Spragues, and Edna let something slip about a buyer. Can't you guys find out if there's a deal pending?"

"Sure, we'll use our infinite resources and unlimited manpower to track down all your wild theories." Michael leaned across the table. "Look Anita, you act like you think cops are stupid because given a choice, we go for the simple explanation, but that's usually how things are. With Regina, there's no shortage of possible perps. Current lovers, ex-lovers—hell, it could have been a stranger she met in a bar who got out of hand, you'll pardon the expression."

"You left out wives of lovers. Edna's strong enough, and she had reason. Where was she last night?"

"On the desk till midnight. Then she went to bed. With Frank. Your basic unprovable, unbreakable alibi. So right now, we're sticking with the most likely scenarios. We had your Mr. Geoffrey Tate over to the station this afternoon. He is one pathetic piece of work. Wasn't too clear on what happened last night, except what he already told us. He's got a pretty good opinion of himself—told Neville if he'd gone after her, he wouldn't have woken up alone. He had no idea what time any of this was. I don't suppose you heard anything, around midnight?"

"No, but I wouldn't have unless they were yelling in the hall. Did anyone talk to Mr. Orton?"

"Seems Orton came down with a case of 'see no evil, hear no evil, write down no evil.' He allowed as how he might have seen Tate and Regina come in together before he went to bed at ten-thirty, but nothing on either of them leaving the building. The M.E. thinks Regina died sometime between one and four a.m.''

"So why does Neville think Geoff did it?''

"Well, Tate is just his first choice. The physical evidence points to him, he admitted they had a fight—but the crime scene guys think she was killed where she was found, and we can't place Tate in the park. He gave permission for an apartment search while Neville was questioning him. We took some shoes and pants, but given his relationship with the victim, you'd expect to find fibers and hair. Jesus, Joseph, and Mary but I'm spending a lot of time in your verstinking building!''

"I think the word you want is *verstunkene*,'' I said. Not that my Yiddish is any more authentic but it comes via Benno, who grew up with the real thing.

Clea and Anne came out of the ladies' room. Clea hit me up for a dollar and made a beeline for the jukebox. She's adept at getting strangers to read her the selections; if that doesn't work, she just pushes buttons. It's all music to her.

Anne pulled a chair up next to Michael. "Are you two solving the crime?''

"Of course,'' I said. "Superior minds at work.''

"So who did it? Colonel Mustard in the Maramay with a pipe wrench?''

Mr. Clark in the park with a scarf? I pushed the thought away for later. "Do you have any other suspects?''

"Yeah, Mark Jenrette turned up in a sweep of the park. When he realized she'd died a few blocks from where he was camped, he totally lost it. We got the works, tears and all.''

"Maybe he really cared about her,'' Anne said. "Did that occur to you?''

"Women. Any time a man cries, you think he's being honest and expressing his real feelings. Let me tell you, Ms. Feminist, men are no different than women. We know how effective tears are, we just don't stoop to those kind of tactics.''

"So what happened?'' I interrupted a budding debate on the differences between the sexes.

"Neville had to let him go. Nothing on him but motive, and a slim one at that—Regina got it on with Frank Sprague, got him evicted, then moved on to Geoff Tate. Myself, I'd go for Jenrette over Tate in the lover department—he's less pathetic. Ah, who knows what turns women on. I'm with Freud on that one." He drained his beer.

"But all that with Regina and Mark happened months ago. Why would he wait so long to get his revenge?" I asked, before Anne could respond to the Freud remark.

"Who knows? We got Jenrette's shoes and clothes, too. It'll take Forensics a few days to go over all of it. Meanwhile we'll give 'em some time to stew before we question them again. A confession is our best bet."

"It seems too obvious," Anne said. "The rejected lover. Who's this other guy you're talking about?"

"Most of the time murder is pretty straightforward. Piss someone off, bam, you're dead." Michael looked around for the waitress.

"My next-door neighbor, Geoff Tate, Regina's most recent boyfriend." I answered the second part of Anne's question.

"Nah, I personally don't think it was Tate. You've got to be pretty determined to strangle someone, I mean to keep going until the person's dead. Tate, he might've wanted to throttle her, but I don't see him carrying it through. Alcoholics come in two kinds, violent or passive-aggressive. The violent ones— they start fights, they go for knives or guns. The ones like Tate, they get belligerent in a verbal way. The foul-mouth talk this morning, that's typical passive-aggressive."

"Careful, Michael," Anne said. "You're starting to sound like a social worker, passive-aggressive! If you don't watch out, you'll be referring to substance abusers!"

"Hey, don't get me started. I'll take a substance abuser over a drunk any day. Junkies, they got a habit, you know what motivates them. Drunks just make a mess. We poured a pot of coffee into Tate, and the main result was he pissed all over the floor around the urinal. I don't know how guys like him get women to give them the time of day."

"I always thought he lured them with coke," I said.

"Yeah, bait, that would explain it. If I was doing the interview, I would've let Tate go, had someone follow him around for an hour. Drunks, cokeheads, you let them have a shot, do a few lines, bring 'em back in before they have too much, and you might get a coherent half hour before they lose interest."

"What?" Anne sat back and stared at Michael. "You mean you would advocate giving someone poison to get him to talk?"

"Maybe that red blouse is for bleeding heart," Michael scoffed. "You don't get it. Alcohol, for an alcoholic, it's like medicine. They don't function without it. Someone like Tate, he couldn't make it a day without a drink. Six hours, he'd be starting to sweat and shake. I guarantee you the first thing he did when he left the station was hit a bar."

"And the police feel no obligation to refer him to Alcoholics Anonymous?"

Even I laughed at that one. "Michael's right, a serious long-term alcoholic like Geoff Tate would need to detox in a hospital."

"Well, I think it's criminal, that the police would in any way condone—"

It was the kind of argument that's really a form of flirting. I left them to it and went to collect Clea.

WE CHOSE A BOOTH inside to wait for Benno. The West End's not bad if you avoid the Mexican food. Benno got ribs; Clea and I split a steak. I call her "my daughter the carnivore"; we both like our meat rare. When she finished her share of garlic mashed potatoes, Clea bounced between our laps and the jukebox. She hit on James Brown, played the same two songs about ten times. The sexy growls changed the mood between Benno and me. He relaxed, glad to find me in one piece.

I took advantage of the truce and turned the conversation to real estate. It made for a neutral topic. The stores on Broadway are like wallpaper; we walk by them ten times a day without paying them any attention. Columbia—the major landlord in

Morningside Heights—takes an active hand in choosing what businesses they rent to. They've let several storefronts go vacant, and we fantasized about what we'd like to have go in—a good shoe store, a restaurant that wasn't geared to student tastes.

I managed, innocuously, to bring up the Bike Building. "I've heard rumors the university has its eye on another SRO. My clients are worried, and I was wondering—your cousin Morris, do you think he might be able to find out if it's Columbia or a developer who's looking to buy it?"

"I can ask him, but it means we'll be invited over for dinner and I'll have to come up with an excuse for not going to Queens," Benno said.

"That's easy, just tell him we don't like to take the subway at night with Clea."

"Yeah, then he'll suggest a Sunday afternoon. I'd rather not get into it, Anita."

"Can't you just make a phone call, and we'll deal with getting together later? It would put some minds to rest—you know how the old people worry," I wheedled. "Besides, what's the good of having a cousin in the business if you don't use him?"

Benno snorted. "You've got to be Jewish, Anita, blood will out every time." But he gave in and wrote down the name and address of the Maramay.

We made it a high-calorie night and stopped at Sedutto's for ice cream cones on the way home. We had the stoop to ourselves. Clea dripped rainbow sprinkles for Barbara to wash off in the morning. It was a start on returning to a world where bodies didn't materialize on a daily basis.

Along with a cheerful nature, Clea is blessed with the ability to slide easily into sleep; she was out before I got done telling the day. Benno brought two snifters of Metaxa into the living room and put on some music. We sat on the couch with the lights off. A quarter moon cast spider plant shadows across our faces. Miles Davis was *Kind of Blue* and so was I.

Telling the day to Benno, I chose my words as carefully as I do with Clea. The last thing I wanted was for him to think I didn't have enough common sense to stay out of danger. Evolved as Benno was, he'd feel he had to put his foot down for my own protection and forbid me to go to Riverside Park.

Not that I was eager to go running around by myself, but if Benno made an issue of it I'd have to assert my autonomy. I could see a pointless argument on the horizon. The trick to male-female relationships in the last decade of the twentieth century, I'm convinced, is to keep in mind what you have in common and take it from there. We both wanted me to be safe.

My worries were groundless. Benno's concern had shifted to my emotional peace of mind. He put an arm around me, pulled my head onto his chest, and let me talk—interrupting with a question here and there, not pushing. When I got to the body itself, I stopped.

Regina Hilton's mortal remains would have to stay in their compartment. I wasn't ready to let the image of her blue skin into the sanctuary of my living room. What I described instead was Mitzi's odd behavior. In retrospect, that muffin of a dog shadow-boxing on her hind legs and barking like a banshee made for a funny story. I laughed until the alchemy of brandy and moonlight brought me to tears. Benno let me sob it out.

We made love that night, and Thanatos ruled. We went at each other like strangers, venturing into hidden places and exploring unnameable fears. Benno fell asleep instantly, still inside me. The night air was hot and motionless when I woke, hours later, sweaty, struggling to push him off.

FIFTEEN

THE NEXT TIME I woke up, it was 9:30 and I had the apartment to myself. I love Saturday mornings—Benno and Clea's special time together, my time alone. They eat a leisurely breakfast, then head off to dance class at Alvin Ailey. I have a second cup of coffee, finish last Sunday's crossword puzzle, water the plants, read magazines. The afternoon is for laundry and vacuuming.

Housework would have to wait this week; the Wilcox sisters were scheduled for discharge at 11:00, which meant there was plenty of time to shower before I went next door to pick up their clothing. Plenty of time to ponder yesterday's events and my conversations with Michael and with Sylvia Chase.

I don't know where other people find inspiration. For me, it comes out of the showerhead. Things occur to me when I stand under a stream of hot water—a new program for the agency, the best way to approach Clea's current growth stage, how to help Benno work through an uncooperative design.

Today's shower brought me not ideas but a desire for the simple explanations to be the correct ones: a fall, a heart attack, burners turned on accidentally. I wanted Regina's murder to have nothing whatsoever to do with anyone whose life touched mine.

IN THE UNOCCUPIED apartment, the air was hot and stale in spite of the open windows. Without the background chirping of Charlie, Bird, and Parker, the street noises were loud, echoey. I felt like a trespasser.

Catherine's needs were simple. She has dozens of polyester-blend, machine-washable pantsuits in various patterns and shades of purple. I had carte blanche to pick whichever one struck my fancy, so I chose a lavender and white houndstooth jacket with lavender pants.

I had some trouble locating the outfit Elizabeth had requested, a yellow and black African-print caftan I'd never seen her wear. For the most part, Elizabeth lives in cotton house dresses, with white ankle socks and open-toed slippers. For excursions to Riverside Park, she exchanges slippers for running shoes and tops it off with an old blue cardigan that lives on the back of her chair.

I finally located the dress in a garment bag at the back of the closet. While I was at it, I poked around more thoroughly for Lillian's satchel. It still wasn't in the closet. I took out clean linens and remade their beds. The satchel wasn't between the mattress and box springs either. I went through the living room again, the china closet, under the sofa pillows. No satchel.

THE SISTERS WERE delighted to see me, the nurses even more so. Elizabeth had run them ragged with imperious demands on Catherine's behalf—an extra blanket, fresh pillow slips, more ice. I called a car service and $4.00 later we were home.

"Oh dear, oh dear, oh dear!" Catherine stopped in her tracks, blocking the apartment door. "The poor darlings—you didn't say—I can't believe—"

"Go on in, Catherine, and stop bleating!" Elizabeth poked her sister with the handle of her cane.

It was my turn to nudge a stuck sister inside. The living room looked exactly as it had an hour earlier. Well, maybe a bit more disheveled than usual although I'd tried to put everything back as it had been. The sisters acted like a cyclone had hit.

Catherine covered the birdcage with an embroidered shawl, rearranged a few throw pillows on the sofa, and sat down with a sigh. "There's no place like home!"

Elizabeth fussed with the mail. "Bills and beggars, beggars

and bills." She added the envelopes to a pile and settled herself in her power seat.

There was no way to do it gently, but I tried. "I'm sorry, I felt I had to mention Lillian's satchel to the police, but we couldn't find it. Then when I stopped by Thursday afternoon to see to the birds, the door was unlocked. Could you check and be sure it's still here? Officer Dougherty told me we should bring it in when you got home."

Elizabeth tsked her disapproval at me. Catherine got up with a sigh and I followed her into the bedroom. She creaked to one knee, lifted the dust ruffle around her bed, and peered underneath.

"It's gone." She made a swipe with her left hand and came up empty.

"Nonsense. You look, Anita. There's a flashlight on the dining table," Elizabeth ordered from the doorway.

Neither the flashlight nor a sweep with the yardstick turned up the black leather satchel. Elizabeth checked the desk between their two beds. Yes, the envelope of cash they kept under the blotter was still there, as was the cloisonné box with their own valuable jewelry, hidden in the bottom drawer.

They had me search the entire apartment, from high closet shelves and the top of the kitchen cabinet to underneath the flowered sofa. Nothing.

Elizabeth called for tea—chamomile and hops to calm our nerves. We sat at the table and tried to figure it out.

"Perhaps the police took the bag," Catherine suggested.

"More like stole it, I should think. I told you, Anita, they are not to be trusted."

"Well, you know, they should have had it anyway." I thought it highly unlikely, although it was the most reassuring possibility—it didn't involve someone breaking in on purpose to steal the satchel. Or leaving the gas on to get the sisters out of the way.

"Be that as it may, they had no right to take it without our permission." Elizabeth added three generous spoons of honey to the teapot and gave it an indignant stir. "I don't like the idea of someone looking under our beds!"

"I *said* we should have given it to Mr. Neville in the first place. He might have found her relations and none of this would have happened!"

Catherine had that right. Which in turn raised the issue of the gas leak.

"Not to change the subject, but do either of you remember what happened Wednesday night?"

They exchanged glances that slid away into the far corners of the room. Catherine got cups and poured the tea. Elizabeth tapped her foot. "Catherine usually wakes in the night at least twice."

"Yes, and so do you! But I never go near the stove. I'm quite steady on my feet. You're the one who needs to hold on for balance, Elizabeth, and you never use your cane, as you should."

"Who was the last one up that night?"

"That's just it. We've discussed it, but we simply do not remember. One of us must have touched the stove, but I'm sure I don't know who. I don't think it was I, but..." Elizabeth's voice was uncertain, worried.

"When I found you, Miss Elizabeth, you were half out of bed," I said.

"It seems to me that I heard the door. You know, the hinge does squeak rather loudly. Catherine was in her bed and I thought, 'What next, am I hearing things?' I was going to see what it was, but I suppose I didn't manage, did I?" Elizabeth frowned. "You don't think someone came in and turned the gas on?"

Hearing Elizabeth say it so bluntly gave me pause to think it through. I remembered I'd had the same experience, the door-knob turning in the night. Was that also someone looking for Lillian's bag?

"But who would want to do such a thing? And Mrs. Raines' bag is missing. Perhaps that was the purpose of the exercise?" Elizabeth, one step ahead of me.

"Miss Elizabeth, did you tell anyone besides me that you had the bag?"

Two worried faces moved side to side in unison. "Not a soul," Elizabeth said. "I believe we had better notify the police. Anita, please dial the number."

Using the sisters' phone was a treat. It was an orchid-pink princess phone, exactly the color and style I'd spent the better part of my fifteenth year unsuccessfully hounding my mother for. I dialed the Twenty-sixth Precinct and handed the receiver to Elizabeth. "Let me have a word when you're done, okay?" I asked. She nodded.

But Detective Neville was not in, would not be in until Monday. Elizabeth refused to speak to anyone else. "Now that the thief has what he wants, I'm sure we're perfectly safe."

I wasn't. "Does anyone other than me have your keys?"

"The Clarks, of course. Mrs. Rearson on the eighth floor, she's deceased several years so I suppose we have those back. Geoffrey Tate had a set at one time, but I believe we retrieved them when he became unreliable. And the Super." Elizabeth counted off on her fingers. "Catherine, fetch the Cherokee basket and we'll see what we have."

The customs of apartment dwellers regarding keys would make a profitable topic for a graduate thesis in urban anthropology. What are the criteria for deciding which neighbor to entrust with a spare set? At what point in a relationship do lovers exchange keys? What if someone chooses you but you don't want to reciprocate? How do you get your keys back if the relationship changes? Not to mention people who refuse to give anyone a key, and risk having their locks drilled in case of flood, fire, or other misadventure.

Catherine lifted a shallow straw basket from the china closet and brought it to the table. Along with rubber bands, postage stamps, paper clips, loose change, receipts, business cards, matchbooks, and a malachite egg, it held several sets of keys, a paper identification tag attached to each ring. I recognized mine, with Gunther, 12A written in my grandmother's formal script, along with Clark, 11B, so the Wilcoxes could feed and walk Mitzi when they went away, and Tate, 12B.

Sure enough, there was also a set marked Rearson, 8C—the unit now owned by Larry Turner. I wondered if he'd changed the locks. It's a funny thing; people often don't. Why bother, if the former occupant is deceased?

"Age has certainly made us forgetful," Elizabeth said. "It's two years at least since Mrs. Rearson passed."

"Not forgetful, sister. You said we should keep the keys until we decided how to dispose of them properly."

"They're metal, why not put them in the recycling?" I asked.

Four eyes looked at me in speechless horror. "Where they might be found by someone on the street?" Catherine said.

As if anyone looking for deposit bottles would know what they were the keys to, I thought, if you removed the tag. "Would you like me to ask Barbara to cut them up with a hacksaw?" I offered. No sense in starting an argument.

"Yes, that might be the thing to do. I thought we returned Mr. Tate's when we retrieved ours from him—or did we? I know I intended to." Elizabeth tapped her foot. "Which reminds me. At one time, the board president kept extra keys for everyone in the building. That would have been well before Mr. Orton's tenure, of course, but I believe the keys were passed on to the new president, should there be a change in the officeholder. Now that I think of it, the practice ended during the unfortunate year that Mr. Malinsky was on the board. He was not trusted. Catherine, do you remember if we got our keys back from the board?"

"Didn't they decide to give all the keys to the Super?" I asked. "I don't remember ever hearing that a shareholder had people's keys." Times had changed, but even twenty years ago, could no one have been aware of the liability implications if a board president had everyone's keys?

"Yes, I believe you're right, Anita." Elizabeth nodded.

"Beliefs and Behavior of Metropolitan Apartment Dwellers

Pertaining to Implements of Access to Domiciles.'' Never mind a thesis, you could write a book.

Not that my behavior was any more rational: On an impulse, I pocketed Geoff's keys along with the Rearson keys. I just wanted them, as Clea would say.

Having dispensed with the key issue, Elizabeth moved on to household management and decreed that the parakeet funeral would be Sunday at 3:00. We were all invited. I went off home to take care of the one chore that couldn't be put off—my family's laundry.

I HAD NO INTENTION of bothering Barbara with cutting up old keys to satisfy Elizabeth's sense of propriety. I planned to throw them out, but not just yet. Those keys provided an idea that hadn't occurred to me when the shower and I put our heads together earlier in the day.

If the sisters hadn't returned Geoff's keys, in all probability they hadn't gotten theirs back from him either. They still had Rearson keys; if their keys had been left in 8C when Larry Turner took possession, he might still have them. I thought I'd return the 8C keys as a pretext to find out if Larry had Wilcox keys. The same with Geoff. If one of them did—well, it was means as well as opportunity.

The contents of the satchel provided motive. Regina was likely to have known about it—she knew Lillian was rich; she told Mar-Lee, she could well have told Geoff and/or Larry. Any of them could have made an educated guess about where to look for the bag.

I intended to ask Malinsky and Orton outright if they still had everyone's keys. If so, I for one wanted mine back. I hadn't changed the locks after my grandmother died; it seemed an unnecessary expense at the time, but now—if she'd given her keys to the Wilcoxes, she might have given them to any number of her other friends in the building. It occurred to me that I'd better ask Benno to replace the lock, regardless.

I put both sets of purloined keys in the junk drawer and took my laundry basket down to the machines in the basement.

Luck was with me. I had the four machines to myself. It was like a Saturday in summer, the building deserted. With the last loads in the drier, I decided to join the rest of the city and make the most of the beautiful weather.

I changed into my sweats and left a note for Benno and Clea. It seemed a good time to get back on the horse—confront my fear of corpses and complete my visit to the Amiable Child's grave.

THE TREES UNFURLED their leaves, turning the promenade into a tunnel of green. Young women in bathing suits the size of toast triangles slowly browned on blankets in the sun. A father in a Mets cap tossed a softball to his three-year-old son, who whiffed mightily with his plastic bat. A black woman in a flowered dress adjusted earphones on a gray-haired white woman in a wheelchair. The elderly woman put a hand on her companion's arm, smiling blissfully to the music.

There was nothing to be afraid of. I walked along the wall where I could look down into the park, keeping my eyes peeled for Mark Jenrette. My feet got reluctant as I approached the scenic overlook.

Yellow crime scene tape crisscrossed from column to column. The litter of leaves and soggy paper had been swept away, leaving the floor clean except for a collection of odd items near the charred fire circle.

Curiosity conquered cowardice and I ducked under the tape. It was an aluminum pie plate with a small, whole cooked fish and a sweet potato on a bed of rice and red beans, a half pint of Georgi, a White Owl cigar in a cellophane wrapper, and a tall glass cylinder with a white candle that had burned down a few inches before guttering out. A tribute to Regina? An offering to some god or spirit?

A breeze that still held the faintest trace of winter blew up off the river. The trees sighed. I heard footsteps. A pair of joggers, Barnard students maybe, white women in neon leggings and gray T-shirts. Their peripheral vision registered the yellow tape and bounced off; their heads never swerved to see what might lie inside the pavilion. Survival in New York is part hawk, part ostrich: Notice everything, make eye contact with nothing. What you don't acknowledge can't hurt you.

I paused at the northern edge of the pavilion. The stairs, too, had been swept clean in the aftermath of Regina's death. No leaves, no condoms, no crack vials. A few cars cruised down the drive.

It's an effort sometimes, not being afraid—even in my own neighborhood. If I don't feel confident about a place, I avoid it. I worked on my attitude. A rabbit hopped under the fence at the foot of the steps. I took it as a sign and went down.

The rabbit was white with black ears and a sprinkle of black spots. Its paws and underbelly were stained yellow-green. This was no wild creature, but some child's once-loved pet. It happens every year, after Easter. A cute baby bunny rapidly becomes uncute as parents deal with hay, droppings, a smelly cage. So bunny gets abandoned in the park, a gourmet meal for the red-tailed hawks nesting in Riverside Church's belltower.

With rescue on my mind, I crouched down and spoke softly to the creature. I held out my hand although I had nothing to offer. The rabbit looked back at me. Its black nose twitched, then it hopped away. It seemed like a dumb decision to me, but considering how the rabbit got where it was, I could see that it wouldn't be in such a hurry to trust a human. I wished it survival.

When I stood up, I was eye to eye with a dark-skinned black man in a San Francisco 49ers warm-up jacket. I stopped breathing and closed my eyes for a second. It didn't work.

"Hey lady, you lose your bunny?" His voice was curious, not threatening.

I took a step back and tried a smile. "Mark Jenrette?" I asked.

It was his turn to be frightened. "How do you know my name?" He took his hands out of his pockets, clenched and unclenched his fists. The T-shirt under his unzipped jacket was red mesh with a white number 8.

"You like Steve Young?" I asked. He nodded but didn't smile. "A woman named Mar-Lee told me who you were. My name is Anita Servi." I offered him my hand.

He took it. His hand was as muscular as Benno's, the palm hard and callused.

I gestured up toward the pavilion where Regina's body had been. "I was the one who found her." His eyes filled. I put my other hand on top of his and patted. "I'm sorry for your loss." Death and marriage, the two occasions when only clichés will do.

He let go of my hand. "You like the 'Niners?"

"I used to live in the Bay Area, and I just can't get excited about the Giants or the Jets." Football, the one guy subject I excel at. "You think Young is a better quarterback than Montana was?"

He glanced down at his shirt. "Young's not as smart, but he runs better. I don't care who the quarterback is, as long as they throw the ball to Jerry."

He stood in the woods on his side of the low iron fence and I stood on the paved path on my side. We spent a few minutes discussing Jerry Rice's hands, agreeing that he was the best receiver the NFL had ever had or would ever see. I asked Mark if he'd played football; he had the size for it, the thick neck and shoulders.

"Long time ago, in college. But I got drafted into 'Nam instead of the pros. San Francisco made me an offer, but time I got out..." he shrugged.

For a man who camped in Riverside Park, he looked like he took pretty good care of himself. He'd shaved that day, and there was an ironed crease in his jeans. "What do you do now?" I asked.

"Lurk in the bushes and scare women and little bunny rabbits." He made a leering, boggle-eyed face at me. "What do you think?"

"I don't know, that's why I asked," I kept my voice even, unintimidated. "I heard you used to live in the Bike Building and Regina got you thrown out."

"They have you outreach workers out on Saturdays now? You tell that Mar-Lee I'm happy how I am. I don't need her bed and I don't need no social worker trying to get me shelters and jobs and all that shit." He took off through the undergrowth, down the slope toward the West Side Highway.

I tried to shout an explanation, but no way was I going to follow him.

Damn. Another thing social work and law enforcement have in common: people have a sixth sense for your profession even when you're on your own time.

I knew how he felt about social workers, though. I always feel like the foster care workers suspect we chain Clea to the radiator as soon as they leave. Seeing it from both sides makes me a bit more hands off than some of my colleagues. The downside is that I'd let Lillian be and she'd died.

THE GRANITE grave marker, a carved urn on top of a rectangular pedestal, stands in a square of iron fence with chest-high, pointed palings. The urn has a convex fluted top like the newel post on the staircase in my mother's Berkeley Victorian. The east side of the pedestal reads:

Erected to the Memory
of an Amiable Child
St. Claire Pollock
Died 15 July 1797
In the Fifth Year of his age

The side facing the river has a verse from Job:

"Man that is born of woman is of
short duration and full of trouble. He cometh
like a flower and is cut down; he fleeth also
as a shadow and is no more."
Job 14:1-2

Someone had put a mayonnaise jar on the pedestal, an improvised vase for a single rose. The rose, dark red, wilted over the edge of the vase. The petals from previous flowers were scattered on the ground, a splatter-painting of pink, peach, yellow, crimson, on a canvas of decomposing leaves.

In a corner of railing at the end of the path sat a tan Dellwood milk crate, situated to give a view of the Hudson River. I wondered if this was Lillian Raines's seat, and if she'd been the one who brought the roses.

I peeled off my sweatshirt, folded it for a pillow, and sat on the crate. The river was a pewter sparkle glinting through the new greenery. The railroad tracks were quiet. The West Side Highway flowed by my feet, visible mostly as motion through the scrim of trees. The cars behind me on the drive blended into the background, easy to ignore.

In the 1790s, this was the edge of a cliff. Over the centuries and with some human intervention, the hillside has moved back from the river. According to the story, St. Claire Pollock was playing nearby, fell down to the river, drowned.

I could sense what drew Lillian to this private place in a public park, a place you could come to remember a son who had died in the fifth year of his age. I wondered how her boy had died, where he was buried, why she didn't leave roses on his grave. Was she institutionalized because she was overcome by grief, or had she been responsible for his death?

I'm as interested in my clients' past lives as in their present problems. It helps me to learn what their strengths are, and people enjoy talking about former glories more than current misfortune. As one wheelchair-bound woman put it, "I used to be a radiologist and now I'm a wreck."

Naomi Spivik grew up in Palestine, her family part of the struggle to establish a Jewish state. Another client's father was an engineer on the Panama Canal. Still another client's father was born a slave, freed by the Civil War when he was six. More than a hundred years after Abolition, she's only one generation removed from slavery. These people are history, alive and breathing. One of my shower-inspired plans was to record their stories in order to preserve them.

And Lillian Raines, was she the mad, alcoholic daughter in a convoluted Faulknerian family? I wasn't making much progress with her history.

A handful of birds pecked around in the petals. Sparrows, maybe; what Benno calls LBJs, "little brown jobs," ordinary as pigeons in the city.

I made a mental list of what I knew about Lillian.

1. At one time, she'd lived in the Bike Building. Now she appeared to be homeless and she sometimes slept in my building, where she died.

2. She was friendly with the Wilcox sisters, who'd given her a key to the building.

3. She liked to sit by a child's grave.

4. She'd had a son who either died at a young age or was alive and well and possibly living in New York City.

5. She had some gorgeous heirloom jewelry, which she left with the Wilcoxes for safekeeping.

6. The jewelry had gone missing after the sisters were incapacitated by gas.

7. She was acquainted with Regina Hilton, who stole from elderly people in the Bike Building and was the girlfriend of Geoff Tate, resident of the building where Lillian sometimes slept.

Then there was Naomi Spivik, also wealthy and also dead, who had had dealings with Regina as well. I should have asked the Wilcoxes if Regina had ever done favors for them as she had with the elderly women in the Bike Building.

Regina, Regina, all roads led to Regina, but unfortunately Regina was dead.

A horn honked on Riverside Drive, scattering the LBJs. Late-afternoon shadows appeared as the sun lowered toward the river. It was getting chilly. The trees moved, and maybe something else? It occurred to me that Mark Jenrette probably wasn't the only person who occupied this territory. It was time to go home.

BENNO COOKED chicken scarpariello that night, a dish to delight his Italian father, make his kosher mother turn over in her grave. I put Clea in the tub and kept her company while all her doll babies got their hair washed. She went early to bed after a chapter of *The Wizard of Oz*. Benno and I watched a video, *Truly, Madly, Deeply*, a romance with a ghost who played exquisite cello music. Your basic evening of domestic bliss. The pilfered keys burned a hole in a back pocket of my mind.

I WOKE UP AT 2:32 and had to pee. I heard voices in the hallway, so I took a look out the peephole. It was Geoff Tate and Larry Turner. Geoff was unlocking his door. Larry had Lillian's black leather satchel in his left hand.

What the hell? I shook my head to clear my brains. I couldn't believe it. Larry followed Geoff into the apartment and the door closed.

I flopped down on the couch to consider the situation. Okay, when Larry mentioned Lillian's hypothetical riches, did he know what she really had? I pondered Larry Turner as stealth candidate for thief and murderer. But why was he bringing the satchel to Geoff's?

I heard their voices again. I tiptoed back to the peephole. They were waiting for the elevator. Larry, empty-handed now, said something about the Marlin. Geoff consulted his wallet and said something I didn't catch. The elevator came; they got on. The light went down the dial to M.

Benno was snoring, loudly. I knew I wasn't going to be able to get back to sleep. I picked up the quilt he'd kicked off in the too-warm night and grabbed my sweatpants and a T-shirt. The snores were still audible after I closed the bedroom door.

I put my clothes on and puddled the quilt on the couch in

some approximation of my sleeping self. I got Geoff's keys and the keys to 8C from the junk drawer. I checked through the peephole. The elevator stayed on M. I left the apartment door unlocked and went barefoot into the hall.

I knew it was a crazy thing to do. I debated calling the precinct, but explaining the whole thing seemed too complicated. What if Geoff came home before the police got there? He'd just deny having the satchel. By the time the police got a warrant, it would be long gone. No, it seemed simpler to retrieve it while I had the chance and turn it over to the authorities later. I could dart in and snag it; they couldn't.

It took me forever to get into Geoff's apartment; I kept unlocking and relocking the top lock before I figured out that he only used the bottom one. I didn't bother locking the door from the inside; I didn't intend to be there that long.

The apartment opened onto a short hallway, with the bathroom directly opposite the entrance. To the left of the bathroom was a walk-in closet, then the bedroom; to the right was the living room, with an alcove kitchen at the far end. A light was on by the couch.

When he moved in, flush with Wall Street money in the eighties, Geoff had the place done over. Everything painted flat white, track lighting, floors sanded and bleached, new appliances in designer stainless steel. His taste in furniture ran to chrome, glass, and red leather. The overall effect was industrial-modern. It hadn't worn well.

The thin, rectangular couch cushions were on the floor. The sofa bed was either half closed or half open; the mattress stuck out of its red mouth like the tongue in a Rolling Stones logo. Various items of clothing—a pair of royal blue leggings, something in a leopard print—were draped over the back of a matching armchair. The smoked-glass coffee table held an ashtray, an assortment of mugs and highball glasses, Chinese takeout cartons, an almost-empty liter of Georgi, a carton of Marlboros, a pile of *New York* magazines.

Lillian's satchel was not sitting anywhere in plain view. The prospect of getting into Geoff's drawers was not pleasant. The top of the desk featured a computer, fax machine, red telephone, and a nest of pens, pads, paper clips, and brokerage statements surrounding a large calculator. I used the hem of my shirt to grab the chrome pulls. I seemed to be making a career of checking out things I didn't want to touch with my bare hands. Checkbook, bank statements, paid bills, letters, a few envelopes of photos; no satchel.

I moved on to the kitchen. The topmost of the three drawers held silverware, angular stainless steel, sleek forks with only two prongs. Then an assortment of gadgets, whisk, corkscrew, skewers, steak knives wrapped in felt. The bottom drawer had dish towels, brand new, red and black. I opened all the cabinets; a few Progresso soups, Saltines, a can of Coco Lopez, plastic wrap. The sink was piled with black plates, bowls, more highball glasses. I passed on the refrigerator.

On the way to the bedroom, I did a quick survey of the bath. Black fixtures might seem like a practical choice, but it's not. Every drop of water leaves a white spot, and pretty soon you've got scum on everything. The black towels were everywhere except on the rods. I took a breath and wished I hadn't. A top note of vomit mixed with mildew and the urine odor that hovers around the toilets of single males.

The bedroom was dark. I reached for a light switch by the door; reconsidered. The track lights seemed like too much illumination for this hour of the night. My eyes adjusted enough to locate a bedside table with a lamp, a space-age halogen thing with an adjustable neck. I turned it on.

The sheets on the unmade bed were light gray with a pattern of black lines and triangles—a practical color scheme for a person with Geoff's evident lack of laundry habits, and the first thing I'd seen in the apartment that I liked. I covered my hand again and went for the bureau. It was gray enamel, and looked more like a filing cabinet than a place for clothing.

This time I started at the bottom. Women's lingerie—stockings, garter belts, satin teddies—then on up through sweaters; shirts, starched, folded, banded from the cleaners; cotton knit polos and Playboys; socks, underwear, condoms, and sexual aids. I'd never seen a French tickler before, but I knew what it was immediately, a rubber-band thing surrounded by what looked like long false eyelashes. The thought of Geoff using it with Regina kept me from touching it.

There was no leather satchel.

I lowered the halogen lamp toward the floor and aimed it under the bed—suitcases and T. Rexes of dust.

I'd just put the lamp back when I heard a key click in the lock—Geoff, not realizing the door was unlocked, had just locked himself out. He turned the knob. When the door didn't open, he kicked it. I turned the light off. Given what was under the bed, it was a no-brainer. I took two steps into the hall and went for the closet.

Geoff gave the key another turn and pushed the door open.

It was a New York situation; I closed the closet door behind me in perfect synchronization with Geoff opening the outer door. If the closet door had been open, the apartment door would have hit it. Geoff went straight into the bathroom—conveniently located between me and escape. If I'd known how long it was going to take him, and how loud the stream would be, I might have chanced it. I cracked the closet door and got hit with the aroma: standing male, open bathroom door.

It wasn't much worse than the smells I was hiding with. The closet was good sized, for New York, which meant there wasn't a whole lot of spare room for a person. I was standing on a pile of footwear, wedged in with an upright vacuum cleaner, a step stool, a folded shopping cart, a tennis racquet, skis and ski poles from a healthier time, and, more unbelievable, an ironing board. The row of suits and jackets I was trying to fade into reeked of cigarettes and aftershave—Old Spice, not my favorite. I was not a happy person.

Without flushing, Geoff stumbled from the bathroom to the living room. He knocked into something and swore at it. The television went on.

I figured I might as well make the best of a bad situation and search the closet. I patted through the jackets and pants, wondering vaguely if Geoff had a gun. All I turned up was a pack of cigarettes and some breath mints.

Given the volume of the TV, I opened the door a little wider and risked a one-eyed look. Geoff had shoved the mattress into the sofa and replaced the cushions. He was stretched out, his feet up, his head at the end farthest from the hall but unfortunately facing toward me. He had one arm behind his head, the other attached to the bottle of vodka.

He let go of the bottle, swung his legs down, and started rooting around on the coffee table. I flinched back into the coats. The TV jumped from murmuring voices to MTV-loud to C-SPAN drone to horror-movie soundtrack. The perfect thing for my nerves.

Geoff settled back, put the remote down, picked up the bottle. Blue shadows flickered over his face. I crossed my fingers, hoping he'd fall asleep.

I crouched down and felt around the floor, wishing I'd taken a Maglite from the junk drawer while I was at it. An inventory yielded a pair of tassel loafers, four running shoes, a box with a new pair of topsiders, two umbrellas, a canvas beach bag, and a pre-cleaners pile of shirts. Nothing that resembled the shape or texture of a leather satchel.

There was a shelf set back above the closet rod, about a foot over my head. In order to see up there, I'd need to either open the door or stand on something. I checked Geoff's condition: still conscious. I held onto the rod with one hand for balance, reached up, and felt along the edge of the shelf.

Scratchy wool, like winter stuff, scarves. Tucked underneath a pile, my fingers encountered leather, a handle. I slid it forward, trying not to bring what was on top down with it. I worked it to the edge of the shelf and pulled.

It came down faster than I expected and thwacked against the door. If I hadn't been barefoot, I would've lost my balance and fallen backward. As it was, a ski pole slid toward the opening. I grabbed for it. My butt bumped the door open.

"What the—"

The blood rushed to my ears. I couldn't tell what Geoff was

doing. I was embarrassed as much as scared—caught in a closet, for Pete's sake! A solid object sailed down the hall and landed with a thunk. A shoe? The carton of cigarettes? Moo shu pork? I pressed back into the jackets, my arms wrapped around the satchel.

"Shit." Geoff's voice came down the hall after whatever it was he'd thrown.

"Queenie? You in there?" He kicked the closet closed on his way to the bedroom and my world went dark.

Why was he calling Regina? A fist thumped against the door.

"Get a grip, get a grip. Regina's dead, the wicked old witch is dead, all dead and gone," he sang to himself. His footsteps passed back into the living room.

I waited about two weeks; nothing else happened.

I WAS JUST ABOUT suffocated by Old Spice when I heard the familiar squeak of my own bathroom door. There's an air passage between our two apartments, big enough to let smoke filter in when Geoff has a cigarette on the can but too small for us to locate and patch. The acoustics were excellent. I heard the splash—Benno taking a leak.

I considered calling out, but what would I say? Honey, I'm stuck in the neighbor's closet, could you come get me?

The closet doorknob turned soundlessly. I peered out the crack. Geoff was horizontal again, his eyes closed. I prayed he was sleeping the deep oblivious sleep of alcohol.

The tricky part would be getting out the apartment door without waking him, because I'd be in full view while I did it. I tucked the ski pole firmly behind the jackets, put Lillian's satchel under my left arm, and made my move.

I forgot Geoff hadn't locked his door when he came in, and I turned the Medeco on top. The doorknob turned; the door didn't budge. I'd locked myself in.

Something hit the floor by the couch. I leaped backward into the bathroom, out of sight. Geoff groaned.

I counted to ten oh-shits before I peeked. Geoff lay still. I tiptoed out, unlocked the Medeco, and was rewarded with a bright slant of fluorescent light. I stepped into it and headed for home.

I slid into my apartment, turned, and locked the door behind me. It was like going from the fire to the frying pan—still too hot for comfort. Benno was sitting on the couch, where my feet would have been if I were under the quilt.

I dropped the bag, quietly this time, on our own jumble of shoes by the door. In the dark, it would have to do. Benno's head swiveled. He stared at me like I was the Lady of the Lake, risen from the depths.

"Hi, honey, I'm home," I said. I kissed him on the cheek.

Benno was not amused. "Yeah, and I'm having a conversation with a bedspread. You smell like an ashtray."

"I had a cigarette." I took a lesson from Clea and went on offense. "You were snoring like a freight train and I couldn't sleep."

"A cigarette? What are you talking about, a cigarette?"

Truth or consequences. "I have half a pack in my desk, left over from when I quit. I put it in my drawer, just in case." It was true; I'm that kind of a pack rat.

"Anita, are you nuts? That was six years ago! Did you save a full ashtray too, in case you needed to roll the butts?" Sarcasm is Benno's strong suit.

"You're right, it was pretty foul."

He was not mollified. "And what the hell were you doing in the hall? Why didn't you go out on the fire escape?"

"You know how loud the gate is. I didn't want to wake you up, opening it."

"I thought I was snoring too loudly to be woken." Sarcasm, salted with irony.

I let it go. "I need to brush my teeth again. Go to bed, I'll be right in."

Under cover of toothbrush and running water, I moved Lillian's bag to the bottom shelf of the linen closet, behind the tablecloths and napkins, until I could work out how to get it to the police without Benno knowing I'd trespassed in Geoff's apartment.

SIXTEEN

SUNDAY IS THE DAY Clea gets to watch television, two whole hours, while Benno and I sleep late. Unfortunately, in spite of my late-night excursion, I woke up at 7:30 with a head full of ideas.

I went back to the beginning. Lillian Raines either fell or was pushed from the upstairs landing last Sunday night. According to Orton's surveillance records, Regina left the building with Larry and Geoff around 10:30 that night and came back by herself, early Monday morning. Which meant that Geoff had lied about their coming back to his apartment together around 3:00 a.m.

It seemed reasonable to assume that Regina knew what was in Lillian's satchel, and that she'd told Larry and/or Geoff. Any of them, alone or together, could have attacked Lillian. Failing to find the satchel in Lillian's possession, they'd tried first my place, then the Wilcoxes. Both of us were known to be friendly with Lillian, the Wilcoxes more than me. Having succeeded, was there a falling-out among thieves and Regina lost?

And what about Naomi Spivik? No one had thought to check her valuables—if anyone even knew what she had!

The immediate question, now I had the damn bag, was what to do with it. In broad daylight, I could hardly face how I got it myself, never mind explaining it to Benno or the cops.

The impenetrability of it all sent me back to sleep.

"WAKE UP, WAKE UP, wherever you are!" Clea Servi, human alarm clock, lay on top of me and put her face on my pillow. "Can we go to Tom's?"

I opened one eye. Objects on the pillow were closer than they appeared to be. I closed it. A little finger delicately poked my eyelid up. "Can we, Mama? I'm hungry for pancakes."

"It's ten-thirty, only half an hour to make it for the breakfast special." Benno poked my butt. "Come on, or they'll run out of hash browns."

We made it with six minutes to spare. Tom's Restaurant, on the corner of 112th and Broadway, is famous on the outside as the place where Seinfeld and company hung out. On the inside it's your basic New York greasy spoon—Greek-owned, iceberg lettuce in the salads, soggy bacon, great French fries, divine chocolate malts. Everyone in the neighborhood comes to Tom's, students, professors, street loonies, cops, doctors, nurses, door men, tourists.

Benno believes the waitresses, middle-aged women with dark eyes and melancholy faces who never talk to the customers, are modern-day Medeas, paroled child-killers. They know Benno as two eggs over easy, sausage, rye toast; I'm scrambled, bacon, Tabasco. Heaven help anyone in the mood for something different. Only Clea rates a smile with her pancakes and sausages.

What sets Tom's apart from other diners is the plants. Boston ferns, philodendrons, spider plants, tall, spiky snake plants, a living wall of green runs down the middle of the restaurant. We slid into a sun-drenched front booth, desperate for coffee. It came on silent feet, along with an extra handful of creams for Clea to drink from the little containers.

"Should we be worried about the Wilcoxes?" Benno asked. "I talked to Barbara yesterday about checking their smoke alarm. She said she did it right after they were taken away Thursday, but that doesn't solve the gas problem. Isn't there a social worker solution you could apply here?"

"They make little covers to put over the knobs, like child guards for adults, but the easiest thing to do is take the knobs off."

"They can't cook if there's no knobs on the stove, can they?" Clea pointed out, correct as usual.

The waitress returned, practicing the lost art of serving a meal in one trip without a tray. She had three plates balanced on her left arm, the coffeepot in her right hand, syrup and hot sauce in her pocket.

"What I mean is take the knobs off at night, and put them back in the day." I turned to Benno. "I don't think what happened was an accident. Their stove has an electronic ignition, like ours. It's hard to unintentionally push in and turn at the same time."

"But not impossible. Remember, your mother filled the apartment with gas a few times when she didn't turn the knob far enough to engage the pilot lighter?"

"She didn't know you have to make it click," Clea said.

"Yes, but she knew she had to push and turn." I hated it when they got logical and ganged up on me.

Benno reached across the table to cut Clea's sausage. "If they didn't leave the burners on, Anita, what do you think happened?"

I gave him the eye signal for "let's not discuss this now," but he misread me.

"Come on, don't tell me you think someone broke into their apartment and did it deliberately!"

"No one had to break in. Do you know how many people in the building have keys to the Wilcoxes' besides us?" I held my hand in front of his face and counted off fingers. "We do, the Clarks do, Barbara does, Geoff Tate probably does, Larry Turner might, either Howard or Malinsky might—"

"Right, Malinsky got tired of pigeon droppings on his windows and gassed the sisters." Benno spread sarcasm as thick as Clea spread syrup. "In fact, maybe he started with the lady of the landing and when he succeeded in getting rid of one menace, he figured he'd try for two."

"He complained a lot about the pigeon poop, you know," Clea added her two cents' worth.

This time Benno caught the look correctly and we both shut up.

WE TOOK THE paisley spread, the Sunday Times, and a Frisbee to Riverside Park. When Benno got tired of impersonating a jungle gym, he played catch with Clea. I rolled onto my back, closed my eyes, and offered up some half-baked ideas to the sun god.

Birdshit was pretty frivolous as motives went, but Benno had inadvertently reminded me that Regina might not be the source of all evil. Take John Clark and Sylvia Chase, for instance. What if Lillian and the sisters knew about them and threatened to tell Margery? Lillian was a sitting duck on the landing, and John had keys to the Wilcoxes'.

And Regina—what had Sylvia said about the coincidence of Regina being involved with John's upstairs neighbor? "I knew it would bring us trouble." Did they want to keep their affair a secret badly enough to kill for it? I went over John's reaction when Mitzi found Regina's body. He'd been quite insistent on accompanying me in that direction, but after we found Regina he couldn't get away fast enough.

Was it acting? The murderer returning to the crime scene to divert suspicion? I could not imagine John Clark strangling anyone. But then, if you'd asked me a week ago if I'd thought he was capable of carrying on a clandestine affair with a stylish blonde, I'd have said no to that too.

Neither explanation covered Naomi Spivik's death, but maybe there wasn't a connection and she just had a heart attack. As Michael said, old people die.

Then there was the ever-popular real estate devil. Benno's Axiom states that there are three possible answers to any "why" question: greed, stupidity, or laziness. Real estate interests in New York City are greed incarnate. I'd find out tomorrow if the Maramay had been sold; Benno wouldn't call Morris at home, when there'd be no escaping his wife, Bernice. As to Regina—Edna had jealousy for a motive; Frank too, for that matter, of Geoff.

In that case, maybe what happened with the sisters was an accident, and stealing the satchel was a crime of opportunity rather than intention.

The Wilcoxes brought me back to Malinsky. Maybe he had some kind of unholy alliance with Larry to rid the building of undesirables. If Larry had gone into the Wilcoxes' to turn the gas on, and seen Lillian's satchel—but then why did he give it to Geoff?

Tree shadows flickered on the inside of my eyelids. Trying to decipher clues and connections is like working a crossword—do what you can until you get stuck, then put it down and come back later.

CLEA INSISTED ON changing into a dress for the parakeet funeral. After playing on the grass, Benno decided he needed a shower. It was as close to an opportunity to reexamine Lillian's satchel as I was going to get; if Clea stayed occupied, I might have all of ten minutes. The other problem was that there was no private place for me to go. Two-bedroom apartment sounds big, but ours is really just three rooms. The bathroom doesn't count, and the kitchen is more like a hall than a room.

I opened the linen closet, figuring I'd just squat there like I was counting place mats. Clea danced out in a red velvet number she'd outgrown a year ago and couldn't get buttoned. I suggested a purple velour dress instead. By then Benno was out of the shower, and that was it for the satchel.

Catherine took the color of Clea's dress as a compliment and slipped her a peppermint. Elizabeth had wrapped each bird in a scrap of dark purple velvet and tucked them into a shoe box, which Clea, under close supervision, was allowed to carry.

It was a dignified procession, down the flagstone stairs to Riverside Drive. Elizabeth took Benno's arm; I got Catherine. We turned north in the park, to the neglected flowerbed at the foot of 113th Street where all previous Wilcox parakeets were interred. Benno did the honors with the trowel while Elizabeth said a few words. Catherine sang a verse of "Amazing Grace." Clea was appropriately solemn.

After the funeral, we accompanied Elizabeth and Catherine on the ritual trip to Woolworth's for new parakeets. They bought three—two green and one blue. Clea was very impressed with the little cardboard carrying cases labeled Live Pet Inside and Elizabeth promised she could have the boxes for her doll babies.

We were invited to share "the funeral meats," as Catherine put it. We brought the beer. They named the new birds Bobby, Blue, and Bland. We all got a little high. Catherine served homemade fried chicken, cole slaw, and potato salad from Mama Joy's (Elizabeth confessed), corn bread, and vanilla ice cream with chocolate syrup for dessert.

"Miss Elizabeth, these drumsticks are so fat and tender," Benno teased, "if I hadn't witnessed the burial, I'd swear I was eating parakeet."

Elizabeth smacked his hand with her fork. Catherine put a Bobby Blue Bland record on the phonograph. She sang along and Clea danced. The side ended with "Ain't No Love in the City." We put our spoons down. Even the birds were quiet, listening to Bobby Blue sing about *when you ain't around*.

It ended the party on a melancholy note.

Which Benno dispelled when we got home by teaching Clea to sing, "The worms crawl in, the worms crawl out, they turn your brain to sauerkraut." She tucked her dolls into their new beds and, in the process of singing to them, sang herself to sleep.

I worked my way through the flowered rayon dresses in my ironing basket, my summer work wardrobe. Benno slept through *Masterpiece Theatre*. I intended to get up in the middle of the night and go through the satchel again. I couldn't set the alarm because it would wake Benno up, but I figured a bladderful of beer would do the job.

IT DIDN'T. Clea greeted us with the worm song at 7:00 the next morning. Her version ended with "they turn your brains to sour cream." Well, it started the week with a laugh. I had to admit

I was apprehensive about what I might find in the hall, especially since there was another Crud Report under the door.

Crud Report 316 from Crusading Crud-Buster
To: All Shareholders, Bored Directors
Re: Less-than-Super-intendant's Duties

It is imperative that no more Crud Creators and Illegal Invaders be permitted to take up residence in our building. To that end, I propose that our Less-than-Super make nightly rounds of the building at 10:00 p.m., midnight, 3:00 a.m. and 6:00 a.m. Our Less-than-Super could continue to sleep during the day and make better use of her nighttime hours.

In addition, our Less-than-Super has permitted an unacceptable amount of pigeon crud to collect on exterior windowsills. As I have previously suggested a well-aimed blast from the hose on a regular basis would prevent this build-up. Better yet, the installation of bird spikes would prevent rats with feathers from patronizing the windowsills of vermin-loving residents and eliminate the problem at its source.

At least one of our Bored Directors is in accord with my suggestions. Now is the time for the Bored Directors to improve the cleanliness and safety of our mutual domicile.

Typical Malinsky. Now I knew what he and Howard had been up to on Friday. If they'd become allies, Barbara was in for a rough road. I folded it in half and stuck it in my bag. Benno had been encouraging me to run for the board in order to add a voice of reason, but it was a little late. The annual meeting and election of officers had been held in March.

The Crud Report bothered me; the attack on Barbara was too personal. If Malinsky had a hit list of residents he wanted to get rid of—

Clea skipped ahead, stopping as she'd been taught at each corner, and held my hand to cross the streets. At least one of us was in a good mood. When I left her at school, Clea was still singing. She'd be a hit with the other kids if not the teacher.

THE THIRD MONDAY of the month means WSCA, West Side Committee for the Aging, an umbrella organization of area agencies for senior citizens. It was a good thing Emma and I alternated representing Senior Services, because she called in sick again.

Actually, WSCA meetings aren't that bad, they're just meetings. I'd get to eat muffins, drink bad coffee, try to stay awake for the educational presentation. The real value, in my opinion, is the opportunity for informal case conferences on difficult clients. Another fringe benefit is maintaining connections with colleagues.

Participating agencies take turns hosting; this month it was at One-Step, officially known as One-Step Legal Services for Seniors, where Dolores Ribera, a former classmate of mine, works. My showerhead had reminded me of something Sylvia Chase said, and I had a question for Dolores.

It was wonderful to be out of the office on a Monday morning. The unseasonable temperature had inspired the lilacs along the Synod House to open early and I paused for a hit of perfume. Lilacs are nonexistent in the temperate California climate; I never get tired of their brief appearance in New York. I cut over to Broadway in order to avoid the twenty-four-hour crack supermarket on Amsterdam and 107th.

One-Step handles housing and landlord-tenant problems and immigration paperwork along with health-care proxies and wills. Two days a week, workers from the city's Human Resources Administration set up on site to process entitlement applications—Medicaid, food stamps, Medicare, SSI, Social Security. The line out front starts at 8:30.

When I got there, everyone waiting outside had made it down the salmon-pink hallway to the receptionist, been assigned a number, and taken a seat in one of the chairs lining the narrow hall. There must have been thirty elderly people, clutching letters and government forms. They'd have a longer wait than usual today, with both social workers in the WSCA meeting.

I threaded my way through the maze of tiny offices to the conference room. One-Step is shoehorned into the back of a building between a Chinese restaurant and a video store, which explains the long hall as well as the pervasive aroma of roast pork. I was just in time to get coffee and nod my greetings to the fifteen or so people in the room.

The presenter was a not-very-enthusiastic middle-aged white man from the city's Department for the Aging who updated us on proposed changes in the Senior Citizens Rent Increase Exemption Program. By the time the City Council enacted anything, it would be something other than the alterations he droned on about. I doodled on my pad and tried to look alert. The man was mercifully brief as well as dull. No one had any questions and a few announcements later, we were free.

Dolores was happy to see me. "Anita! All week I've been meaning to call you!"

"Yeah, me too. Did you ever have a client named Lillian Raines?"

"I swear, Anita, you must be a mind-reader, she's who I need to talk to you about."

"Did you know she died last Sunday night?"

Dolores crossed herself. "What happened to her?"

I gave her the official version, with a detour to include Regina Hilton's shenanigans in the Maramay, where Dolores also had clients. If any of them had been victimized by Regina, no one had mentioned it to her either.

"The poor woman! I don't understand why the police are not investigating—no, I do understand. Just another old person. Have you spoken with the family?"

"They haven't found anyone. That's why I'm wondering, did you guys do a will for her?" I crossed my fingers.

"No, really, you are psychic. A week ago Friday, she signed it." Dolores snapped her fingers. "Oyo, that explains it! It was a funny thing, you know. The lawyer is supposed to keep the original, but Ms. Raines wanted your boss to have it. Then she didn't want to carry it with her all weekend. She said she'd come in Monday, but she didn't show. I thought she just changed her mind and decided to let the lawyer keep it, but I was going to ask you to have her call me, just to be sure.''

"Do you know why she wanted Emma to have it?"

"She made Emma the executor. Mr. Douglas, the lawyer, he said it wasn't unusual for the executor to keep an original will if she wasn't a beneficiary. He had me do a mini mental-status evaluation of Ms. Raines, which she passed with no problem, so he did it the way she wanted.''

"Is the lawyer here?"

"No, he's on vacation this week. Now, where did I put that will?'' Dolores shuffled the piles on her desk, exhaled a soft stream of Spanish that started with *Madre de Dios* and ended with *hijo de puta.* She finally located a dark green folder and took out a vellum envelope. The gothic script read "The Last Will and Testament of." "Lillian Raines" was typed in small caps underneath. *Yes.*

Dolores tapped the envelope against the edge of her desk. "I wish Mr. Douglas was here. Do you suppose I should give it to the police? Just what I need, on a Monday, too.''

It was not exactly my better nature who suggested that Emma should have it instead, and volunteered to deliver it to her.

"Anita, you are an angel. My eight scheduled clients and my five walk-ins all thank you from the bottom of our hearts.''

Rarely have I felt so guilty for doing someone such an appreciated favor. I bought my conscience off with lunch from Blimpie's. I hate to admit to patronizing a fast-food chain, especially one with such an off-putting name, but I have a serious jones for their tuna sandwich with everything.

I WONDERED WHETHER Emma was aware of the responsibility Lillian had given her, and what Regina's involvement was. I was almost ready to turn the whole thing over to the police. I'd worked up a story about getting the satchel from a client who'd sworn me to secrecy. Like all good lies, it was loosely based on truth. I might hint that the "client" was one of the Wilcox sisters, and invoke confidentiality if asked directly.

I headed back to my apartment to eat my messy sandwich in private and have another look at Lillian's baubles. I had plenty of time before my standing 2:00 appointment with Mrs. Lord; it wouldn't do to miss her two weeks running.

GOING HOME IN the middle of the day is like going to work on a weekend—you're in the right place at the wrong time. On weekdays, the retired and the unemployed linger in the halls, UPS and Meals-On-Wheels make their deliveries, the mail carrier visits with the Super while sorting the mail.

Howard Orton was at his post in the window, keeping an eye on the street. I waved and smiled, aware I'd be an entry in his notebook: "Mrs. Servi home alone midday." I'd have to ask Michael if he'd seen any commentary on me, along the lines of Regina and the whore of Babylon.

It occurred to me that Benno's joke about Howard as a blackmailer might not be so far-fetched. Barbara had seen John Clark and Sylvia Chase strolling in together while Margery was out of town—surely Howard had also. I wouldn't put blackmail past him, not for money so much as morality. He's the kind of man who can't stand anyone to cross the line of propriety but keeps porno magazines under his own mattress. I rode up in the elevator, imagining secret vices he might have—a penchant for panty hose, masturbating into stray socks from the laundry room.

SEVENTEEN

THE TULIPS ON Lillian's landing were starting to droop. Faint riffs from Bobby, Blue, and Bland came through the Wilcoxes' door. A trace of cigarette smoke in the hall said Geoff Tate was awake.

My living room was full of midday sun. I put up water for coffee and made the rounds of the houseplants while I waited for it to boil. Watering plants is a form of meditation for me; I let my mind drift, settle, calm.

Along with the apartment, I inherited my grandmother's collection of African violets. The rosettes of velvet leaves aren't much to look at, but boy do they bloom—burgundy, magenta, violet frilled with white, pale orange, deep blue. They crowd the windowsills, softening the ugly bars of the child guards and the grate across the fire escape.

The kettle wailed. I carried the will into the kitchen and contemplated steaming it open, reading and resealing it before I turned it over to Emma. I poured water through the coffee filter, turned the will over in my hands, held it up to the light.

My good angel won the battle, at least temporarily. I decided to go for gold and look at Lillian's jewelry first. I slid the satchel out from under the pile of linens and put it on the table, got my coffee and a handful of napkins. I unwrapped the sandwich, took a bite, undid the buckles on the satchel.

The plastic kit of toiletries was missing. In their place was an accordion file, dark brown with a red string clasp.

My mind went blanker than meditation ever got me. I took

the file out and hefted it in my two hands. Sirens wailed down Riverside. I unwound the string and lifted the flap.

It was divided into two sections, one of photographs and one of papers. I emptied the section of papers, spread them on the table. There were eight dark blue passbooks from a bank in Asheville, North Carolina, all with balances that hovered just under the FDIC limit of $100,000. I looked at the dates; the most recent deposits had been made in the late eighties. I was no genius at mental math, but with interest all the accounts held more than they were insured for. Who on earth kept that kind of money in savings accounts? It was a sizable chunk of change, for a woman who slept in a stairwell.

There were two legal-size envelopes paper-clipped together, one yellowed and stained, the other a bright new white. I opened the older one first. It yielded a birth certificate for one Thomas Jefferson Tate, born March 17, 1942, at 6:32 a.m., in Asheville, North Carolina. Two tiny footprints, toes round as inky pearls, stood in the bottom right corner. Mother's maiden name: Lillian Raines. Father's name: Jefferson Davis Tate.

Tate. It had to be more than coincidence. I stretched my mind around the possibility that Geoffrey Tate was related to Lillian Raines. And the names, father for the president of the Confederacy, son for a founding father of the Union. I wondered which parent was responsible for the generational shift in ideologies.

The newer envelope also held a birth certificate issued by the state of North Carolina. This one was for a boy named Geoffrey Lewis Tate, born March 17, 1942. Father's name: Jefferson Davis Tate. Mother's name: Erica Fraley. There were no baby footprints on this one.

Stamped in the upper right corner were the words Second Certificate. You might think it was a copy of the original, but as a future adoptive parent I knew those two words would be the only indication that this document was not the one issued at birth. Everything on an adopted child's birth certificate reads as if the adoptive parents gave birth to the child. The date and place are of the child's actual birth; parents are recorded as they were when the child was born; the child's name is the one given by the adoptive parents. The owner of this second birth certificate had been adopted.

It was the first piece of information that explained anything. Lillian slept in this building because her son lived here.

But who put these papers in the satchel? What did Larry Turner have to do with it?

It raised more questions than it answered. Family secrets tend to do that. My father's listed on my birth certificate as "Deceased"; my mother would never tell me so much as his name. It made me wonder if she'd lied, and he was still alive.

Did Geoff know Erica Fraley wasn't his birth mother?

I refolded the birth certificates and put them back in their envelopes. At least these were questions Clea would never confront. One good thing about adopting through foster care, you know who all the players are. We'd met not only her birth mother and father, but also two half brothers and a niece. If she ever has a desire to see them, we know who they are and how to find them.

I took a sip of cold coffee and reached for a fat, cream-colored envelope with a twist of baby-blue satin ribbon around it. It held five smaller envelopes, each with a matching notecard inside. The first card, white with a blue border, was engraved in a raised, spidery black script. It announced the birth of Thomas Jefferson Tate.

The other four envelopes were pale ivory. Their cards, engraved in a less formal font, were invitations to the first, second, third, and fourth birthday parties for T.J., as he was called from the second invitation on. The address was given as the home of Davis and Marion Tate, in Asheville—T.J.'s paternal grandparents, presumably.

There was one more legal-sized envelope, addressed to Lillian Raines, Parkside Manor, Asheville, NC, postmarked November 8, 1948. It held several sheets of paper, stapled across the top, that read: State of New York, County of New York, Final Decree of Dissolution of Marriage. Jefferson D. Tate, Plaintiff, against Lillian R. Tate, Defendant.

There they were, the documents that made up a life. Or rather, four lives.

I took out the photographs, turned the file upside down, and shook it. A piece of paper, folded to a two-inch square with worn edges, fell out. I opened it carefully, afraid it would shred in my hands. It was a death certificate for Thomas Jefferson Tate, dated July 17, 1947. The fifth year of his age. Cause of death was given as "Drowning by Misadventure." A thick, anguished NO was slashed across the page.

Good lord. Lillian Raines had told the truth—not only had her husband stolen her son, he'd gone her one further and arranged for his second wife to adopt the child.

I TURNED TO the photographs. A stack of five-by-seven-inch black-and-white studio pictures were stuck between the covers of an old-fashioned cardboard frame. Two color-tinted studio portraits faced each other—the same pink-lipped boy in the sailor suit as had been in the locket, and a wedding picture from the thirties or early forties.

The dark-haired bride, in a full-skirted gown with long lace sleeves, held a cascading bouquet of roses. Her lips had been reddened and the flowers tinted a delicate peach. A swirled pool of lace filled the bottom of the frame. She looked directly at the photographer. Her expression was tranquil. The groom was a tall man in a white naval uniform, with yellow hair and a fuzzy oval of paper where his face had been erased.

Lillian and Mr. Tate, I presumed.

The five-by-sevens were other poses from the wedding—the couple with their attendants, with both sets of parents, with a flower girl and ring bearer. The whole nine yards of marriage, and in every one the man's face had been obliterated.

Two square ivory envelopes, dated 1942-45 and 1946, contained deckle-edged snapshots. They were snatches of a happy childhood—the infant T.J. in Lillian's lap; as a potbellied toddler squinting into the sun on a beach, a bucket in each hand; riding in a wagon pulled by an older man; on a wide front porch with his arms around a dog; the same porch with Lillian in a swing chair, T.J. standing serious beside her.

In the second envelope, T.J. held his mother's hand, sat in her lap, peered out from behind a chair on the front porch of a white house, posed with a cowboy hat, chaps, and six-shooter. The faceless man appeared only once, T.J. riding his shoulders. Clearly, an adorable and adored child. I put the photos away and wound the red string around the button clasp.

I FINISHED MY sandwich but the tuna did nothing to improve my brain function. I emptied the satchel. No one had sucked up the cough drops. I gave St. Anthony credit for Lillian's papers finding their way into her bag, but as far as I was concerned, St. Nicholas hadn't exactly cleared up the matter of her child.

I opened the red leather case with the man's jewelry and broken pearls. I wound the Patek Philippe. The second hand ticked around, so I set it to the correct time. I stroked the pearls, cool as silk under my hot fingers.

I closed that case and opened the blue plush one. The wedding set was there, along with the opal, but the emeralds were gone. The diamond solitaire caught the light and shot rainbows across the sunny apartment. I couldn't get it past the second knuckle of my ring finger. I closed the box and put everything, including the accordion file, back in the satchel.

Hoping nicotine would do what caffeine hadn't, I made an honest woman of myself, at least in Benno's eyes, and got a stale cigarette from my desk. I unlocked the burglar gate, perched on the fire escape windowsill, and lit up.

The accordion file had to have belonged to Lillian. Did she give it to Geoff, to prove she was his mother? Could she have hidden it somewhere, like at the Grave of the Amiable Child, where Regina or Geoff or Larry had found it? The kicker was that only Geoff could have added his own birth certificate—so he knew what was in the file. Had he known before Lillian died or only afterward?

When you get stuck in a crossword puzzle, it usually means

you've interpreted a clue incorrectly. The best approach is to erase the whole area and start over. The implications of it all were too confusing. I'd done what I set out to do, found evidence to motivate the police to do a real investigation. It was definitely time for them to get involved.

I stubbed the cigarette out and made another cup of coffee. This time the imp of temptation won. The vellum envelope was sealed at the narrow end; fifteen seconds of steam, and it was open.

The gist of the Last Will and Testament of Lillian Raines, whereby she revoked all prior wills and codicils, was that she gave and bequeathed "all my tangible personal property to my beloved son, Thomas Jefferson Tate." She went on to "nominate and appoint Emma Franklin, Executive Director of Saint John Senior Services, to be the Executor of this Will," and to leave one quarter of her estate to the agency.

The meaning of the words seeped into my brain, water through coffee, and darkened my thoughts.

A quarter of Lillian's assets was a lot of money, especially for an agency as small and precarious as Senior Services. If Emma had known the terms of Lillian's will…the size of that bequest presented a fairly substantial conflict of interest.

The last page had Lillian's lacy signature and those of the three witnesses, including Dolores, who attested that "The Testatrix was…in the respective opinions of the undersigned, of sound mind, memory, and understanding and not under any restraint or in any respect incompetent to make a will."

For an elderly person, competency can be a shifting state. Dolores had done what I would have, in the situation, but she didn't know Lillian was leaving the bulk of her considerable estate to a person who might be dead, and she hadn't seen those photographs of the man with the erased face. A case could be made that "of sound mind, memory, and understanding" Lillian was not. As for restraint—why had Lillian chosen this particular time to make a will? And why so much money to Senior Services? I didn't want to follow that thought any further, not at all.

I slid the stiff pages back into the envelope, wet my finger with tap water, and ran it over the flap. I added the will to Lillian's satchel and rebuckled it.

It was just past one o'clock. I called the precinct. Miracle of miracles, Inez came to the phone. She and Michael were just going to lunch, they'd meet me at work in fifteen minutes to pick up the satchel and the will. Let Neville sort it out, he was the professional.

"I am sure Michael will be glad for the excuse to see your beautiful assistant," Inez said. I thought so too.

I DON'T KNOW WHAT impulse made me call Anne to say I was on my way in. At the time, I thought I was doing her a favor by alerting her that Michael was coming to the agency, but my guardian angel may have had a hand in it. Her, or Lillian's avenging spirit.

On the off chance Geoff would see me on the way out, I put Lillian's satchel into a canvas tote bag. The top part stuck out, but it was better than nothing.

Barbara Baker was in the hall when I opened the door, busy with yellow bucket and mop. "Hey, Anita, I heard you were the one put those flowers up there. I didn't know you had Mexican blood," she teased me.

"I didn't want to chance her ghost floating around," I said. "You know, like what happened to the Wilcoxes."

"I'd rather have ghosts than some of the live ones we got living in this house, but it isn't any ghost has it in for those two. You see the latest Crud Report? 'Bird spikes will prevent rats with feathers from patronizing the windowsills of vermin-loving residents,'" Barbara quoted. "The weasel doesn't come right out and name anyone, but we all know whose sill he wants spiked. That man hates everything alive."

"You think Malinsky had something to do with what happened to the sisters?" I asked, as if I hadn't had the same thought myself. But as soon as I said it out loud, I realized he would never have left the gas on in the Wilcox apartment—as an ex-firefighter, Malinsky of all people knew the danger of explosion from a gas leak. No way in god's brick city would he risk blowing up the building.

Barbara stuck the mop in the bucket and wheeled it toward the elevator. "What do I know? I'm so busy sleeping all day and patrolling the halls all night, I don't have time to speculate. Sometimes I'm sorry I took this damn job. George just shrugged off Malinsky, but he gets under my skin. I'm telling you, we got plenty of undesirables in this building, and they don't sleep in the halls."

Barbara dropped her voice. "Did you hear the commotion on the stoop last night?" She pointed a thumb toward Geoff's door. "He got into it with Larry Turner. I don't know what-all it was about. I thought I was going to have to call the cops to break it up, but Howard beat me to it. Time I came upstairs, Howard was whaling on both of 'em with his cane. You should've seen him, hair flap flying!"

"I didn't know Howard had it in him," I said. I would have shared Barbara's amusement if I hadn't suspected what Geoff and Larry were fighting about. I shifted the canvas bag around in front of me and clutched it to my chest.

"You okay, Anita?" Barbara cocked her head and examined my face. "You seem a little out of sorts."

The elevator came. I shrugged and held the door open for Barbara to wheel the bucket in. "I'm just tired."

"It's predicted to rain this afternoon. You had enough sense to put your briefcase in a bag, I hope you shut your windows. I don't need you calling me to do it later since you're here now."

So much for getting back to work with time to spare. I let the elevator door go.

THAT'S THE OTHER SIDE of summer, afternoon thunderstorms. No matter how blue the morning is, it can pour on a dime. The rain comes from the west, across the Hudson, and the winds are something fierce.

If we leave our windows open, we get lakes. If we close them, the violets go limp with heat prostration. I've gotten into the bad habit of calling Barbara from work if a storm blows up. I felt guilty trading on our friendship, but this was the first time she'd complained.

I had my purse over my shoulder, on top of the canvas bag, and I was scrabbling around for my keys when I bumped smack into Geoff Tate.

I stumbled backward, trying to swing the bags around to my back. My right arm got tangled in the straps. I dropped the keys.

Geoff grabbed for my elbow. "Hey, Anita, take it easy. I didn't mean to scare you."

I managed to stay upright and pull away from him. My heart was tap-dancing like Clea's little feet. I made my voice assured, confident, and looked directly at him. "I was just startled. I didn't hear your door open. Barbara said it's supposed to rain, so I'm going to close my windows."

I noticed Geoff had trimmed his beard. His hair was damp, freshly combed, and parted on the left side. He wore a light-weight khaki suit with a pale yellow shirt and a striped tie, diagonals of brown, yellow, green. The man didn't look bad, all cleaned up.

He bent down to retrieve the keys for me.

I kept the canvas bag with Lillian's satchel anchored behind me with one elbow and held out my hand for the keys.

Geoff held them up, just out of my reach. His face turned evil. "What you got there, neighbor?" He peered over my head.

I reached for the keys. "I'm late for work, so if you don't mind…"

"But I do mind." Still dangling the keys, he moved toward me. My alternatives were limited. Up the stairs, the only exit was to the roof. Down the stairs, he'd chase me. I played my strong suit and used words.

"Why are you teasing me? Please give me my keys so I can get to work."

Geoff shook the keys in my face. I grabbed for them. He slipped them into his jacket pocket and advanced on me. I retreated and hit a wall. I had my purse and the satchel wedged behind me, my body between Geoff and the bag. I shoved him away. "Leave me alone or I'll scream!"

Geoff put his hands on my arms and leaned toward me, using the weight of his body to pin me to the wall. His face was inches away from mine. "Yeah, you go ahead. Your friend Larry won't hear you."

They tell you to make noise if you're attacked, but they don't say what to yell. I hesitated, thinking Fire! Rape! Or simply Help! In that instant of hesitation, Geoff put his lips over mine and kissed me. I froze. All words fled. My only thought was Old Spice, why does a man with a beard use so much Old Spice?

Geoff slid his lips up to my ear. "Now give me the bag, beautiful," he whispered.

I snapped out of it faster than Sleeping Beauty, twisting and wriggling. It didn't faze him. He gripped my two hands in one of his and wrenched my shoulder forward.

I pressed against the wall to protect the bag.

Geoff slapped me. My head banged against the wall. "You didn't have enough?" He put a hand under my chin and bent his head for another kiss.

This time I was expecting it. I bared my teeth. Geoff opened his mouth wide and covered my lips with his. He slid his hand down and squeezed my breast.

His fingers feeling for my nipple acted like a dose of adrenaline. I went for him with all I had. I pushed with my elbows, butted him with my head, tried to knee him in the balls.

"This bag is evidence and I'm taking it to the police." I was panting mad.

Geoff tucked my hands under his arm, forcing me sideways against his chest, and felt for my breast again. I curled forward to keep him away. The straps of the tote bag slipped down on my arm. He waltzed me around so I was facing him. He slapped my face again, hard. The blow knocked me upright.

Geoff yanked the bags off my arm. He dropped my purse

on the floor and lifted Lillian's satchel out of the canvas bag. You could have driven a cab through his grin.

"Larry Turner, he's good. I never suspected the two of you were in it together. I bet your husband didn't either."

I lunged for the satchel, got my arms around it, and held on. "The police know everything and they're on their way over here right now."

Geoff laughed, but his hold on the satchel was dead serious. He pried my right arm away. "You're full of shit, Anita. Larry didn't know anything and you don't either."

Geoff yanked the satchel up and out of my arms. I made a leap for it.

He turned his back to ward me off. I jumped on him, riding him piggyback with my arms around his neck. He bent over, then straightened with a sudden jerk. I lost my hold and fell over backward. My head cracked against the floor. I saw a thousand points of white light.

All the self-defense techniques I learned were aimed at getting away from an attacker, not being one. I curled onto my side. He could have the damn bag.

Geoff snagged my purse from the floor and stretched its long strap between his hands. "This'll do. I've got places to go, people to see. I guess you're coming with me. Shit, I wish I'd had you instead of Larry." He rolled me onto my stomach and knelt on my legs. To my great relief, he went for my hands instead of my neck.

To my greater relief, two voices speaking a melodious French emerged from the elevator. They turned shrill with alarm and one of them switched to English. "What is this? You leave her alone!" It was the opera singer.

Geoff tried to haul me up by the wrists. The strap he'd been tying came loose. I fell forward and my head hit the floor again. Stars came out and danced around the walls. I lay still. The voices swirled around me and disappeared.

Gentle hands rolled me to my side. I opened my eyes. The stars faded. The opera singer helped me sit up. A woman with hennaed hair and penciled eyebrows spoke agitated French over her shoulder.

The singer shushed her. "Are you all right?" she asked me.

I nodded my head up and down. My jaw ached but other than that I seemed to be okay. I stood up, tucked my hair back in place. "Where did he go?" I asked.

"Mr. Tate? He ran down the stairs. What a welcome to the Big Apple my friend has had!" She took the handle of a large wheeled suitcase. The other woman had a makeup case in one hand and a tan leather duffel over her shoulder. "Please, won't you come in for a moment?"

I didn't have time for pleasantries. "No, but I need you to do something for me. Call this number—" I got a Senior Services card out of my purse. "Tell them to send the cops over here right away. Tell her I said it's Geoff Tate, and hurry!"

The elevator was still there. I got on and jabbed the button for 1. I felt the back of my head. There was a slight bump.

I had to know where Geoff was going. He didn't just have Lillian's satchel and her will, he also had my keys—the one thing a New Yorker hates to lose. They're like an 11th finger, an extension of your hand, always there, hard to replace. Work keys, mailbox, desk, bike lock, Benno's shop... If I waited for the police, he'd disappear.

The elevator descended at its usual slow pace. I bent and flexed my legs and tried to be patient. I crossed my fingers that Howard was on the alert. When Michael and Inez showed up, he could tell them where I'd gone.

Sure enough, Howard was sitting by the open window.

"Which way did Geoff go?" I called up to him.

Howard pointed right, toward Riverside Drive.

"Which way did he turn?"

Howard started to give me an argument. "Which goddamn way did he turn?" I screamed.

"North, Anita, and that's no way—"

"Tell it to the cops," I said. "When they come, tell it to the cops." I took off down the street. Places to go, people to meet—north on Riverside?

EIGHTEEN

GEOFF WAS ALMOST three blocks ahead of me, on the sidewalk side of the street rather than the park side. He'd paused to light a cigarette in front of one of the ornate apartment buildings lining the east side of the drive.

I wiped at my mouth with the back of my hand. I could still feel Geoff's lips, the prickle of his beard on my face. I took a lipstick out of my purse. The eyes that looked back at me from the little mirror were totally calm and collected, my usual self with no trace of fear or indecision. I applied a coat of dark pink.

Geoff had started walking again. He swung the satchel, moving like a man with plans. I crossed Riverside into the park, where I could watch him without being obvious.

I stayed back about a block. The afternoon crowd set a more leisurely pace than the morning people. An elderly Chinese couple walked arm in arm, black women pushed white babies in strollers, college students ate lunch on the benches, a late-sleeping homeless man's feet stuck out of his blanket nest. Good thing I was wearing a black rayon dress instead of something bright. What with the people, the trees, and parked cars, I was well shielded if Geoff happened to look back.

He was headed in the direction of the scenic overlook and the Amiable Child. North just didn't make sense; there was nothing up here but park. People to see. I thought about Larry Turner. From what Geoff said, probably not. Mark Jenrette?

Someone else was involved, that was a safe bet. Although— Geoff was stronger than I'd given him credit for. He might also be smarter. I'd assumed Regina was the mastermind, but Regina was dead. What if Geoff had silenced her?

Goose bumps crawled up my neck. I hung well back, thankful for the activity in the park, and kept my eyes peeled for a blue and white patrol car.

Geoff cut across the street to Grant's Tomb and went straight up the wide allée of granite squares toward the monument. The double row of trees was still bare, leafless.

To the north, the sky was an ominous dark gray; in the south, it was blue and sunny. There was an odd, clear cast to the light, a hush of stillness. Only the very tops of the trees bent silently under the gathering wind.

At the point almost opposite the scenic overlook where Regina's body had been, Geoff's pace slowed. I crouched between a light blue Toyota and a black minivan. The stone eagles on either side of the broad steps raised their wings as if to swoop down on him. The fluted columns of the overlook pavilion, still wrapped in yellow tape, were thin imitations of the fat Doric columns under the portico of General Grant's final resting place.

Geoff headed around the east side of the tomb, and disappeared from my view.

I crossed Riverside and climbed the shallow granite stairs from the street. The tomb is surrounded by an undulating mosaic bench. I paused in the shelter of a tall brown tile man. His blue eyes watched over the courtyard.

For all that Grant's Tomb is a national monument, it's not a place many people visit. Two Japanese men in suits took photographs of each other next to a rising sun, a dove with an olive branch in its mouth. A stout white couple in matching plaid jackets joined the audience of penguins watching an Eskimo catch fish in front of her igloo. Their solid backs looked like Scottish slipcovers.

The tourists weren't much camouflage for my New York black. I drifted toward the rear of the tomb and caught a glimpse of Geoff heading for the stairs. I faded behind an ample woman with hair like Tammy Faye. The Japanese men followed the benches north.

I made for a low spot, stepped on a yin-yang symbol set in a spiral of red tentacles, and went over the wall behind the mosaics. An unpruned hedge of some shiny-leafed shrub ran along the wall and formed a narrow crawl space where there didn't seem to be any broken glass or piles of excrement, human or otherwise.

I could see through the hedge better than I could through the tourists, but Geoff was somewhere outside my field of vision. To the north, lightning flicked. I counted, sixteen oh-shits, before the accompanying growl of thunder.

Where was Geoff? I craned my neck but I didn't dare stand up. Even more important, where were the cops?

I did a kind of three-point crouch-walk to the corner and peered out. Geoff stood not ten feet from where I was hiding, waiting to cross Riverside—heading toward the grave of the Amiable Child.

Was the answer still there? But he continued north, passing the path down to the stone urn.

I STOOD UP AND shook out my skirt. Geoff was about two hundred yards ahead of me. I skirted the fenced area around a nondescript tree, the gift of a Chinese dignitary, and trailed along through a derelict playground at the northern end of the monument park when I heard the splash of running water.

A man on a bench, sleeping under cover of a cardboard box, was urinating without getting out of bed. New York; you can't make this stuff up. I was uncomfortably aware of two cups of coffee making their way into my own bladder.

Where the two lanes of Riverside reunite at the north end of the monument, the drive becomes an elevated roadway, supported by a steel-arched viaduct soaring above the gritty reality of 12th Avenue and the West Side Highway.

I watched Geoff from the high ground of the swing sets. I had a vista all the way to the George Washington Bridge.

A hundred yards from where I stood, a matched pair of

stairways descend from the Heights to West Harlem. Geoff paused at the head of the western stairs, put his fingers in his mouth, and whistled—two shorts and a long.

Lightning bolted across the sky to the north. This time the thunder was only nine oh-shits behind.

About halfway down the steps, there's a high, arched pedestrian underpass. The western stairs continue down; the eastern stairs branch right to a schizophrenic off-shoot of Riverside Drive that manages to be one-way in two different directions before it wanders across 125th and becomes 12th Avenue. The windows of a modern high-rise, Columbia housing, look down over the eastern stairway.

Geoff went down the stairs. What the hell? No white man in a suit and tie and his right mind would go down there, not even in broad daylight, let alone with a satchel of antique jewelry.

A few cars went by. None of them were New York police blue. I trotted down the grassy slope to the eastern staircase.

Weeds grew in the cracks of the stone steps; vines curled over the parapet walls. The stairs were an obstacle course of unidentifiable, flattened articles of clothing, a car headlight, handlebars and one tire from a child's bike, a bottle of orange juice, pieces of cardboard boxes, brown shards of broken beer bottles—not to mention the usual litter of lavender-, red-, yellow-, blue-topped crack vials.

I kept an eye out for syringes. The vault of the underpass came into view. I heard Geoff whistle again. The notes echoed in the vast, tile-roofed space. The gathering clouds reflected in the blank eyes of the high-rise windows.

I made my way through the underbrush to the massive stone wall supporting the drive and edged down the steep slope to a cluster of young ailanthus trees, newly in leaf, by the mouth of the archway.

This vast underpass is a kind of no-man's-land, owned and ignored by the city. It would be the ideal place for a homeless encampment if university security didn't do regular sweeps to prevent anyone from spending extended time there.

Which doesn't stop the street people from using the area to make their toilettes and transact other private business. Judging from the caliber of unbroken beer bottles—Heineken, Bass, Guinness—the students who lived in International House, a block south, also had their uses for the high-roofed space.

I stuck my head around the corner. Geoff was silhouetted at the far end. He put the satchel down between his legs, like a man waiting for a subway train, and lit a cigarette. Given the distance—about a hundred yards—I wasn't worried about being seen. The cigarette smoke wafted my way, a delicious contrast to the pervasive urine-and-excrement aroma.

I was really coming up in the world, career-wise; from investigating things I didn't want to touch with my bare hands to lurking in closets and foul-smelling shrubbery. Thunder growled, ominous as the monster music from Geoff's television.

"All right, all right." A new voice, soft, husky. Silhouetted against the western end of the underpass was a tall, skinny man with a ponytail and beard, in a long coat. Sam Katz.

"Hey, Uncle Sam, what took you so long?"

"People around."

"Down below? I didn't see anybody."

"You don't know where to look. Let's go in." He held out a hand, ushering Geoff into the vaulted space like it was his living room.

I kept one eye where I could just see them. Sound was no problem; the curved tile roof amplified Sam's whispery voice. They stopped about midway down. Sam perched on the side of an overturned shopping cart.

"I got you these."

Geoff took what Sam offered. He rocked it back and forth in his hand. I heard the faint rattle of pills in a plastic vial. "Valium. Jeez, you really knocked yourself out. I need Ambian, Xanax, something with a little more kick."

"That's all I had left. The pills were Regina's gig. I don't do that part."

"Sure you do. Just like the last batch, only you gotta be

careful not to scare the next old lady to death." Geoff snickered. "It's like killing the goose that lays the golden egg."

"Listen, man, that was the only time. I don't go into their rooms."

Geoff opened the bottle, shook out a pill, and swallowed it dry. "Yeah, whatever. Give me the money." He held out his hand.

"I got fifteen hundred." Sam took an envelope out of his pocket.

"That's all? You ripping me off, Uncle Sam?" Geoff put the envelope in his inside jacket pocket without looking at what was inside it. "Regina said she'd get three thou, and the freaking lawyer wants two. I need the rest of it!"

"She's not me." Sam gestured at the satchel between Geoff's feet. "You have more."

Geoff hauled him up by the front of his jacket. "Listen up, Uncle Sam, I know you kept back a thou. Cough it up or I'll rat out your skinny ass for croaking that old lady."

Sam let Geoff hold him by his shoulders. His arms hung at his sides, neither resisting nor yielding.

"Don't threaten me." Sam kept his voice a level monotone. "You killed your own goose, man."

Geoff dropped him. "Regina had a big mouth. All right, you forget what you know, I'll forget what I know."

He paced the length of the tunnel. I flinched back from the opening as the squeak of new leather shoes approached.

"I need a drink. My nerves are shot, and we got another problem."

That would be me.

The footsteps turned and headed toward Sam in the middle of the tunnel. It was time to get out of there. I stepped backward up the slope. I'd gone about four feet when I slipped on some foul wet rags and landed on my butt. A miniature avalanche of dirt slid onto the path.

"Get out of here, Ray," Sam raised his voice. "Find someplace else to keep dry."

There was no Ray at my end of the tunnel. The wall of

windows watched my predicament without comment. A cab went down the hill, so close I could see the gold earrings on the female passenger, and was gone before I had the wit to leap out at it.

Using the wall for support, I levered myself upright. The back of my dress was a mess. I didn't want to think about what I'd sat in.

There was silence in the underpass. I edged my face around for a look. Geoff and Sam stood shoulder to shoulder at the western end, staring out at the incoming weather. Their voices were too low for me to make out what they were saying.

I figured I was better off staying put than tackling the slope again. I was wearing leather-soled sandals, fine for work but not bushwhacking up a muddy hill. I squatted down, thinking maybe I could relieve my bladder without the men hearing me. That's one advantage of dresses; you just hold the crotch of your panties to one side and do it.

But then I heard the metallic jingle of keys. I knelt forward and risked a look.

They'd come back to the middle of the underpass. Sam put something in his pocket. Geoff sat on the shopping cart, put the satchel on his knees, and undid the buckles. "Okay, it'll have to be the diamond. Get it in twenties, I don't want any— What the hell?"

I kicked myself for a fool.

Geoff held up a white envelope with ornate lettering. "Hey hey, I just got freaking lucky." He slit the will envelope open with his thumb and unfolded the stiff sheets of paper. Sam stood over him, hands in his pockets.

Praying for a downpour, I bent over and slid my sandals off. If I didn't have to worry about making noise, I could manage the scramble up to Riverside Drive. I'd flag down a car, any car. A middle-aged, middle-class white woman in distress— someone would stop for me.

My left foot had fallen asleep. I bent and flexed my ankle, trying to get rid of the needles and threads.

Geoff read the will, the delight evident on his face. "I'll be damned, the old hag did what she said.'' He tapped the envelope against his hand.

"Get my nosy neighbor out of the way and I'll give you double what we agreed on. I wish I knew how that bitch came up with the will!''

"I need something up front,'' Sam said.

"It'll take time to settle this estate shit. I need my lawyer to deal with this.'' He put the will back in the satchel.

"I'll take the jewelry.'' Sam's voice stayed level but there was something in it that stopped Geoff.

He laughed nervously. "Yeah, okay, you could have the watch.''

Sam put out a hand and gripped his wrist. "All of it,'' he said.

Geoff tried to pull away but couldn't. Sam stared him down and let go.

Geoff reached in the satchel and took out the blue plush jewelry box. Sam put it in his pocket.

I stopped watching and leaned against the granite wall. The sky had turned the sick yellow-gray that precedes a downpour. I'd lost track of the lightning and thunder count, but even in the gloom under the trees in the shadow of the viaduct I could tell it was close.

I caught a flash of light and started counting. One oh-shit, two oh-shit, three— Oh shit. The squeak of Geoff's shoes was headed in my direction.

NINETEEN

I SLID TO A CROUCH in the shelter of the ailanthus. I put my head on my knees, held my breath, and made myself small and dark and invisible. Lightning cracked, loud and close, the thunder right on its heels.

"Shit!"

Startled, I looked up. Geoff had dropped the satchel. He bent to pick it up and looked right into my face.

I knew how it felt to be a small animal caught in car headlights.

"Goddamn it! Sam!" Geoff lurched over the low iron railing. I swung my sandals up at his face. The momentum sent me into a slide and I sat down hard. Geoff hauled me up and handed me, kicking and squirming, over the railing to Sam.

This time I had no inhibitions about yelling my head off. Those apartment windows were my best hope. "Help! Let go of me! Help!"

Sam twisted my right arm behind my back and marched me into the tunnel. "Be quiet," he said.

I screamed again. He jerked on my arm and I shut up. I was caught, pinned, no longer wriggling.

"Please stop, you're hurting me." I made my voice calm, casual, friendly, the opposite of how I felt.

"You won't run," Sam told me. He eased my arm down slowly, laid an almost gentle hand on my shoulder for support, and let go. I had to blink back tears. I cradled my arm and took a few deep breaths.

Geoff dropped my sandals and purse at my feet. I didn't

dare bend over to pick them up. Self-defense classes tell you to give the attacker what he wants, to scream and struggle, to run away. In this case, what they wanted was me. Screaming and struggling hadn't worked, but I could still run.

Yeah, my fight-or-flight response said, Who are you kidding? There's two of them. How far do you think you'd get?

My struggle with Geoff in the hall had been brief and furious. I lost because he outweighed me. Sam Katz was something else again, strong and purposeful, emotionless.

I know women who carry Mace, pepper spray, whistles. I wasn't one of them. I considered, briefly, trying for an empty beer bottle. My attitude toward weapons is, anything I tried to use could be taken away and used on me. I let go of that idea, too.

In spite of the self-defense classes, what I've always believed will save me is words. Words are the tools of my trade; I use them to help people find their way through to the other side of a bad idea. I straightened my dress and tucked strands of hair back into my bun, trying to regain my composure if not my dignity.

Sam stroked his beard. I had a feeling words would not cut it with him.

"What'd you do, Anita, follow me out of the building?" Geoff asked.

I nodded. In counseling, you take your cues from the client.

"I can't figure out what's in it for you." Geoff patted around at his pockets, found a pack of cigarettes, and offered me one. I accepted. Sam took a book of matches out of his pocket and lit my cigarette.

"Thank you." I gave him a smile. If you can't escape 'em, join 'em.

Geoff shot Sam a look and lit his own cigarette.

"I work at St. John Senior Services," I said. Geoff had read Lillian's will. I made the statement open-ended so he could build on it.

Geoff snapped his fingers. "You're a sly one, Anita, Goody

Two-shoes sucking up to the old lady for her money, you and your playmate. Jeeze, Larry worked me like a pro."

Okay, he thought Larry and I were coconspirators, and we'd double-crossed him. I didn't think I could go anywhere with that. My plan had to get us aboveboard, out of the tunnel. His inheritance was the real stake, and he needed Emma to get it.

"The executor of the will, Emma Franklin? She's my boss." Keep him talking, buy myself some time to figure just the right angle to hook him. "Regina went to see her last week and offered her the satchel if Emma would cut her in."

Geoff snorted. "You think I'm just a stupid drunk, don't you, but I know when I'm being shined on."

"I'm telling you what I know. They were up to something behind your back."

"No freaking way. Regina had biiiig plans and a big mouth to go with them, but she couldn't do shit without me. I needed that inheritance. Damned if I was going to marry that slut so she could spend it for me." He narrowed his eyes at me. "I'm not too sure I want to donate any of it to charity, either."

A flash of lightning lit the tunnel and froze us in a tableau of concentration, smoke curling above our heads, three brujos cooking up trouble. Thunder cracked on the heels of the light. The sky opened, one of those ten-minute Manhattan downpours that render umbrellas useless.

Curtains of rain closed the tunnel off from the outside world. I crossed my fingers that whoever Ray was, he or some other stray would pop in for shelter. No one did. A fork of lightning stabbed into the Hudson.

"So both of you killed Lillian Raines?" In a perfectly pleasant, conversational tone, I completely overplayed my hand.

Geoff slapped my face. My head hit the wall. I slid into a crouch, curled around my knees.

Geoff grabbed my hair and jerked my head up. "Freud should ask me what women want, I'll tell him—they want to know who's boss."

"Leave her alone, man," Sam spoke. He hooked a hand under my armpit and hoisted me up. He felt the back of my head, tenderly, but I flinched. "It'll make a bruise." He turned to Geoff. "No more of that. No marks on her."

"Huh?" Geoff stared at him. My thought exactly.

"It has to look like an accident. If you beat her up, the cops'll be all over here like gulls on a dump." Sam didn't raise his voice or change his inflection. "Especially after Regina."

Great, my defender was a sociopath. I recalculated my options. Fight or flight were no more possible now than they'd been ten minutes ago, although I was prepared to go for Geoff with elbows, knees, teeth, all I had, if he touched me again.

"Watch her. I'll be right back." The rain had eased up. Sam went out the west end of the tunnel, down the stairs.

THE IMAGE OF Geoff Tate as pathetic lingered in spite of the slap. Maybe it was arrogance on my part, or denial, but I was still confident I could outwait, outthink, outsmart this man. "Never provoke an attacker." I remembered that advice, too. I hoped I could lull him into thinking he had me intimidated into obedience.

I made my voice small and meek. "You didn't have to hit me. I was just curious about how the lady of the landing died."

Geoff stared past me, his mind somewhere else. "She came to my apartment last Sunday, to show me my baby pictures, she said. She knew my mother's name, her maiden name, but I thought she was trying to scam me and I closed the door in her face. Then Regina told me about the jewelry. I didn't believe her. Sleeping in a goddamn stairwell, what could the old lady have? The Tate diamonds?" Geoff shrugged.

"You didn't know she was your mother?" Fools rush in.

"I know who my mother is!" The look in his eyes scared me more than the slap. "I tried to show the old bat a picture of me with my mom and dad. We had to go up top to use the light by the roof door. She called my mother a whore."

Geoff scowled. "She told me she left everything she had to me. She started patting my face and talking baby talk. It was gross. I pushed her away. She fell over backward, down the stairs." Geoff shuddered. "She had a goddamn hard head. It didn't even knock her out. She grabbed at my leg when I went by."

"Lillian Raines bled to death," I said. "You left her on the landing, and she bled to death."

"What was I supposed to do, call an ambulance?" Geoff snorted.

"That would've been nice." The sarcasm went right over his head.

"Besides, Regina went up to check on her and she was alive. She gave Regina that file of papers to prove she was my mother."

Right, I thought, that's what Regina told you.

I had one track of my mind alert for Sam. With him gone, if I kept Geoff talking, got him distracted with his feelings... Call it an occupational hazard of the helping professions: we care. We're trained to fix people who are hurt, broken, confused. To do that, sometimes you need to know how a person got that way in the first place.

"I saw the two birth certificates. Geoffrey Lewis Tate, it has 'Second Certificate' stamped in one corner. That's the kind of certificate they issue when a child is adopted." It was a loaded piece of information and I delivered it as compassionately as I could.

Geoff gave me a withering look. "You really do think I'm stupid. The only thing those birth certificates prove is that there's a lot of in-breeding down there in North Carolina. Two boys born on the same day, some cretin in the records office put my father's name on both certificates."

"Don't you think it's a pretty incredible coincidence?" I got ready to move. "Lillian Raines knew your mother's name, and she came looking for you in New York. Why do you think she—"

"You women, you don't let up. My mother died two years ago. She was beautiful and sweet and gentle. She was not a lunatic bag lady fixated on a dead baby." Geoff's eyes were clear, and full of malice. "Regina didn't shut up about it until I shut her mouth for her, and you're next."

I bolted for the street.

TWENTY

I DIDN'T GET FAR.

Sam was just outside the east entrance. I practically skidded into his chest.

This was a clear case of frying pan to fire: much worse.

Sam twisted my arm, the other one this time, behind my back. It's an amazingly effective hold. He applied a slow pressure that had me panting with pain.

Geoff joined us. "Hey, it's about time you made it back."

"So I see," Sam said. He dropped my arm with a sharp, downward motion. I stumbled forward. Fire shot up my shoulder. I couldn't stop an involuntary squirt of urine.

"Get back inside and get your shoes. You too, asshole." Sam checked the blind eyes of the apartment building. He reached into his coat pocket and handed Geoff a half pint of vodka. "I thought you might need this."

If there was irony in Sam's voice, it went right over Geoff's head. His Adam's apple bobbed, four swallows. "So what's the plan?"

"Drown her."

"In broad daylight?" Geoff asked.

Good question. Geoff was right, I'd equated drunkenness with stupidity. My estimate of his intelligence rose, but not by much.

"There's a place we won't be noticed. We'll feed her some of your stash and let her get relaxed. Although it would take less time to block her air until she's almost out. Either way, by the time she comes to, she'll have lungs full of water. No bruises, a simple suicide."

The sun came out. Each drop of water on each green leaf in front of me glittered and winked. The river, my future grave, sparkled a welcome.

ACTUALLY, I'VE ALWAYS wanted to swim in the Hudson. I grew up with the Pacific Ocean; large bodies of cold water appeal to me. Hot, humid July afternoons, a river practically on my doorstep—if it weren't for the pollution, I'd have sneaked in long ago.

Plan B arrived, full-formed. I'd jump in the river and swim off before they had a chance to throw me in.

Sam was advocating suffocation, if Geoff had the stomach to hold me. "No pills to trace. You did Regina, you can do this," Sam said, in his level voice. "All right, man. Let's get to the river. I have plastic bags."

Geoff swatted my behind with the satchel. "I'm ready."

I had a quarter second to contemplate running before Sam took my arm.

His grip was all bone and sinew; even without twisting, his hold immobilized me. "Take her other arm, Tate. Here we go, three companions."

The rain had stopped. A fine frizz of split ends curled in Sam's beard.

I made myself heavy, my feet reluctant. The stairs were mostly dirt and frost-heaved stone, easy to stumble on. Being small definitely had its disadvantages; they simply carried me down. I almost didn't care. My shoulders ached. The need to pee was a sharp pain.

THE STAIRWAY dumped us onto St. Claire Place, a two-block stretch that runs under the West Side Highway and connects the Hudson to a stray tendril of Riverside Drive. It's a turna-round for the 125th Street buses, a pit stop for cabbies. Being named for the Amiable Child, St. Claire Pollack, did nothing for its ambiance.

Blank windows watched from the Columbia building. Shouting would be futile. Sam turned us toward the Hudson. Riverside Drive soared overhead on the graceful steel arches of Olmstead Bridge.

They marched me across the northbound off-ramp and under the lower overpass of the highway. Cars hitting a metal expansion joint ka-thumped above us. We skirted a huge puddle, passed a plastic-covered mattress-and-cardboard sleeping shelter, crossed the southbound ramp. No cars exited or entered.

Even if they had, the few drivers who get on or off here speed past with their doors locked and their eyes on where they're going. The spot Sam had in mind was perfect for his purposes. Riverside Park and most of the West Side Highway are built on landfill, what was dug out of the subway. Huge boulders, a rip-rap of Manhattan schist, line the water's edge.

Marginal Street is the apt name of the road along the river's edge. A narrow esplanade with a strip of grass and a few trees in round cement planters are all that remains of the old piers. People sometimes duck through a hole in the chain-link fence to fish from the cement embankment.

In the aftermath of the storm, no one was around. Sam herded us down over the wet rocks to the water line.

"Sit," he said.

"Are you nuts? On this mossy shit?" Geoff complained.

"Yeah, man, you want to keep those khaki pants clean. Use this." Sam handed him a plastic shopping bag.

If he was being sarcastic, I missed it too. Mostly I was thinking about how badly I needed to pee. Nothing like an immediate problem to distract from less imminent troubles.

They still had me by the arms. They sat; I sat. Once we were down, our feet inches from where the muddy water lapped the rocks, we were blocked from view by the rise of the ramp to the left, the concrete wall to the right.

The river was fairly high, and probably ice cold with snow melt. I noted the tide coming in; at least I wouldn't be swept out to sea. That's another thing that's kept me from an illicit swim, the currents. The Hudson is a tidal river, with a strong inflow and a tendency to odd eddies.

The spot couldn't have been more public, or more private. We sat in full view of the warehouses and apartment buildings across on the Jersey side. If anyone noticed us, they'd assume we were up to no good—sex, drugs, drowning—and pass by without a second look.

A car went up the on-ramp behind us. I caught a glimpse of back bumper.

Sam laughed, a short, dry sound. He let go of my left arm and directed Geoff, "Move her forward. Get in back of her and use your arms and legs. Your body weight."

Closer to the water was where I wanted to be. I bumped along on my hands and butt, a boulder away from Geoff. Sam came after me quick as a cat and put his hand on the scruff of my neck. I froze, a kitten in its mother's mouth.

"Give me your purse," he said. His eyes never focused on my face.

"Why?" I stalled. I wanted the rhythm to be mine, not his. I learned that from football—if the defense disrupts the offense, mistakes happen.

Geoff scooted forward on his plastic bag. Sam scraped me back up over a smaller rock and deposited me between Geoff's knees. Geoff put his legs in my lap and wrapped his arms over mine, pinning me down.

"Hold her," Sam said. He put the palm of his hand under my chin and tipped my head back against Geoff's chest. I couldn't get my mouth open. "This is how it works."

Sam pinched my nostrils closed and cut off my air. I panicked. I kicked and thrashed from side to side, with no thought whatsoever for conserving my energy. I wouldn't have lasted long.

Sam let go. I gulped air and stopped struggling. Irrationally, what I wanted most was to pull my skirt down.

Sam rocked back on his heels and held his hand out for my purse.

I had the strap over my neck and across my chest. "How do you expect me to get it off with him holding me?"

Sam nodded to Geoff.

Instead of letting go of my arms, Geoff pulled me up so I was sitting in his lap. His heart thudded against my back. I was enveloped in Old Spice. He put his lips to my left ear, took my earlobe into his mouth, nibbled.

I pulled away and head-banged his chest.

"Ow!"

"Don't get started with that, man," Sam said.

Geoff caught the contempt in his voice and let go of my arms.

"Don't suicides usually write a note?" Geoff asked.

"Not always." Sam, his hand in a plastic bag like a glove, deposited my purse on a protected piece of ground. "She's too distraught for a note."

Geoff had his ankles over mine, and I was just too far from the water to dive for it. I slid a little forward, as if to get out of his lap, and Geoff slid with me. I needed to get in while I was still breathing; if I fought, Sam would cut my air off again. I was going to need all the breath I had for the icy bath.

Sam saw what I was up to. "Get your arms around her, man. Hold her with your weight. Lucky she's so small."

I gave up on false pride and whimpered for mercy while I tried to implement another piece of self-defense advice: if all else fails, make a stink. Vomiting is good; a bowel movement can put a quick end to rape. Of course, they do warn you that grossing out an attacker can backfire, but I had nothing to lose.

As full as my bladder was, a lifetime's training made emptying it in Geoff's lap difficult. But I needed Geoff's involuntary reaction of disgust to loosen his grip.

Sam squatted next to me and reached for my chin. It suddenly got very easy.

"God damn it, she's pissing on me!" Geoff shoved me toward the water and scrambled backward, knocking Sam off balance in the process.

Propelled by the unexpected push, I flopped into the river face first. It was colder than anything I'd ever been in.

A hand grabbed my ankle and held on. I struggled to roll over in the water and come up for air.

I lifted my leg and slammed it down sideways. The hand let go.

I kicked out from shore and came up gasping. The ice cold wet stopped my heart, but not the pain shooting up my left leg. This was not the swim I had in mind.

The current was gentler than I'd anticipated. I treaded water, trying to get my breath back. A hot liquid bathed my legs. My brain cleared.

I hadn't given enough thought to how I was going to get out once I'd gotten in. A four-foot concrete wall stretched several hundred yards to the north. Sam and Geoff crouched on the shore, watching me.

The current carried me very slightly upstream. I'd have to swim as far as the Fairway parking lot before I'd have a shot at being noticed. If I didn't get going, hypothermia would finish the job for them. I put my breaststroke to work.

"Stand up, you bastards, and say your prayers!"

I rolled to a backstroke. No. 8, Marky Mark, stood in a batter's stance, a long metal pole over one shoulder. He swung it back and forth, eyeing an easy pitch. Geoff grabbed for the pole on a forward swing and missed.

Sam went for Mark's legs and brought him down to his knees. Mark swung the pole again and caught Geoff in the belly. The impact hurled him into the water, a perfectly executed bunt.

Geoff went down and didn't come up.

I thought about changing directions to head downstream for where he'd gone in. The chill had set into my bones and it took all my energy just to stay above water.

Sirens shrieked somewhere above me. They brought the edges of a ringing red oblivion with them. I fought it off and let the current carry me.

TWENTY-ONE

A NICE WHITE LADY threw me a piece of foam that smelled like dog vomit. Two men with a yellow rope finally realized I wasn't able to do anything with the loop they threw me. My brain was no more than a recording device for what was happening to my body.

A black man took off his shoes, put his wallet and keys in them, and lowered himself into the water, swearing a blue streak. I felt the rope prickle under my arms, the concrete scrape up my thigh, the hands hauling me like a beached whale onto dry land.

I kept expecting the lassitude I'd heard came with hypothermia. I wanted to be warm, to float off into the golden glowing sunshine. When I did finally drift away from my shivering cocoon of skin, I got hauled back by the nose.

Waking up to an ammonia ampule is about as nasty as it gets. I coughed, choked, gagged. My eyes watered. My teeth chattered like castanets on amphetamines.

It was Hotkowski again. He apologized profusely as he ripped my dress down the middle. Like cops, paramedics come in pairs; why did I always get stuck with the junior member of the team?

Hands rolled me to my side and wrapped me in something dry and soft. Hotkowski tried to put an oxygen cone over my face. I retched up coffee, tuna, river water. He wiped my face and got the mask under my chin. It was a start on improved relations. Maybe I'd lend him some mascara for the mustache.

I tried to drift off again, but every sound in the air around me seemed to have settled into my head. An urgent female voice, the babble of the parking lot crowd, car horns, radio static, more sirens.

Michael's face floated into view and chased all the noises away. I started shaking.

"Hang on, lady," someone said. I was jolted over and up, into an ambulance. The world suddenly got much smaller, heavier, brighter. More blankets piled on top of me. This time I succeeded in leaving.

THE NEXT THING I knew, I was sandwiched in warm plastic bubble wrap. A Filipino nurse murmured soothing syllables while she attached something to my chest. Other hands rolled me onto my side and inserted something in my rectum.

I was lying on the nubby green couch of my childhood. My mother took the thermometer out of my behind and said I had measles. I clutched my blankie and told her I didn't want measles. She put a cool cloth on my forehead and sang *hush little baby, don't say a word.* The heat on my cheeks told me I was crying.

Two disembodied voices circled my head. I caught "heart arrhythmia" and "100 percent oxygen." I realized I was breathing warm air. I started to feel again, and it wasn't pleasant. Never mind needles and threads; I was being triple-stitched with fiery lace. I closed my eyes and followed the nurse's voice to warm tropical waters.

Then Benno was there, stroking my cheek. "Speak to me, Anita of my heart, tell me you're okay."

I opened my mouth but my teeth started dancing and I couldn't get the words out. Warmth was flowing into my other hand from a tether attached to an IV pole. I told Benno I didn't want the diamond ring, I wanted the mockingbird. The voices above me got anxious about "core temperature" and "moderate to severe hypothermia." I let them worry about it and surrendered to my mother's off-key singing.

THE NEXT TIME I came back, I was swaddled in warm blankets. My mother was gone.

Benno squeezed my fingers. "Hey, honey, are you back with us?"

I realized I was in a hospital bed surrounded by striped curtains.

I opened my mouth and words came out. "I swam in the Hudson."

"So, what, you couldn't wait for summer?" If Benno was joking, it meant I'd live.

I shivered. "I swear, I'll never be warm again."

"As God is your witness?" Benno grinned. "Want a sip of hot water?"

The inside of my mouth tasted like mud. Benno hit a button and my upper half tilted toward vertical. "Hot water, is that all I get?"

"It's all you deserve," Benno shot back. "What the hell were you doing, Anita?"

I knew his sharpness had more to do with relief than anger, but knowing didn't help.

"Oh no, don't start crying, you'll set off one of these machines. I'm not mad at you, Anita of my heart, I just—"

But I *was* crying, I couldn't help it. Benno located a tissue and mopped at my face. "It's okay, we'll talk later. Here, drink your water." I sipped.

Michael's head appeared around the curtain. "Yo, Social Worker. I'm here to officially see to your health and well-being." He nodded to Benno and pulled up a chair. "Anne Reisen's here with your daughter. I'll sit with Anita while you go see them."

Warmth spread up into my cheeks. Benno kissed my forehead.

The ailanthus trees I was hiding in swayed like the eucalyptus in my mother's backyard. The ground was damp from a spring rain. I didn't want to go into the tunnel in my bare feet because of banana slugs and their slime trails. I went looking for my mother to pour salt on them and make them fizzle up and dissolve.

A brown-skinned woman with a worried face appeared at my side. It was Dr. Diane Lorenzo. I figured my mother sent her and I asked her for the salt.

"You're a little confused right now, Anita." Dr. Lorenzo watched the television next to my bed even though the picture was nothing but spiky green lines.

The striped walls wavered again and made me dizzy. I closed my eyes and went into the house to stand over the heat register and get warm. My skirt billowed up. The heat flooded my crotch and I remembered peeing in the river. Benno took my hand and pulled me back to shore.

"She seems to be drifting in and out," he told Dr. Lorenzo.

Her answer involved observation, antibiotics, admission.

I let Benno deal with it. I wanted sleep and heat and no watery dreams.

I had the sensation of floating down green corridors, of elevators sliding open and closed. I woke up when they tried to ease me from one bed to another.

"Where am I?"

"From the sound of it you're body surfing in the Pacific," Benno said.

I had an IV in my hand, oxygen tubes up my nose, and something heavy taped to my chest. People bustled around and sorted out my attachments. I let them tuck a warm, glowing blanket around me. I closed my eyes and went back to sleep.

WHEN I WOKE UP, it was dark outside. Michael was dozing in the visitor's armchair by the window. I stared at his blue uniform and remembered everything that came before my swim. I wished I hadn't.

Michael's eyes opened and caught me staring. "Welcome to New York City," he drawled. "Or are you still a California girl?"

New York, where sarcasm is an art form. It wasn't funny but I tried a smile.

"Benno went to get some food, he'll be back soon. Anne took Clea home. Now we're alone, you want to tell me what happened?"

"Why are you here?" I asked.

"It's just a formality, ma'am." Michael tipped his hat. "In case you have anything pertinent to say before Neville comes by to interview you."

"Is Geoff okay?" I asked.

"Last I heard, your Mr. Tate hadn't come up for air."

"And Sam Katz?" I needed to know what the police knew so I could figure out how much of my own idiocy I'd have to confess.

"Collared on the spot, along with your avenging angel, Mark Jenrette, who swears he was defending you. Neville's holding him until you confirm his story."

"What did he say?"

Michael narrowed his eyes. "I'm supposed to be asking the questions here."

I let a shiver start at my toes and work its way north. There was a sharp ache in my left leg, a duller ache between my shoulders. The memory of my arms twisted behind my back brought another kind of shiver.

"Okay, okay," Michael took pity on me. "Jenrette says he saw Katz and Tate carry you down to the river and toss you in. He picked up a piece of metal signpost and, he says, accidentally sent Tate in when Katz attacked him. Katz went catatonic and wouldn't say a word. He's on his way to Bellevue for psychiatric observation. Your turn."

"They didn't throw me in, I jumped. Sam was going to cut off my air…" I wasn't shivering, I was burning up. "Why is it so hot in here?"

Michael put an ice chip in my mouth and I swam off.

When I surfaced, Benno was explaining aspiration pneumonia to Detective Neville. I didn't stay for that conversation. Benno left and a different cop in uniform took Michael's chair. During the night, nurses came and went. Thermometers beeped in my mouth and were withdrawn. Neville asked my mother why I wanted salt. Emma told me not to worry about coming to work, there was no money to pay me.

Just before dawn, I came fully awake. The sheets were damp and tangled. The uniformed cop, a sympathetic black man with a mustache, called the nurse for me. I made a fuss about the catheter and the nurse took it out and helped me to the bathroom while an aide changed the sheets. I fell back into a dreamless sleep.

A SMALL CADRE of doctors gathered around my bed and told each other alarming things about the potential of bacterial contaminants downstream from the waste disposal plant. I told them I was hungry and I wanted to go home. They informed me that I had aspiration pneumonia and would not be going home until tomorrow, if then, but I could have clear liquids along with more antibiotics.

The cop made a phone call and told me Detective Neville would be by soon. I called Benno for sympathy, but he turned traitor and told me the doctors knew best, he had to get Clea ready for school, I should go back to sleep and he'd come as soon as he could.

They brought me a tray with red Jell-O and lukewarm tea. The cop, whose name was Pettiway, fixed the tea with milk and two sugars for me. It helped.

It was a good thing, having Benno there. Interviewing me in my husband's presence had the effect of making Neville go easier on me than he wanted to—that, and the fact that I acted like I was still fuzzy in the head. Plus Benno heard enough to satisfy him without asking any questions of his own.

My brain was working well enough to realize that Geoff was the only one who knew I'd ever had Lillian's satchel in my possession, which meant I could keep my escapade in the closet to myself.

I explained about the will and confessed, with much contrition, to the sin of curiosity—steaming it open. When I saw Geoff in the hall with Lillian's satchel, I'd done what I could to alert the police and then followed him. For good measure, I threw in something about thinking I'd seen Larry with the satchel the day before.

I told what I'd overheard in the tunnel, and in the course of things implied that the will had gone from my possession to the satchel when I was bargaining for my freedom.

Not that I needed anyone to hammer home the foolishness of what I'd done, but Neville and Benno lectured me in two-part harmony.

Then Neville added, "So, Mrs. Servi, it seems we were both right."

I opened my mouth to point out that I was righter than he was—Naomi had been murdered. Benno's glare of warning brought me to my senses. Never say "I told you so" to the police.

"Yes, you've handed us a nice bit of motivation. Unfortunately, Mr. Tate and Ms. Hilton are not here to explain themselves. With this information, however, the public administrator will attempt to locate surviving relatives. If no one surfaces, your Senior Services may inherit the full estate. Yes, it all works out nicely for you."

Benno put my mouth to better use than I was about to, and kissed me. "My wife, the heroine!"

Husbands can surprise you. In the face of Neville's insinuations, he chose to protect me by being proud. Neville's remark, however, cut close to the bone of truth.

God bless hospital routine. An aide came in with towels and a washbasin. I groused at Benno for not bringing me a night-gown and he and Neville took their leave. Nothing gets rid of a husband like whining.

The bed bath wiped me out. I fell asleep with Emma and sins of omission nagging at the hem of my fading consciousness.

I SPENT THE MORNING drifting in and out of a debate with myself about what I'd left out of my story. Seeing Emma and Regina together, what did Neville need to know about that? Neglecting to mention certain things isn't the same as lying.

I don't believe in keeping secrets from one's spouse, but in this case—what good would it do to tell Benno I'd broken into my neighbor's apartment? Would he be hurt if he knew? No, but I'd never hear the end of it. However I sliced it, I was on the slippery slope of situational ethics.

Which got me pondering Sylvia Chase and the rules of extra-marital affairs. John Clark lying to Margery, was that a sin of omission or commission? The unfaithful rationalize that what you don't know won't hurt you. What they really mean is it won't hurt them.

Secrets have a way of backfiring. Look at Lillian. If her family hadn't put her away; if her husband hadn't lied to her…

And if Lillian had told someone she'd found her son—but that train of thought led to Emma, where I couldn't go yet.

TWENTY-TWO

I WAS DEBATING between more weak tea and salty beef bouillon accompanied by orange Jell-O when Emma walked in with a cappuccino and two croissants.

"I thought you might appreciate this." Her smile was concerned, but her eyes didn't quite meet mine.

I didn't care what she'd done, the smell of that coffee absolved her. I held it like a chalice in my two hands.

"I owe you more than a cup of coffee, Anita. May I?" Emma raised the lunch tray.

I nodded. She moved the tray to the windowsill and sat in the visitor's armchair. I dipped a croissant in the coffee. It was heavenly.

"I had a long conversation with Detective Neville yesterday afternoon. He shared the contents of Lillian Raines' will with me. I told him I was aware that Mrs. Raines intended to make a bequest to Senior Services, but I was unaware of the size of her estate."

I noticed the care with which Emma chose her words.

"At the time I spoke with him, immediately after Mrs. Raines died, that was the truth. Then a young woman gave me some additional information and made me a proposition."

"Regina Hilton," I said. Emma nodded.

"Did you know she was the woman who'd been stealing from the old people in the Bike Building?" I interrupted.

Emma looked directly at me. "No, but I suspected as much. Regina said she was approaching me on behalf of Lillian

Raines' son. Lillian had told him she'd made a will, but he didn't know where it was. She thought I might have it."

"You knew she'd found her son?!?"

"Anita, please. Detective Neville has already impressed on me that I share the blame for what happened to you. If I had known the son was your next-door neighbor, that he lived in the building where she died—well, hindsight is perfect."

I realized it was as close to an apology as I was likely to get.

"You know, I think, something about our financial situation. The cathedral is again threatening to cut our budget. I have been working on a grant proposal, but…" Emma stood and went to the window. "I am not a writer. Oh, a letter on behalf of an individual client, yes, but I'm a social worker, not a fund-raiser. The only reason Senior Services functions so well is that the Cathedral provides our funds and lets me do what I'm best at."

"But aren't they always threatening to cut the budget?"

"Certain members of the board would like to see the youth services program expand, and with the dean about to retire… Of course, I did not have the will. Regina informed me that Lillian Raines was worth quite a bit. She wanted me to petition the court on behalf of Senior Services. The son, according to Regina, was reluctant to step forward due to considerations about adverse publicity should it become known that his mother was a mentally ill street person. She refused to tell me who he was, but she promised to arrange for me to examine the documents that proved the relationship. In exchange, she offered me twenty-five percent of the estate, plus any legal expenses I would necessarily incur."

"I saw you and Regina together that night," I said.

"Then you found her body the next day, and I didn't come to work…" Emma was pretty quick on the uptake. Fever and all, I blushed.

Fortunately, she was amused. "Give me some credit, Anita. I would never have accepted her offer. Having heard her out, however, I needed to consider the lengths to which I was willing to go to keep Senior Services operating. I didn't come in on Friday because I wanted to rework the grant proposal. I finally wrote it with a focus on the clients as individuals in need rather than 'the agency as service provider,'" she mocked the jargon. "It's a much better piece of writing. I sent it out yesterday, so we'll see what the New York Foundation thinks."

We let it go at that.

THE DOWNSIDE of living and working in the same neighborhood is the blurring of boundaries between personal and professional. Once the news got out, I had visitors. Fortunately, Barbara was first, with a bag of things Benno had asked her to bring.

He did better than just a nightgown and sent over my main comfort item, a dark green quilted satin robe that had been my grandmother's.

Barbara studied me. "You look like last week's leftovers." She got me to the sink and washed my hair for me, talking the whole time. "The building's all in a tizzy. Cops crawling everywhere, including the garbage I had ready to put out this morning. They were looking for that pair of shoes that jammed the compactor Friday morning."

"Did they find them?"

"Oh yeah, they found 'em. Geoff Tate's nasty old loafers. They were also asking about some satchel-thing belonged to the lady on the landing. They were after Larry Turner in particular, I don't know why." Barbara paused. "Would that be what you had in your bag Monday afternoon?"

It was more than fever flushing my cheeks.

"Okay, you don't want to talk about it, that's your business." Barbara, trying to get the pathetic plastic hospital comb through my hair, gave a vicious tug.

"Ouch!" If I hadn't told Benno, how could I tell Barbara? The sins of omission were coming home to roost.

"Sorry, I forgot how tender-headed you white people are."

"Never mind, I'm a sick woman."

"You got that right." Barbara put a fat French braid down the right side of my head.

"Thanks, Barbara. I feel better with my hair clean."

She finished braiding in silence and left me to sleep. The second braid was tighter than the first. I had to trust that our friendship would hold as well.

BETWEEN THE ROBE and the braids, I was not only presentable but elegant for the afternoon contingent of elderly visitors.

Sylvia Chase brought parrot tulips in a plastic vase and stayed a brisk ten minutes to report that Mr. Patel's surgery had gone well. Mrs. Lu's offering was a bottle of white ginger bath oil. Ruth Goldfarb showed up with a pink azalea. Then Catherine Wilcox, bearing a box of Mondel's chocolates large enough to make everyone happy.

It was a good thing they all had each other, because I kept drifting toward sleep on the haze of their voices, querulous, shocked, smug, gossipy. The weather had turned cold again. Woolworth's was going out of business. Frank Sprague bribed Sam Katz with drugs to get rid of the old people in the Bike Building. Edna Sprague paid Sam to kill Regina because she was Frank's lover. Regina was two-timing Frank, and her other lover tried to kill me because I threatened to tell Frank about him if she didn't stop stealing from them. I didn't have the energy to correct any of it. Later.

WHEN I WOKE UP AGAIN, Clea was eyeing me critically from the foot of the bed.

"Barbara did them crooked." She climbed up and tugged on the left braid.

I got my arms around her and hugged.

Anne laughed. "Looks like you're feeling better."

It had been a good sleep. My body still ached, but I was neither cold nor sweating.

Clea gave me one of her patented five-second hugs before she squirmed off the bed to show me the fruits of her afternoon in the office. A police car, a blue river with me swimming, a woman with witchy hair that was also me, a rainbow, and a flower for good measure. Anne got to work with Scotch tape and decorated the walls.

Then my dinner tray arrived. I'd been promoted to solid food, road kill with gravy. Fortunately Benno arrived with Chinese take-out, making my bed the center of another party. A doctor stopped by, declined a sparerib, read my chart, and decided I had to stay the night. Benno, now that he'd had a full day of child responsibility, agreed reluctantly.

He took Clea home around 7:00. Anne stayed, totally unrepentant for having told people I was at St. Luke's. In my opinion, the hospital was the least restful place I could be.

It got even less comfortable when Michael arrived, out of uniform but still wearing his cop attitude. He shooed Anne out without remarking on her outfit—grays and blacks, to match the cloudy sky and return to winter temperatures.

"Yo, Social Worker, you look like you'll live. Nice robe."

I smiled innocently. The storm clouds were all Michael's tonight.

"Look, I read your statement this afternoon. There's one little inconsistency."

"Only one? Considering my state of mind yesterday, I'd be surprised if there *weren't* any gaps." I knew what was coming.

"I didn't say a gap, I said an inconsistency. Actually, Inez was the one who noticed. When you called the precinct, you told her you had Raines's will *and* the satchel. But in your statement, you said Geoff had it and that was why you followed him."

"It was." Benno, Barbara, now Michael. My rationale for not telling the police was the Fifth Amendment, protection from self-incrimination. I still thought Benno was the only one who had any right to know.

Michael considered me. "The bag was presumably stolen from the Wilcoxes on Thursday. You had it Monday afternoon. Inquiring minds might want to know how the bag got into Geoff's possession."

Exactly what I was afraid of. "Then inquiring minds are doomed to disappointment. Inez must be mistaken about what I said on the phone. All I had was the will."

Michael didn't like it. "Don't play cute with me, Anita. I'm here asking you, I haven't said anything to Neville yet."

"Are you going to?"

"I should. I didn't come here to get you in trouble, Anita, I just wanted to know."

"I can't tell you, Michael. I would if I could, but I can't." I loaded my voice with sincere regret, and changed the subject. "So are you going to put me out of my misery and tell me what you found out?"

"I gotta hand it to you, Social Worker, you got balls. Let me get Storm Clouds before she starts raining on me."

THE UPSHOT WAS, the police dusted Naomi Spivik's room for prints but didn't get anything they could use. With only my word for Sam and Geoff's conversation in the underpass, it wasn't enough to charge him with Naomi's death; they'd have to settle for nailing Sam on attempted murder for me.

"Yeah, he'll spend a few years in a funny farm upstate, take his meds, and be just fine, so they'll discharge him, send him back on the streets. We've got a great system here, if you're criminally insane." Michael snorted.

The Wilcoxes, however, wound up on my side of the balance sheet. A set of their keys, complete with Regina's prints, turned up in Geoff's apartment.

"No prints in their apartment, though. It's a moot point, was it Geoff or Regina turned on the gas. At least Regina goes down as a solved homicide." Michael patted his pockets and withdrew a folded piece of paper. "I almost forgot, I brought you a present."

It was a photocopy of a fax of a newspaper item dated July 18, 1947. The gist of it was that the rescue squad had responded to a boating accident on a private estate near Asheville. By the time they arrived, the child had been pulled, alive,

from the water. No names were mentioned, a nod to the priv-
ileges of wealth in those days.

"It's ironic, isn't it?" Anne said. "He was saved from
drowning as a child, but his fate finally caught up with him."

IN MY DREAMS that night, my mother and I stood on a cliff
overlooking the Hudson. Lillian Raines's body lay between us
on a marble slab. Clea and a little boy in a sailor suit were on
the river in a rowboat with Neville at the oars. My mother
wanted to talk about my father, but I had to get down to the
shore and make Neville bring the children back. I called and
waved, but he rowed them further from shore. Clea waved back
and blew me kisses.

TWENTY-THREE

WEDNESDAY MORNING, Benno and Clea took the day off to spring me from the hospital. They got there just in time to save me from lumpy wallpaper paste and curdled yellow glop with cardboard bacon.

I could have done without a wheelchair, but Clea insisted on pushing me. Benno and I did a dismayed-but-proud parent look. From wanting to ride in a lap to piloting—could adolescence be far behind?

They let me walk the three blocks home, Clea carrying Sylvia's tulips. The weather was April overcast with a chill wind blowing up off the river. I had my winter coat, but a glimpse of the Hudson brought the cold back to my bones. I felt a new appreciation for Brighton Beach, only an hour and a subway token away.

AN ELDERLY WHITE WOMAN in a wool coat waited on our stoop. A claw went up my spine and clutched the base of my neck.

"Be polite, Anita, it's Mrs. Katz," Benno said.

So it was, in a navy coat and matching knit hat. I thought about Sam being released from the prison hospital and coming home to Mama. The claw didn't let go.

Clea bounced ahead of us. "Hello!" she chirped, oblivious.

"Such a big girl, to carry the flowers!" Mrs. Katz spoke to Clea. "I'm going to see my son. He's in the hospital, you know. It's so far away, over to the Lower East Side." She made a tsking sound.

I stopped on the sidewalk, a step below her so we were eye-to-eye. She examined my face. "Yes, you're Mrs. Gunther's granddaughter. A lovely woman, always a pot of coffee on the stove. And your little girl, such a pretty thing."

She smiled. I smiled back. I had my child, healthy, happy, intact. Her child would never be a comfort to her in her old age. I had an urge to apologize to her.

As if she'd read my thoughts, she said, "Children, they always disappoint you. Your grandmother, what she went through with your mother! But grandchildren are a blessing. Mrs. Gunther was lucky to have you."

She cupped my chin in her hand, a gesture so like Sam's that I jerked my head back. She reached out again and lay her hands on my cheeks. "You have such a face, a beautiful Jewish face! Look, here is my taxi." She raised her hand, signaling the driver.

EMMA HAD GIVEN ME the week off. The next morning, Benno took Clea to school on his way to the shop. I read yesterday's paper and did the breakfast dishes. Then I went up to Broadway, bought two red roses, and withdrew $100 from the bank.

I walked down to Riverside Park and headed north. The weather was still cool but it was definitely spring, the sky bright blue, cloudless. There was a green-gold light under the trees.

The police tape at the scenic overlook had been replaced by a metal barricade. I paused at the top of the steps, looking for the rabbit. It didn't appear.

At the grave of the Amiable Child, I took the wilted rose out of the jar and put my two roses in. I sat on Lillian's milk crate and waited for Mark Jenrette. He didn't materialize either.

I thought about the stories people tell each other and the secrets they keep. I thought about my father until the chill started to reclaim my feet.

In the Jewish tradition, I picked up a round pebble and added it to the pedestal under the stone urn.

When I got home, I called my mother. It was time to ask questions.

THE GOOD AND THE DEAD

A BEN NEWMAN MYSTERY

True-crime writer Ben Newman has a talent for re-creating murder, though until now he's viewed homicide only as an outsider looking in. But suddenly bodies are turning up in his suburban Philadelphia hometown. And he knows each and every one of them—they were all classmates at the same elementary school.

What secrets lie behind the innocent facade of childhood in this small, tightly knit community? As corpses and old memories come to light, Ben is reconnecting with the past...and getting worried about his own future.

SEYMOUR SHUBIN

"Shubin keeps his winning streak going..."
—Tony Hillerman

Available October 2002 at your favorite retail outlet.

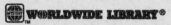

WSS436

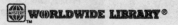